Faerytale

The Greatest Tale Never Told...
Book One

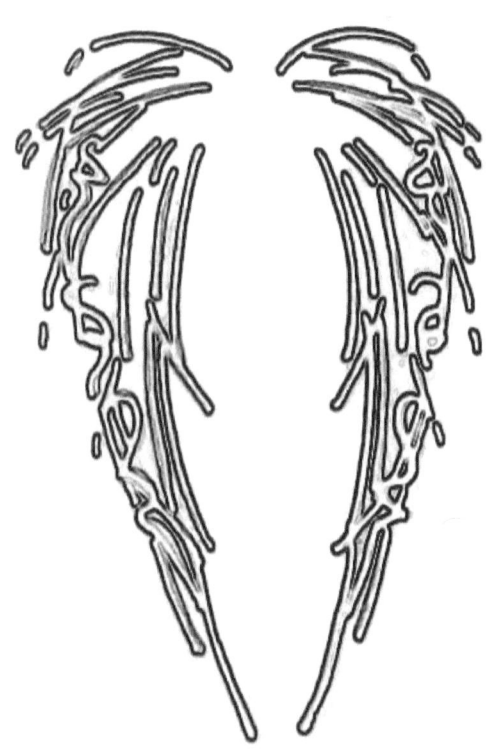

Dedicated:
To God, who opened my eyes, my heart and my mind
to beliefs and the true teachings of the soul. To Michael, who
dealt with two "rambunctious tricksters," Blyss
& Stv, as it took me "forever" to finish my manuscript.
To my mother, Denise, for instilling in me her beliefs and insights.
To Brent, Colt & Kelly, who have shared my visions of this
world. To Cheyenne, my own definition of rare
magick. To ᓭ, my ᓭ aunty, who understands the unusual.
To my friends, old and new who helped see
me through, and to the rest of You, my love . . .

Aelfwynn

Faerytale, The Greatest TÁle Never Told . . .   *Book One*

Copyright ©2011; by Aelfwynn MacGregor, AMB
ISBN 978-0-615-46244-8

Front Cover Photo: © Freesurf69 | Dreamstime.com (Castles of France)
Front Cover Concept: by Aelfwynn MacGregor, AMB & Keltik Faith, CSM
Inside Title Design: ©2011; "Wings & Shield," Aelfwynn MacGregor, AMB
Back Cover Concept: by Aelfwynn MacGregor, AMB & Keltik Faith, CSM

Lulu Distribution Services

Visit me on Facebook at: *The Realm of Faerytale*
or contact me at TheRealmofFaerytale@hotmail.com

Chapters

Chapter	Title
Prologue	
Chapter 1	Instincts
Chapter 2	Fear
Chapter 3	*Once Upon a Time . . .*
Chapter 4	Company
Chapter 5	Vigilance
Chapter 6	On Their Knees...
Chapter 7	Drifting
Chapter 8	Time
Chapter 9	Memories
Chapter 10	Awakening
Chapter 11	The One
Chapter 12	Origins
Chapter 13	Believing
Chapter 14	Knowledge
Chapter 15	Guardians
Chapter 16	Allies
Chapter 17	Epoch
Chapter 18	Traditions
Chapter 19	Birth Right
Chapter 20	The Garden
Chapter 21	The Gift
Chapter 22	A Burning Question...
Chapter 23	Elements
Chapter 24	Childhood
Chapter 25	Destiny
Chapter 26	Darke Ones
Chapter 27	Shattering
Chapter 28	Finding Courage
Chapter 29	Without Fear
Epilogue	In the Beginning...
The End	*... Happily Ever After*

Foreword

God is with us always; above, below, all around and everywhere in between.

Aelfwynn

Heat

I felt fear as he approached. Not of him, but that he might turn the other way. That I might never know him; that he might leave me to myself. But his steps came closer, and I burned at his very sight. As he finally arrived, he reached close, running his long and graceful fingers over the skin of my hand, of my inner wrist, curling, tingling pleasure, following in their wake. Then his fingers found their way upwards, along my arms, across my tender shoulders and neck. The burning continued; the intensity building stronger. My emotions were a whirlwind from the effect he was having on me.

They ended their assault just under my chin. I could feel the thickness, molten gold that scorched my insides in deep pleasure. My heart beat out a fierce rhythm against my ribcage, a tune as old as time itself. Tilting my chin upwards, my eyes closed on their own accord. *"I could just smell the aroma of him, pine, woodsy . . . and something else."* I thought just before his lips descended to claim mine. What was fire before was now a raging inferno. The response to his arms wrapped around me, his grip strong, but pleasurable, the pressure of his lips on mine, dizzying. As the assault continued, the intensity increased. I could feel the velvet caress of his tongue as it slid across my swollen, silken lips.

I sighed in pleasure, a moment of weakness, and his tongue dove deep, a caress of velvet on velvet; my initiation into the physical aspects of life, a blazon web of temptation. A mating of intensity so complete, that I could feel myself burning in the depths. I could feel the heat as it spread out twofold, the first, from our joined lips, the second, from my middle. Deep within my core, the muscles bunched and released, shooting outward in ripples of tension and flames. A deep pulse, a liquid heat as it raced outward. As it spread, it fed the inferno of my desire higher, the two sensations, waiting to join, to mate and burn me into cinders.

My mind racing, my heart beating beyond ability, I waited for the explosion, for my life to end on such a wondrous eruption. My thoughts were beyond me now, they were consumed. There was only us, only us and the passion. His hands continued their work, his assault along my flesh now. Quickly, through a thickened haze, I realized that we were bare, his fingertips running across my sensitive, hardened nipples. Our union broke, as his lips descended lower and his tongue took its turn below at my silent torture.

I could feel him consuming me, knew that we were no longer each other, we were quickly becoming one. Pulling his lips free, a trail of liquid fire followed as he brought his mouth to my ear.

"I claim you now, but you must offer yourself willingly. Will you be mine?" His voice was thick with passion.

I felt the heat burn even higher, felt as it completely consumed me. "I claim you." The words a mere whisper as they worked themselves out, between my moistened lips to consume us both in the savage heat.

Mid-May 2012

Instincts
(1)

"It had started out as a simple, normal day. So blessedly normal, until..."

The broadcast today was far greater of a concern than any of the previous had been. What had been taken in humor and lightheartedness now rang with a sense of fear for the unknown. The incident today having managed to leave nearly the entire world reeling. Now, the question of reality was something that teetered on the edge itself!

For several weeks, reports of mysterious goings-on's had been reported on the late night shows after the news. Mostly spoofs that gave people a good laugh, or cry, depending on your humor. People reported incidences of seeing interesting animals around their homes, giant birds in the sky and strange noises in the day as well as the night. One story had even covered a group of teenage boys who claimed that garden gnomes had come to life. Chasing them in the fading light of dusk. All that humor had come to an end, as a breaking news report had begun this afternoon. By the evening, it had escalated to the only thing on all channels.

"What had started out as a normal day of little league soccer will forever be remembered as the first day of the end of our reality." The once quirky, Becca Devlin reported. "In Central Park, around 2:30, a disturbance began. It was witnessed by nearly a hundred people. Caught on tape, all appears fine at first. Then, a disturbance begins along the side of the field." She shuddered as she finished her lines.

I must admit, I was intrigued by her reaction.

"It was there that large shrubs and overgrowth served as a barrier between the field and the park. The initial disturbance was not caught on tape, but what followed was. The images you are about to see are violent and brutal in nature, they should not be viewed by a younger audience." Devlin disappeared to be replaced by a sunny scene of Central Park, a soccer field in motion, children racing, a ball flying and parents yelling.

Watching as the footage started. Out of view, you could hear cracking and swishing noises, when suddenly, the camera shifted off to the side of the field and it appeared that something large was trying to get through the thickened brush. The effect was terrifying as all hell broke loose, many guttural screams, all in unison, rent the air. Watching transfixed and mortified, the people on the TV began grabbing at their noses and mouths. It created the impression that something was giving off a horrendous stench. Breaching the overgrowth, terror of a new form arrived. Literally.

I could feel the goose-bumps as they rose along my flesh, the ice cold tingle traveling up my spine.

The hideous creatures, no more than four feet tall, burst through the overgrowth. They were terrifying. So many of them coming through the brush it was impossible to even begin to get a count of them all. The game stood still as the people observed the strange sight. No one moved or responded, minds frozen in disbelief. Then the attack began. The "Goblins," as they were referred to after the initial report, attacked without mercy. The small creatures were dressed in rags. Their skin was a pallid shade of green. Scraggly, coarse strips of hair standing on end and rows upon rows of sharp and jagged teeth could be seen as they yelled their cries of attack. They ran across the field, carrying crude weapons that resembled swords and daggers. It quickly became apparent what they were after.

The chill raced along my spine once again and the hairs on my neck were coming on end.

The children were easy prey as the goblins reached them. Pulling them onto their shoulders, attempting to haul them back to the overgrowth from which they'd come. Chaos truly erupted when the dumbfounded parents finally responded to the threat. They rushed from the sidelines. Grabbing anything they could to use as weapons, their desperate attempts to rescue their children, a terrifying and brutal encounter to watch.

As the violence escalated, it became harder for me to keep my eyes on the flashing scenes. It was viciousness like I'd never seen before. Blood was flowing unstaunched from the wounded. But soon, the parents scored a victory. The sounds of police sirens could be heard in the background of the recording. The loud sirens appeared to be the best deterrent. The goblins grabbed their ears, screaming in pain. They let go of their prey and ran for cover, retreating back to the overgrowth, none of the children having been lost.

As the police searched, the paramedics went to work on the wounded. The parents suffered several serious wounds, although none were life-threatening. Several children had received deep lacerations from the claws of the goblins that had required stitching. The worst wounds were maul marks, as it appeared that the goblins were attempting to feed, right then and there, on the frightened children. The father in charge of taping the game had managed to record the entire event. The only break in footage, was a moment of static, as the man recording began to race to the scene, in an attempt to rescue his own son and he accidentally knocked the camera over. The rest of the footage was recorded sideways, but it was all there, in all of its frighteningly clear detail.

It was quickly broadcast on all the local channels, from there, around the world in a matter of minutes. In one day, the boundaries of reality and fantasy had crossed and it appeared to be a living nightmare.

*

"It wasn't that the violence surprised me, really." I shook my head, saddened at the realization that I'd actually just had that thought. *Unfortunately, it seemed that the world had been turned upside down as of late. Violence in homes and schools had been escalating without warrant, the abuse, wars, famine and genocide. How had we come so low? The atmosphere the world over was that something was getting ready to blow. And I was terrified that we would not survive the eventual outcome. Even nature had taken a turn on the wagon wheel. Strange weather patterns beginning and continuing. There was that freaky tornado in New Jersey and the month of hail storms in Australia. That was just two to start! Apparently, nothing was too impossible anymore.*

"Oh my God! This is not right, so not right!" Watching the broadcast again, finally getting all of the information, seeing everything in its brutal detail. I turned off the TV as it began to repeat once more, no new news having been added. Glancing in the mirror over the fireplace, I saw the fear in my own violet eyes, my normally apricot skin, an alarming shade of pale. Stepping back, the gravity of the situation sinking in. This was something from out of a dark faerytale. The oddity of it, striking closer to home than I could of imagined.

My life was a faerytale, at least, the basic aspects of it were now. To be honest, it was one of my own making, as an author of fantastical novels. But that had only been for the last several years. What had come before had been the nightmare for me, another tale entirely. Now, who needed the mundane of real life, when the imagination was so potent?

How many people did I know, truly, who could say that their ability to be imaginative and creative was their staple in their profession? Were able to recreate this world from scratch and survive on those concepts and images? I knew that that answer was small, nearly nonexistent. *What, a handful of writers and movie stars?* I really thought about that for a minute, and then I laughed, a quick break from facing reality . . . for a moment.

Well, there were always meteorologists. I thought. Glancing out the window only proved it. They had predicted hail all afternoon and not one speck had been seen. *Meteorology was one profession, where a college degree was mandated and earned a large salary, yet the majority of the time their predictions were just that, predictions. Accuracy for them was an illusion at best. The everyday farmer seemed to have a better understanding of the weather, than the professionals. I guessed that's what happened when all of the learning was in the classroom and not the out of doors anymore. The experience of real life was missing. The deep down gut feeling that you felt to the bone.*

But my truth, my reality, was that my career screamed magick, and I loved the idea of it. But this was no laughing matter. Actual creatures of the faery realm, something that was not supposed to exist, seemed to be popping up all over the world, my world. Something like this should not be happening. This was something that no one could believe that they were seeing, much less experiencing. Disbelief etched into every single face that I'd seen on that television. And even more, it has also been confirmed that the sightings were not just limited to America anymore either.

Additional reports had come in from Ireland and England, a videotape reporting on "Gremlins" coming from both places, though these didn't seem to be getting as much coverage as the Central Park Incident. They'd been taken as a hoax. Nothing more than humorous, until New York had aired and they'd been broadcast as well, no one had been hurt in either of those cases, only massive outbreaks of fear. But it showed that the incidences were spreading, and as they spread, they became more real and more dangerous. Innocent people were getting hurt now.

Realizing that the danger could be as close as my own backyard, I quickly ran through the house, closing all the windows, locking all the doors. After all the years of living in the city with my adopted parents, I thought that I'd finally found a place to be safe, but I was wrong. I realized now that living in the country, only meant that there were less people to hear us scream.

"Whoa!" I shook my head. *"What in the hell was wrong with me?" This was not me, not any longer. Irrational fear, looking over my shoulder . . . if locking the doors made us feel safer, then I would lock them. But blatant paranoia was something else entirely!"* The thought made me sad, but my resolve stood firm. Before I went any further, I had to ground myself, step back from all those old fears, those old terrors. I was an adult now, no longer a victim. I could face this, as I had faced everything else. I took a deep breath and cleared my mind.

* * * * * *

After the first report had aired, my Editor had called.

Thinking back, Catherine and I had become fast friends, due mainly to the fact that my novel had been one that she'd been unable to put down upon reading, something that had truly intrigued her. Up until I'd moved to the country, we had often spent Saturdays shopping together in the city. She'd become more of a sister than a friend and boss. Now, it seemed that the only time we were in touch, was the quick infrequent phone call. Talking to her earlier, we'd both decided that it would be safer for my daughter and me, to not be so secluded, so alone. So I'd made arrangements to leave and head for the city . . .

*

"Angel, I think it would be best if the two of you come to stay with me for a few days. You know that you're family. It's been too long since we've really been able to catch up." She'd said in her best, *"I'm the Boss"* voice. "Also, I'm worried about the two of you." Here, her voice had cracked slightly. "I don't know what I'd do if anything happened to the two of you."

I really thought about that. *For some reason, the idea of leaving the house seemed right.* My instincts were one of the few things that I could depend on, that little voice inside of my head that spoke so clearly, sometimes, too clearly. *Secretly, I had often wondered if I wasn't just a little bit crazy. I'd taken enough in this lifetime to have slipped a little bit. But no, the voice was always right . . . in the end.*

"I like the idea of coming for a visit. With everything that's suddenly going on, I'm worried about Caitrin. I don't want her to be affected by all of this. There could still be another explanation for what's happening." *"Not very likely!"* Was the comment I thought to myself. "We'll leave tonight and be there in a couple of hours. We'll make a time of it, for Caitrin. How about some fattening Chicago style pizza, or the such? It's just been a while since we've really had fun, really let go."

"I know what you mean, it all sounds wonderful. So long as you're footing the bill," Catherine laughed, "best friend for not, I remember how expensive your tastes can run,"

"Deal!" I'd hung up the phone after finalizing our plans. It was nice to realize that after depending on myself for the past several years that I could put aside the old fears and truly trust someone else. It truly felt comforting.

Getting back to the packing, letting my mind drift. It was not surprising that I ended up thinking of the past. *It seemed that lately my thoughts kept taking me in this direction, bringing up the forgotten images, the indistinct voices. It was painful for me, but the first seven years of my life were nothing more than a blur. Just the vague thoughts that filtered around the edges, always there, but not enough to focus on. Sometimes I felt ancient, far beyond what my twenty-three years had taught me. I felt like I'd stepped out of the pages of time itself and been left stranded in a time that didn't know me. But I also knew that there was nothing that I could really do about it.*

It was the years that had followed those with my adopted parents that haunted me; those that made me wish that it was them that were forgotten. I'd spent these last six years attempting to correct the damage that they'd inflicted upon me with their controlling ways. Their ways so strange, that the ability to function as a normal person, day to day, had become as challenging for me as an asthmatic had gasping for air! But enough of that, I could spend the rest of my life, trying to rationalize why they were, the way they'd been. To forget them, that was the greatest service that I could do myself.

Wash them away from my memories, from existence . . .

Fear
(2)

My life was now my own. I'd walked out the door and out of their lives. I'd disappeared without a trace, or so I'd thought. I'd kept hidden, kept my identity and age a secret. Being seventeen, I still wasn't legal, but I was fortunate that I had always looked older, so no one really asked. Especially when you had the means to always pay with cash, my own cash. Not a penny from them. Never having deep roots, always moving around and never trusting anyone, the money was good, but even it got low with the extra measures I'd had to make to ensure my identity was safe. Six months, that was all I needed and it had been worth it, worth every penny spent.

I'd learned more about myself than I'd ever dreamed possible. I was talented. Spinning a tale and illustrating a book in no time at all. My imagination had now become my salvation. On a whim, I submitted a sample of my work for a magazine contest, and I'd won. The money was good, so I'd continued. This realization made me a hefty profit a little over a year and a half later, when I submitted my first novel and it'd accidentally ended up on Catherine's desk. Her response had been nearly instantaneous. It allowed me to support myself and put down roots, permanent ones. I'd already had my daughter by then, she'd only been a few months old. But my life had changed irrevocably. Now that I was the mother, I finally understood and I would never let her down.

*

It had been my pregnancy that had changed everything for me. It had opened up my mind, allowed me to view the magick within me, to see things in my head, in a depth that often went beyond the ability to see things in the real world. My pregnancy had opened my eyes and my heart to the ability of real magick. I could not really be sure how to describe it, only that it was true. It was almost like an alternate reality, a world of my own. I was able to create an entire world from scratch. It had depth and vibrancy. I could create the characters and give them souls. They took flight and came alive. I was the outside observer, watching the day to day. Even if I stepped away, I could come back and see the way the world had progressed in my absence. It helped me to see my own world in a unique way. Now it influenced the way that I lived. My life now depended on the very imagination that had been denied me as a child. My soul had obtained freedom on a level of extraordinary.

I knew that I was sound, at least, in mind. I had serious issues. I was damaged goods, I knew that and I understood it. I had forced my way out of an abusive situation, but that did not make the evidence any less damning. Neither, did it make me a better person for allowing it to happen in the first place. I knew that I had been young, but I'd also known that what they'd been doing was wrong. How do you wrap that around yourself when you're no more than a child? But I worked for a change, and now, here I was.

I had someone to care for other than myself. I found a way, I was still struggling, but I knew that I didn't have any other options anymore. My daughter came first. She was the future, my future. Between my imagination and keen instincts, I was creating a safer world to live in, for myself and her. I never wanted to imagine her having to go through the things that I had been forced to endure. So, I left nothing to chance. I was a survivor. My soul had been scorched with all that it had been through, and it allowed me to avoid the danger of smoke now, before the flames.

* * * * * *

I had a second sight and right now, my defenses were up. This latest incident on the news filled me with a numbing terror. The idea that a Magickal Realm was real was absolutely amazing, the fact that terrifying things were emerging from it, was paralyzing!

I came back to myself for a moment. *"Damn it! It's just not possible! Things like this . . . they just don't happen!"* The thought kept racing through my mind. I could feel the line of worry creasing my brow as I continued packing.

Like a religion, everything that I thought and felt, went into the books that I'd been writing for years. *What bothered me most was that the creatures in the park today, were nearly identical to the ones on my illustration board upstairs in my study, locked up tight. They were only waiting for me to complete my newest tale. The similarities were just too much to be called coincidence. Nor did I believe in them. It left me hanging in limbo, without any answers. And that left me wondering . . . could I possibly have some type of knowledge about a magickal world that I've never been aware of, until now?*

*

I recalled Catherine discussing the newest book with me. She was as suspenseful as the rest of my readers, waiting for its completion. Her questions ringing in my ears . . .

"Your last five novels have all progressed in a sequence of age. They are some of the greatest sagas of the Magickal Realm that have ever been written. You cannot just leave me hanging like this! I need to know what's going to happen! Come on, give me something?"

I'd laughed. Catherine in charge was nowhere near as intimidating as Catherine on a mission for information. "Catherine, where is the professionalism?" I'd laughed.

"Professionalism went out the door after I read the first line. Talk!"

I gave in, slightly, just giving her a taste of what was to come.

"Then this next book should have you totally hooked." I said. "This one, my sixth, is going to be the darkest yet. Some will face challenges never imagined, while others, others will find that they believe in things beyond their knowledge, their understanding. Even I don't know how it will end, or how many more there will be afterward."

What I had not said was that the battle just kept playing out in my mind, the beauty of my created world and the horrors of it. Could I truly have more of a connection to some unseen world than any of us realized could be possible? I didn't know. But I wished I did.

Caitrin was my most avid critic, as they were tales that I told her for bedtime, though they were edited for her. Her nightmares would never be because of me. I laughed, and then scowled again. This was ridiculous. "Damn it! How is it possible that something from my own nightmares, something that I've never told anyone, has come to life? It's just not possible!" I said loudly, this time.

"You know it's true." The words suddenly popped out of nowhere. I almost screamed. God how I hated it when that happened. *My little voice, little indeed!* I glanced quickly to see if I had bothered Caitrin, but she was fine. *I really must be upset, I never swore!* I really needed to know what was going on. Was I even ready for the answers?

I shook my head and yelled at myself. *What we really needed was to leave. Soon.* I was just stalling with all of this confusion. Not wanting to face change again. The apprehension and fear was creeping along my spine now. We needed to get out of here. My duffel was almost packed and Caitrin was asleep on the couch. She lay there, blocking out the world, sleeping as only the innocent could do.

Shoulders squared with my determination, I carried my bag out to the car at a swift pace when suddenly, a wave of dizziness overtook me. The world quickly went dark as I lowered myself down onto the curb, my bag forgotten for the moment on the sidewalk beside me. The world around me disappeared. This was a warning, something else that I was familiar with, something that I had long ago learned not to fight, because it would come regardless. So I gave in. The dizziness passed, though my vision did not clear. Instead, the world of gray emerged, along with a pair of aqua colored eyes, ringed in silver. A feeling of true unrest shuttered through me.

Those same eyes had haunted me for years, they were something from my past, I was sure, but that was all I was sure of. They were as much a part of the mystery of my youth, as everything else was. They held knowledge thought, as well as sadness. It had been several years since I'd seen them last. But their warnings were something that crossed my mind continuously. They steadied me now, offering what they could and I knew that it was time to leave. We were no longer safe here. I cleared my head from the vision the best I could, and headed back into the house. Picking Caitrin up from the couch, I prepared to carry her out into the night.

She sighed as I lifted her, her eyes opening only a small way. "Are we leaving now Máthair?"

Looking down at her, smiling in return. From the first moments of her ability to speak, she had called me by it, never even having heard the word previously, its meaning, apparently running soul deep. "Yep, it's time. We'll see Aunt Catherine in a few hours. Why don't you go back to sleep and I'll wake you up when we get there?"

Her smile could light up the room. "Sounds like a plan." A small yawn on her lips as her eyes drifted downward again. I'd never understood how I'd been given such a miracle as her.

There was lightning in the sky as we reached the car. The lightning cast an eerie green glow and the air smelled of ozone. A shiver of dread crept up my spine as I fastened Caitrin into her booster seat, her eyes never once opening, and her sleep, peaceful. I waited, knowing that the coming storm was preparing to descend upon us. "I'll keep you safe. No matter what, I'll make sure that nothing harms you." I said quietly. I swept my hand across the curls on her forehead, pushing them from her eyes before leaving to retrieve my duffel.

The fear of going out into the night was strong, but the fear of remaining in the house was much worse. Caitrin did no more than shift in her sleep as we backed out of the driveway and into the night. The destination was set in the navigation system. I vaguely knew that we would start heading south. But I really was not familiar with the route, as we usually took the shorter one, unfortunately, so was everyone else right now. Mass evacuations from the rural areas had been happening since early evening. So, I would follow the new directions provided for me. Traveling south would require us to travel through the least dense area of the surrounding woods. As we left the trees behind, the old Toil Bridge would provide a way across the ravine. I smiled to myself, *"Toil & Trouble."* Every time I thought of the bridges name, it conjured up images of witches brewing their latest concoctions.

"Hum." I said in surrender. Only several more miles after that and we would reach the limits of the small town that we resided in.

Needing a distraction, I went to turn the radio on. But the idea of hearing more of the earlier story had me quickly pulling my hand back from the dash. Instead, I reached up to grab a CD from the overhead console. Smiling, I slipped in my favorite Celtic selection and it began to play. As the melody started, it washed through my ragged nerves, a soothing balm that evoked visions of green cliffs and seashores. Helping me erase some of the fear and frustration that I was experiencing. I looked in the rear view mirror as I settled back in. The words to the wordless song, filling the car as I sang a tune forgotten by time itself. The only break in the music, the crack of lightning as it raced across the night.

My God was she beautiful. I thought to myself as I checked on Caitrin in the rearview mirror. Her white blond hair, it was more silver than gold, hanging in ringlets around her dainty face. Her skin was the palest of alabaster, with a quirky pink smile. Her eyes were one of her most unique features, their color that of purple lilacs. Her features were finished off with her ears. They were quick with their upturned ends. She was definitely unusual, my little "pixie," and my miracle. I knew that she disturbed people at times. This tiny, perfect little porcelain doll that spoke with a near adult's clarity and perception. Her view of the world was unique, as was her insight. It was going to be interesting, to see how she would be handling school. *We'd be finding out soon enough, or more so, how they would be handling her.* I relaxed more as my thoughts drifted and the drive continued in near peace. My music, a comfort to my soul as it followed the car through the long stretch of dark road ahead.

One song began to blend into the next as the navigation system beeped to let me know that we were coming up to our first marker. The area was peaceful, but it was also very dark. I noticed that the wind was picking up and the leaves were whipping in response. No street lights were along this stretch of private property and the full moon, circled by a red halo overhead, could not penetrate through the treetop canopy. It seemed impossible to believe that evil was stalking the land. But I myself had seen evidence of it today. I was not taking any chances with my daughter's safety.

The need to get away was beginning to overwhelm me. It had to be forced back down so that I could focus on the road ahead. Watching as the old elm tree came up on my left. From here, I would know to watch for the fork in the road. Ahead of me, I could see twigs and loose debris sliding across the road as we continued onward.

I nearly jumped out of my skin when my cell phone went off! Laughing at myself, I grabbed for it. "Hello?"

"Angel, its Catherine. I wanted to make sure that you'd left safely? It's getting late and I hadn't heard from you yet?"

"Sorry about that. I got out later than I'd intended. Everything's going fine though. We should reach town in a short while and from there, it will be easier going. Having to travel through the dark has never really bothered me before. But with everything that's going on, I really wished that I'd put more lights up on the southern portion of my property. I'm just so jumpy!"

"It's amazing, the things we regret once we know that we needed it and didn't take care of it!"

"OK, smart ass. That's enough from you." I said with a laugh. "I don't think any of us could have foreseen anything along these lines."

I watched as the second marker approached. Suddenly, the fear started to rear up again and I was forced to roll my neck on my shoulders to relax. Looking back up at the rear view mirror, I expected to see something, but there was nothing there. *It felt like there was something there, watching us, something just beyond my range of vision. It was like we were in a race for our lives.* I couldn't really understand it, or shake the feeling. My heart started accelerating, my palms getting sweaty, and I jumped a mile again as Catherine's voice returned.

"Hello! Are you still there?"

"Yes, I'm here. Sorry about that. I just thought . . . ?"

"What? Is everything alright? I'm really starting to get worried about you!"

"Yeah, everything's OK. I think my imagination is just getting the best of me." I laughed. *My imagination. . .* Driving, I took to the right of the fork, keeping to the directions. "You know how I am." I finished. A loud bolt of thunder rocked the air. I could feel the earth shift, watched as the scene in front of me shifted before coming back to center. I was pretty certain that the lightning had made contact somewhere out there in the stretch of darkness.

"Maybe I should start driving and meet you. That way, it will be a shorter trip and I'll know that you're safe sooner."

"There's no need for that Catherine. I'm making good progress. I just overreact sometimes. I'm getting close to the bridge and the town is not far afterward. I'll see you soon, the drive into the city from there won't be more than two hours at most." I said, trying to placate her.

"If you're sure . . . ?" She asked hesitantly.

"Absolutely! There's no need for you to have to be out here as well. We'll see you soon..." I was just preparing to hang up the phone . . . when the sky around me lit up. Like the lightning before, it zigzagged from sky line to sky line, but the color was an eruption of blue, then purple, a tinge of silver following in the rear. The wake of the lightning was ripping the sky open like a wave, before it disappeared again. Looking behind me, my attention was immediately drawn to an intense glow from the rear view mirror. "Oh my God...!" I felt fear as it twisted within my stomach and took hold.

"Now I know something is . . ." Catherine's voice became lost in the reverberations of the wave.

"I can see flames coming from behind us. It's coming from the direction of my home! I think that the last lightning strike might have hit close to the house. I can't be sure though!"

"My God, it's a blessing that you weren't still there! What are you going to do?" She asked worriedly.

Shaking my head, I just sighed. *All of our belongings, everything I had worked years to attain, gone.* "It's too late to go back. I'll call the fire department and phone it in. There's nothing I can do right now, going back could be too dangerous. There's only the one road, if the fire spreads quickly, we could become trapped. It's just not worth it."

"Are you . . . are you going to be alright?" Catherine questioned again, the worry overly evident in her voice now.

"What choice do I have?" For a moment, a savage frustration raced through me. "It's not like I haven't lost everything before and had to start over. At least Caitrin and I are safe. That's all that matters. I have to let you go, I'll talk to you soon." Hanging up the phone, calling 911 was the next step. I left the information anonymously.

As we continued to travel, more of the road became visible, the glow behind us continuing to grow stronger. The treetops overhead were becoming more spread out. *Soon.* I thought. *We would find safety.* After several minutes, the bridge came into view. The years had given it a decrepit appearance, though it had recently been confirmed, by the city architect, to still be structurally sound. *Tonight, under the red cast of the full moon, it appeared dark and foreboding.* Before I had time to really think more about it, the tires hit the gravel at the start of the bridge.

The wood slats began to creak as the tires drove over them. The moonlight shined down through the cracks between the boards overhead and allowed a stunted view of the sky, as we made our way slowly across, a large groaning noise and movement from above caught my attention. Quickly, I slowed the car and watched to see if I saw the movement again. Sure enough, the light in front of us was blocked out by something on top of the bridge. I debated for a moment. *Wondered if the local kids were playing a joke?* I started to laugh at myself. *I wanted to believe that it was nothing.*

Then a sudden loud crack startled me from my thoughts. A huge hole appearing in the top of the bridge as wooden debris came raining down onto the slats in front of us, through the gaping hole, dropped down nothing less than a ten-foot monster, the sight nearly undoing me. Reacting quickly, I brought the barely moving car to a sudden halt. There had to be a way to escape. Oh my God, Caitrin could not get caught up in this!

The horror of what was in front of us, only matched the view of what was coming up from behind. The light at the back of the bridge became blocked as another one, as what I could only describe as a troll, as large as the first, closed in from the rear. Ten feet of ragged, filthy fur, with teeth hanging down to well below their huge jaws, the abominations were covered in the matted hair, a shaggy monster with long arms that ended in claws. From both ends, we were boxed in. I looked desperately. We were already halfway across the bridge. We had to keep moving forward, it was the only way. There was still enough room if we could just get around it quickly enough. I took a deep breath, said a quick prayer and slammed down on top of the accelerator. It took a moment for the car to catch up to the initial momentum; when it did, it took off like a mini rocket. I prayed we cleared the troll. It had to weigh at least 600 pounds.

At the sound of the tires on gravel, the troll swung fully around. *It was much quicker,* than I'd thought, *than should've been possible.* The car smashed into it, much like hitting a small tree. The effect was no different. The troll stood its ground, while the front end of my car buckled. The temporary distraction had the troll looking at me like I was a fly to be swatted. I definitely felt like the fly. Felt the queasiness as it washed through me. I knew that our chance to escape had passed, that I'd failed miserably at it. Suddenly the troll screamed as if in pain.

Dear God, what had I done? Had it only now, felt the damage I'd inflicted upon it?

The scream it released, was loud enough to wake the dead, that, with the combination of the impact, it didn't surprise me to hear Caitrin call out in a sleepy and confused voice.

"Máthair?"

I looked back at her. "Shh . . .!" Putting my finger to my lips. I had no idea what would happen if we made any more sudden noises or movements.

The moment was lost however, for the infuriated troll did the only thing that it could think of to get rid of the painful and annoying thing that had hurt it. It picked up the car as if it were a child's toy, hurling it through the gaping hole in the ceiling. Wood fragments splintering all around us, the car plunged down into the dry ravine below. The last thing I remembered was the sound of Caitrin's scream, as it pierced the night . . .

*

Before the car reached bottom, a blinding white light of high intensity burst forth from within the car in every direction, so bright, that the trolls themselves were pushed back from the wreckage, blinded. A moment later, the car struck bottom and a fire ball blossomed, engulfing the car and shooting heavenward. The only sound that remained was the rush of the flames.

*

They arrived moments later. The rush and hum of their wings the only announcement of their presence. Two broke off to take care of the dazed trolls. They fought swiftly and hard, the battle only lasting minutes. The two remaining flew straight, arriving at what was left of the car. Fear fueled their search of the smoldering remains. They had felt the magick. They had felt it and been pulled by it, as it had raced out through the night. Faery magick was not possible in the Realm of Man. There was only one possible explanation. They had to hurry, so much depended on them finding her still alive!

But the wreckage was pure destruction! The chance that anything had survived would be low. The fact that two cracks had appeared in the same area was an unknown anomaly. Thank the Creator that they had been where they were needed this time. They moved as quickly as they could, shifting through hot and charred metal. Even from the distance, they could "feel" the others coming. The darke faery, the soul sucking vampires would be zeroing in on the burst of magick, the same as they had. They pulled back what remained of the interior of the car and were momentarily dumbfounded at what they beheld, a girl, no more than a child, asleep upon the ground. She was surrounded and protected by a magickal circle of leight, peaceful and alive.

ZackaRAy recovered quickly, the knot of fear in his belly, pushing away at his astonished and sluggish mind. He was reaching down to touch her, when a moan of torture reached his ears. He swung around and began to search for its source. Off to the side, he discovered another body. Upon the ground, lay the wrecked remains of a human form. He knew that it had been female, he could tell from her essence. But all that now remained were raw and angry burns, the majority of flesh, removed and wasted, the pain of her reeking through the air. Tingles of pain and repulsion raced across his skin. He was forced to steel himself in order to remain in her presence.

"TazaRine, we need ta get these two away as quickly as possible! We must get them back ta thee safety of thee Stronghold walls. You take thee wee one and I will follow with tis one." He said as he motioned to the woman on the ground. "Thee darke ones are almost upon us." He finished.

"Do you think it is worth taking her? She is near death." TazaRine asked quickly.

"As long as there tis any life left in her, I would na leave her here ta face them. Leaving her here, they may attempt ta stay. If we take her, and they follow us, thee shimmer should have time ta heal and they will na be gettin' through. Either way, she will be needin' help immediately!" He said fiercely. "They have nothin' here ta help the poor lass."

The other nodded his assent and took off in flight with the child and the remaining faery. Turning, ZackaRAy removed his cloak and used it to place around her form. *"Healin ta be."* The magick imbued within it would offer her some comfort from her pain, though not enough. Praying for speed, they were off, the sound of his wings a frantic hum in the night. Looking back over his shoulder, he could see the darke magick as the others came nearer. He faced forward and moved with speed that bordered on invisibility. *Soon.* He thought. *Soon, I will be home.*

*** ⊃C ***

... I was drifting through swirls of mass, substance ... drifting ... my thoughts whispered to me. A swirl, a swish and the grey mist pulled me down, and I was gone...

Once Upon a Time
(3)

"Once Upon a Time... the Stronghold of Ainys'Dai rose high above the earth, nestled amongst the foothills of the Rain'Dai Mountains. The Sanctuary of the Leight was a brilliant gem. The sky pure and blazing in azure, the mountains fell next from the heavens. The deep shades of sapphire and amethyst covered only at the tops by the pristine white snow. The trees of pine began midway down; like a dark emerald that lightened as it reached the less condensed woods to the open fields. The lake's deep crevices gave way to its teal appearance and tide.

Everywhere, beauty still held a foothold, the blemishes of mankind unable to cross the boundaries of the shimmer, the earth here, still unpolluted and pure. Here lay the largest Stronghold of the Faery Leight. For nearly a thousand years, the Darkeness had once again taken hold and spread out across the Lands of Magick. Already the number of Strongholds had fallen to a count of but a few score. Those that remained, remained strong, though they were few and in between.

The battles between Leight and Darke raged, the loss great on both sides, but only truly felt for the Leight. The Leight succumbing to the wreathing Darke as it wound its way in, capturing the soul, shredding it with its depravity. Their numbers were dwindling and the Prophecy was now more important than ever. The faery suffered greatly with their inability to easily reproduce. Their numbers were falling and there was no way to rebuild them.

Long ago, humans had lived long lives, lived well into their hundreds. Not as long as the faery though, they who lived to be thousands of years old. In exchange for shorter lives, humans were given the ability to have multiple children. Faery were unique. They were capable of bearing a single faeryling between soulmates. Even then, the death of an Elder would awaken the soul of a faeryling to creation; always keeping a balance, always keeping life. Now, with the plague of the Darkeness, faery were fading before their time. Faerylings were not awakening and their end would come by extinction if nothing else . . .

ƆC

I could feel . . . swirling, tingling . . . then, then there was nothing, nothing more . . . I sighed into the darkness as it swept me away . . .

ƆC

Caitrin stared out at the view opened up to her, the world unfolding through the high tower window. Smiling, she dressed quickly in the clothes they had provided her and she thought about her arrival the night before. *Remembering was an amazing thing. She had never imagined anything as beautiful as this place. It all seemed like a dream, a dream of magick.* Shaking her head, she thought of her new friend and her smile grew larger, *this was a wonderful world . . .*

*

...He had watched her as she had walked cautiously around. He could not see her face, but she was tiny. He could see the nearly white, curly hair. It hung to just past her shoulders, bouncing as she moved in a cautious manner. He had heard of her arrival not long before, others whisperings had reached his ears. He had come to look for himself. To see if what the others had said was true.

She stood in the hallway, as she had no doubt been instructed to do. Waiting, she did not realize that she was being watched . . .

*

Caitrin was lost in her wonder. She was in a castle! A real castle! Her Máthair would never believe this. And the faery, they were real! All of her Máthair's stories were real. Glancing from side to side, she looked at the pictures on the walls, the huge candles that burned brightly, casting a great glow. She was going to love it here, she only hoped that her Máthair would be here soon to be with her.

*

He watched as she began to move, running her fingers over the tables, the books and statues that sat upon them. They probably felt cool to her touch. He wondered what she was thinking. *She was so quiet, especially for one so young.* He was tempted to approach her, just to get her to turn around, so that he could see her face. He stepped forward unconsciously, his thoughts taking precedence over his caution, when he caught himself and stopped.

His abrupt movement brought him in contact with a chair, though the contact was slight, it still made a small scuffing noise. He looked up as she swung around, the light from the candles casting a glow upon her features . . .

. . . His heart stopped within his chest! He could feel his old knees trying to give, his own weight too much for him to bear. *It wasn't possible! NOT possible! Flesh and bone, a ghost brought to life.* His mind lashed out in denial and fury in response . . .

*

Caitrin startled at the noise. Turning quickly, she saw another faery, this one older than those she had already met. He stepped forward and abruptly stopped. His face was nice. She could see that he seemed surprised. His hair fell in long waves and his eyes held sadness. He looked at her with a dark intensity and then, it was gone, replaced with confusion. She startled at the change that came over him so quickly. Most would have missed it, but she didn't. She smiled up at him, instantly deciding that he was hers.

"Hello, my name is Caitrin." She said.

His heart stuttered to life again, his blood moving within his limbs. He smiled in return, his features shifting and changing in the blink of an eye.

"I am RandelfSon." He replied, his voice quiet, yet rough.

She offered her hand and they shook. It seemed like a good fit. She looked back up at him, "It's good to already have a friend." She said with a smile.

* * * * * *

Caitrin smiled now at the memory as she looked out over the thriving courtyard view. *He was indeed her friend.* She thought as she watched the morning awaking.

* * * * * *

She was not the only one, viewing the scene of the coming day. Gable stared out across the land, the morning view from the uppermost tower, allowing him with his sight, to see the very boundaries of his broad Stronghold. The shimmer held strong, the magickal boundary between realms a constant reminder of their duty. The outside Realm of Man kept ignorant from the Realm of Magick, kept safe. This was his domain, passed on to him through the blood of his fáthair, not more than a few centuries ago.

Leight was the strongest here. The Darkness had not been able to take hold. From shimmer to shimmer it was protected and preserved. His Kind, within these walls, remained pure. Even he was not sure how much longer that was to last. Daily reports came to him of the destruction and loss. This plague was quickly corrupting the hearts of the Leightened. It found its way in through cracks in their resistance, using their own fears against them, weaving into his Kind; their souls, homes and Keeps. So much of the Magickal Realm had been lost, the earth darkened from the evil that resided within it now.

The beauty and even sorrow, offered him some comfort. Some semblance of what could be considered normal, right now. But Gable's mind raced regardless. He had awoken in a sheen of sweat, his heart beating a rhythm of intensity and his body . . . *aroused.* It had been years, years since the dream had come to him, had awakened in him the sensations of desire. He still felt her touch, felt the caress of her warm, gentle hands as they traced along the muscles of his shoulders, chest and thighs, the rippling of his body in response. Sense the smell of her, it was consuming him. He could feel her passion as she wrapped her fingers around the solidness of his rigid heat, a mere moment before burying it deeply within her warm, welcoming body.

Holding his seed, promising him the life of another, only to awaken alone, cold in the cooler morning breeze. He sighed in his frustration. *Why was he being punished so? He didn't think that he would ever have an answer, at least not anytime soon.*

"A thabhairt dom neart." He said, *give me strength.* Breathing deeply, he pushed it aside, all of it, to focus on what was important right now. His mind went through the dilemmas of the days ahead. *The news from ZackaRAy had been bad. The Stronghold of SarinA had fallen. The survivors were being moved. Even now some arrived through the high southern gate. Their numbers had suffered another devastating blow. The causalities, the loss, the numbers were beginning to stagger him. He held on, his faith strong. But even that was becoming a struggle these days.* Though he was greatly troubled, his mind began to travel down another path. It was what ZackaRAy and his garrison had brought back with them that now filled his thoughts.

Gable turned away from the window and concentrated his attention on CalOwAy. The other had entered a few moments ago and had left Gable to his thoughts. It was custom to do so, to wait until he was ready to be spoken too. *CalOwAy was one of the few that could have gotten away with interrupting him though.* He smiled now to himself. *It seemed that the Elder was now, not paying any attention to him. Deep thoughts seemed to permeate his countenance. Gable was not sure if it was from recent events or not, but CalOwAy absentminded was a side of him that Gable did not see often.* The thought did have him cracking a smile, a small laugh escaping him. He coughed, in a way, to cover the act. One did not disrespect an Elder. Though CalOwAy was a respected one, Gable thought of him more as family. He offered him his greatest respect and honor. As head of the ArtimA, *the Healers,* his knowledge and insight made him one of the most regarded faery alive. Gable needed him now. He put all pretenses of humor from his thoughts. *They would need to come up with a plan on how to proceed with the Chosen One.*

Gable had never expected her to be so young, or so small. *More like a "pixie."* He had as an afterthought. This left him at a loss as to how to train and prepare her. With CalOwAy having been gone for several days, attempting to provide care for the survivors of SarinA, he would have to be brought up on current events of the Keep.

Gable thought back to the conversation he had had with ZackaRAy the night before. His warriors had been returning when intense faery magick had shot out through the evening sky. They had been aware, for some time now, of unstable shifts in the shimmer that were causing cracks to form within it. They usually healed quickly. So far, only small creatures were able to slip through the cracks. This development had kept many of his warriors busy, as they attempted to protect the humans and keep them safe until the cracks had time to heal. This time, they had not been so lucky, the cracks had strengthened, ripping the realm open as if a ragged wound.

He thought about what ZackaRAy had said, as he relayed the information to CalOwAy. "My warriors returned only yesterday, in the early morning hours. There was a large crack in the shimmer that allowed two trolls to pass through the evening before. Then it sealed itself before my warriors were able to intercede. They watched helplessly, as the trolls went on a rampage against several humans. Suddenly a second crack appeared as intense faery magick ripped through the night. It allowed four of my men to enter into the Realm of Man. There they discovered a smoking inferno, caused by the two trolls that had come through the shimmer before them. ZackaRAy and TazaRine broke off to check the wreckage, while the other two made quick work of the trolls themselves. After which, they found the survivors of the troll attack. They worked quickly to get them both back here. They were lucky. The Darke had been right behind them. The shimmer remained open long enough for them to get away and it kept the Darkeness from crossing over as well. "

"So, there are two here. Was there anything else left behind, any evidence of the magick that occurred?" CalOwAy asked.

"First, the troll's interaction was uncontrolled. Before the two that survived, they attacked and there was one casualty, an innocent caught up in the rampage. Second, the trolls came upon the next of the motor vehicles that the humans use for transport. These were the two that survived, the ones brought here to us. Third, the trolls were destroyed by magick, we are not sure of the extent of their exposure. Though, to any who come upon the scene, it will most likely appear a double motor vehicle wreck with no survivors. As it is, the Realm of Man is already beginning to realize that we are here. What they find, if there is anything, will probably only feed that knowledge."

"The first survivor was a human child, a small girl?" CalOwAy asked.

Gable nodded. "It appears that the other one might be the máthair. We are not sure yet. The girl's trust has not yet been completely earned, especially when we are so different from her. But she does keep asking for her máthair, so we assume that she is her."

Gable thought of the two survivors. One lay now in the healing Atrium. She held onto life with a ferocity that did indeed seem to be inhumanly possible. Her strength and resistance to death was awe-inspiring, though her wounds were of the worst sort. "Of the second, so much of her body has been ravaged by the flame, that the other ArtimA feared that the "healing" itself would kill her, so damaged was she. But still she has hung on, fighting in a way that few of us have ever seen. I am told that her mind has receded in upon itself. It is not able to deal with the pain and the agony. But it will not release its grip. So the others healed her, what they could, while you were gone, offering her as much oblivion from the pain as possible. Still, she has not awakened."

"Well, there is not much that we can do about the exposure to the humans. This was bound to happen eventually. Things are beginning to move much more quickly now. As to the máthair, if the damage is as bad as you say, this can be expected. She might never awaken. It is something that we will have to watch and see."

Gable continued on. "The human child," here he felt a twinge in his chest and rubbed at the unfamiliar sensations; "she was found unharmed, encased within a circle of some of the strongest magick. It appears that this was the magick that cracked the shimmer a second time and pulled the warriors through. They moved quickly getting both of the survivors here." He paused a moment, not even sure himself at the words that followed. "It seems that the Prophecy has finally come to pass, the Daughter of Man has arrived."

"It has been a long time coming Gable. Now that she is here, are you ready to face the task set before you?" Concern overly evident in his features.

"Ready? That really is the question. We have waited so long for this, yet it feels like we did not have enough time, while waiting." He shook his head, turning around. "We need for her to be ready. But I had not anticipated her age. I knew that she would be young, but so young? She is only maybe four or five years and her size is abnormally small. We need to prepare her. We have planned for this for centuries. We need to refresh ourselves with the training course that was created long ago. We will probably need to update it, add things in that we have learned, remove things that we know are no longer important."

He turned back around to face CalOwAy. "Battle and skill is something that is second nature to me, but to a human child, and with no wings? How could any of us really have foreseen something like this?"

CalOwAy felt for the young leader, the weight of his responsibilities, those that had been thrust upon his shoulders, at a much younger age than any other Faery Leader previously. But CalOwAy understood him. A faeryling or child was out of the scope of Gable's understanding. Training of warriors began at a young age, but they were mostly male. The fact that the girl would have no previous training in magick before she began, made him wonder how much of a hindrance it would be? This was something that they were all going to have to approach delicately. Too much depended on this to allow uncertainty. He cleared his throat.

"I think that we should handle this much the same way that we would approach the teaching of any faeryling. We can edit the teaching, as you said. Advance different areas of it that apply. We can go by the "tips of our wings," so to speak. This should not take us too long and it will allow us a short amount of time to make adjustments for us as well as for her."

"How long do you think we have? She has had no training, so we will be working from the beginning." Gable asked.

"We could have days or we could still have years. We will just have to pray that we have enough time to prepare. I can not see the Creator giving us less than enough time. We will discuss, the other Elders and I, and we will begin reviewing the text to determine that best way to handle her education and course in magick, before turning the reins over to the TA Archers to teach her. We will leave the training and fighting to you and the other warriors, of course." CalOwAy placed a comforting hand on Gable's shoulder. "We will work together Gable. This has all been foreseen by the Creator. Hé would not set us the task of her training if Hé thought that we were incapable. It is her time now."

Gable nodded to him. Her training was going to be something that they were all going to have to adjust to, himself the most. No one other than CalOwAy would be aware of his unease though. They would find a way to make it work; of this he had no doubt.

"Where is the child now?" CalOwAy asked.

"She is with MadaREn. I believed that she would be more comfortable with a female presence. Both seemed to take to each other pretty quickly and MadaREn was honored to have the chance to take care of the girl." Gable said. "It was odd, when they met. It was like two old friends that had been separated and reunited. I was glad for the quick friendship, honestly."

"It is good that she feels that she is welcome, that she can fit in with ease."

"Then that will be our goal." Gable said with the determination on his face, written in granite.

ᗡC

I drifted as if in the clouds, feeling unattached from everything. It was like my mind was free to wander. I gazed all around me, but I could not see my body, I could only sense myself. All that I was was what I felt. My existence had become a kind of total oblivion, a silent hum that seemed to fill my entire being.

"I didn't think that I was dead, but I did not feel alive either..."

Company
(4)

Caitrin tip-toed carefully down the long hallway, it was still early, and no one had come to her room to awaken her yet. If she was going to find out about this place, she would have to be *"quick and quiet,"* at least, that was what they always said, in the stories her Máthair told her. She peeked out around the corner and moved quickly to get down the staircases, almost out of breath, but her heart was racing with excitement when she reached the bottom. She'd managed to make no sound. She saw two faery (*Amazing!!*), cross her path before it was clear again for a break-a-way. She ran quickly, covering her own mouth to keep her laughter and excitement contained.

The enormous front door was slightly ajar; she pushed just enough to allow herself through. The courtyard was amazing. Here, faery were moving about but so were other creatures. She watched as small winged beings, flitted through the trees and others that resembled . . . *elves,* she decided, were sitting on the tops of small wagons. The wagons were being pulled by animals that she did not know, could not even begin to recognize. She'd have to ask her máthair about that. They were pulling the wagons out through the gate, full of what appeared to be barrels of food.

Walking steadily, she continued on exploring the courtyard at her own pace. It was endless. There was no way that she would be able to see everything today. So she decided on what to look at first. Off to her right were a cluster of buildings. They were all gathered together, blending around the side of the castle and back. There was a long walkway that led to a huge tower, towering high above the other structures. Behind all of this, sat woods. Shifting to the left was a divided area, to the right side of here were several other buildings, all set in a circle type of formation, but these were all much smaller. Behind them were more woods as well as a flat open field. Here a large group of male faery were . . . *fighting. Wow!* She probably should have been scared, fighting was a bad thing. But right now, it was all just too wonderful. Turning her back to them, she looked to the area to the left of the field; here was a building unlike the others. It was set back to the side of the castle, wrapping back in on its left side. A lot larger than the others, it was a . . . *a barn! That meant animals!* She thought to herself. *Animals were what she loved.* She raced forward, as quickly as she could. Barely acknowledging the great wall that surrounded it all.

She noticed the doors of the building stood open, it was easy to see within. And the smell, it was pretty much the same as she remembered from back home. The sight took her breath away. There were horses everywhere. One right after the other, there were so many that she could spend the entire day getting to know them and she would still run out of time. She jumped up, screaming in delight, unable to contain herself.

"Yeah hoo...!"

"Who's there?" She heard the question coming from a stall within the barn.

"It, it's me . . . Caitrin." She said hesitantly, her heart suddenly pounding in her small chest.

"You came to see me!" She could hear the surprise and happiness in his voice, as RandelfSon left the stall and the safety of the barn to greet her.

"Are you here often?" She asked, scratching at an itch on the tip of her upturned nose.

His smile was huge. "I am always here. This might as well be my home."

She laughed at that, imagining him sleeping in the hay with the horses. "That's funny! Why would anyone sleep in a barn?" She asked, suddenly curious.

He smiled in return. "Because, they are usually better company than any of the others I know." He added as an afterthought. "But not any longer."

ꓛC

. . . All around, I was surrounded by lights, a pulsating bliss of soft colors and hues. I felt comfort and no fear. Off to the one side, I could sense turbulence. There things appeared darker, and . . . off. I could sense fear and pain, though I did not understand what they meant, or their reasoning's. I wasn't sure what was there, only that I did not, was not, ready to face it. It was so simple to just turn back to the comfort and listen. There was nothing and everything, all at the same time. I could not really recall. It was just peace and emptiness . . .

ꓛC

After CalOwAy left for the evening, Gable finished up with his work and made his way down to the child's chamber. He entered quietly, knowing that she should already be sleeping. MadaREn had made sure that the child was well cared for and it seemed that Caitrin was more than comfortable in her presence. MadaREn had let him know that the young one had had a day full of exploring and that RandelfSon had taken an immediate interest in the child as well. This had stunned him. Nothing ever seemed to pull RandelfSon out of his deep recession. But she was unique, so he was probably just as curious as everyone else was bound to be.

Gable looked down upon her. She slept on bedding of the finest feather pad. In the light cast from the candles, it struck him that she almost appeared to be faery. The pale skin, the vibrant hue of her eyes and the glow of her nearly white hair, even the rise of her ears were all distinct. The lack of wings was her greatest disservice. But the Prophecy was very detailed in the fact that this child would be human. Furthermore, there was no way that a faery could have fáthaired her. The shimmer had only just begun thinning, and until recently, it could not be passed through at all. Still, the coincidence of her looks whispered in his raised ears.

He continued to watch her for a while. Her sleep was peaceful though she had already been through so much. Much more than any young one should have had too. This was something that he had not seen for a while, innocence. Actual innocence as it was meant to be. Faerylings here were so rare, only a few had been born in the last twenty years. They were protected and sheltered in an attempt to keep them safe. Seeing the peace of this child, affected him in a way that he could not have imagined.

He knew that his life had become hardened by the constant battle. That was not to say that he could not enjoy the good things in life. It was only that they were so rare, far and in between. He felt a sudden twinge in his middle, his gut clenching in an unfamiliar sensation. It came from within and was as foreign to him as these humans. It provoked within him, a need to protect. He startled at the realization. He had never felt anything so strong before. The emotion, *consuming.* The child had to be responsible for it, there was no other explanation. She had the ability to free his Kind from the evil that they had been fighting for so long, that no one even remembered what it was like before the Darke. Yet, even for all his devotion to the Leight, he had no idea how one child, one so small, was going to face the Darke and free them from their imprisonment. He knew that his obedience was to the Creator, he only prayed that the way would be shown, for he was still unsure of where that path was leading. *He knew that it was only his faith that was required, but still, it would be nice to have a little more insight into the process.* He silently laughed at himself. *Here he was, acting like a human. Impatient!*

He sat with his thoughts a while longer, wondering what the future held in store for them when he noticed the child turn in her sleep. She cried out suddenly, incoherent words from her sleep glazed mind. She then called out for her máthair, seeking comfort. Before he realized what he had done, he had crossed the room and offered his hand to the sleeping child. She pulled it close to her face and snuggled back in. He actually felt a shudder ripple through his being. His heart, something that had never truly been touched, thawed and in its place…was her, *her essence.*

The shock of it sent waves of amazement rocketing through his warrior's body. This child had to be of strong faery magick to reach a place that was only reserved for his own Kind. *She had found a way into his heart. In less than the span of a heartbeat, he realized that he had fallen in love with the child.* He knew then, that it would be his duty to insure that she succeeded in her destiny. He stayed close for a while longer. With her falling back into a deep slumber, he freed his hand and pulled her covers up to her chin. He would insure that she succeeded . . . and he would make sure that she survived...

Vigilance
(5)

By the next morning, word reached Gable that the Stronghold of SosallEe was in danger of falling. SosallEe was a main waterway Stronghold. Water had a powerful magick, and losing it to the Dark*e* would be devastating. Several fa*e*ry were discovered to have been infected with the Dark*e*. Gable prepared his men as they might be needed to defend the Keep in the event that the dark*e* fa*e*ry arrived before the cleansing was finished. This was the break that they needed. If they could defeat the plague before the dark*e* ones arrived, there would be a huge possibility of saving many lives. Gable was finishing the packing of his battle gear when CalOwAy knocked on his chamber door.

"Come in."

"I have heard the news. You called for me?"

"I need you to keep things in order here while I am away. If your services are needed, I will send the others here to you. How are the other ArtimA doing in their preparations for Caitrin?"

"Well. In our enthusiasm, I must admit that we have jumped quite quickly into the Archives. Much of the text is viable. It has only been a short span since the last time it was revised and there are only a few things that will have to be adapted to suit her."

"That is excellent news! While I am away, I want you to talk to the child. Try to gain her trust. I have explained a little to her, but I did not want to rush into things and frighten her. I need you to try and gain her confidence. If you can start training while I am away, it will help me immensely when I return and begin to instruct her in battle."

"I will do as you ask. What about the other, the máthair? I have checked on her myself. The healing was done well. It will offer her several advantages to normal human healing but, her condition is still not the best of circumstances."

"Continue your vigilance. I have complete trust in you CalOwAy. We will discuss more when I return. I hope to be gone no more than a few days. I think time will be on our side for once. I leave now; the others are ready as well." Gable replied, as he placed his sword in his scabbard and finished his instructions.

CalOwAy stared at the warrior that he had known since fa*e*ryhood. He was the full definition of a Fa*e*ry Warrior. What all young warriors envisioned being one day. There was no doubt to the terror he could inflict if necessary. CalOwAy only felt pity for those that had to be stared down, when those eyes became cold and violate. Evil should have no chance in the presence of Gable. He might have been an avenging Ang*e*l. But CalOwAy wished that it was only so easy.

"Return safely Gable. May the Creator be with you."

"Hé always is." He replied as he walked out the door, his faith and confidence squaring his shoulders.

* * * * * * *

They road hard, needing to cover as much ground as they could. There was a chance, a slim one, that they could make a difference this time. If they could only get there fast enough, they might be able to stop the death of thousands. It was a hard day of travel, nearly twenty-three hours nonstop to reach the end of their course. Gable looked around him. He had brought one hundred warriors with him through the shimmer, another hundred were to meet with them at SosallEe. They had the advantage. They were going to use it. The ride was long, but something they were used too. The signal was given and the two groups converged onto covered ground, shortly away from the shimmers entrance. Most of the area was open ground and water, so they had to come through in a condensed area of hills and tall wild grasses.

"TazaRine, how do things look?"

"From all signs, the Stronghold is still solid. Our warriors are on the walls, the all clear posted on the pennants. DariEan is approaching now, we will have the signal any moment to approach or prepare for battle." They didn't have long to wait.

A long, drawn out whistle, holding a whip at the end, heralded the faery to enter safely by DariEan's command, the Guardian of the forces here. Gable road out at the front of the others, to meet the ruling family at the gate. From his vantage, he could make out the confines of the Keep. The Keep was much smaller than his own, but the beauty and comfort were still very much evident.

"Welcome Gable, it is unfortunate that it is under such circumstances." DariEan, joined by Etinnin, the Overseer of SosallEe said.

Gable nodded in acknowledgment to DariEan. "What are the circumstances? I still do not have a full understanding of what we are facing here."

"I will explain." Etinnin took the lead as they walked around the Keep.

"Two days ago, word was sent to us of a family on the outskirts who were acting strangely. They had holed up in their cottage, refusing visitors. A neighbor thought them sick and sent for the ArtimA to come and help. They refused her entrance as well. It was then that it was brought to my attention. We took no chances; several of the warriors entered the cottage by force. That was how we found them; there were three of them by then. All infected with the Darke plague. Another had apparently joined them in the previous hours."

"What have you done with them?" Gable asked.

"They were quarantined to a cottage a little ways closer. The other one was burned. No one was allowed in and no one out. We know that the infected do not require food and water the same as us, so we allowed no entrance. No fear of spreading the plague."

"You did well. My warriors will attend to this now. What of others, have any others been detected or suspected?"

"I called a census as soon as we realized. All have been accounted for except for several that are away at this time."

"Excellent! Take me to the cottage." They moved quickly, leaving the confines of the inner Keep walls.

*

They wasted no time, arriving at the cottage in little less than an hour. Gable was impressed by the care and precautions that Etinnin had taken. The cottage was surrounded by two concentric sets of guards, eight in all. The first circle had four posted at the four directions, then next, had four posted at the corners, a tightly knit knot on two separate levels. They stood back only shortly, as we approached.

"How do you wish to precede Gable?" TazaRine asked.

"Directly. Trying to question that first two will be worthless, as we have learned in the past. However the one that is newly changed, he may yet have retained enough of himself to answer our questions. We take the least violent attempt first."

The door was unbolted, the light allowed to shine into the darkened room. Gable could make out the three tied to chairs, secured in their imprisonment. "Bring me the one who was changed last." Etinnin pointed him out to TazaRine, and the faery was quickly brought before him. Gable studied him carefully. He was definitely fresh. His skin pale, but his hair still a shade of auburn and his eyes, not yet changed from their blue hue. But the wings were showing, a darkened gray tinge beginning to wash through them. "What is his name?"

"SaInE." Etinnin said.

"SaInE, are you able to understand me? Do you know what is happening to you?" The faery was shaking, he kept his head bowed low, avoiding the contact of eyes. Gable was preparing to ask him again, when a sound drew his attention.

"Yes . . ."

"Are you still able to feel the leight?"

"I feel it, feel it draining from me." He looked up then, the blue of his eyes, already dimmer than they had been moments before. "You must kill me, I will not suffer this plague on anyone else."

"Do you know what happened? How it was brought here?"

He groaned for a moment, apparently lost. "It burns as it travels and slithers threw the skin, it burns like fire through the veins and blood." He went back to moaning and Gable gave him another moment, his body beginning to shake, as if cold. "It was the female. She was suffering. Her mind was ill at ease. It had been ever since her young one was taken from her, nearly six years ago."

"In the morning, several days ago, she went down to the river, alone. When she came back, there was something wrong. But her mate was not sure what. He commented on it to me that evening. Then I returned yesterday and . . . something was very wrong . . . not even close." His words losing some of their fire from before. "I could tell right away, but they attacked. Then, the next thing I knew, I was burning . . . the fire horrendous! Now you see, here I am. Death . . ." His words hung there, his head returning to its downcast position.

The horror of the truth faced them and there was nothing anyone could say.

"SaInE?" Gable started. The faery did not lift his head. "SaInE?" He tried to question again. A rattling sound came in waves as the faery began to shake worse. Suddenly, he lifted his head, his eyes closed. The rattling stopped, and his eyes opened. Gone was the blue, the brilliance. Instead, deep black pupils stared back at him, the leight gone from view.

A twisted smile formed on Its lips. Before It could utter a word, the slice of TazaRine's blade removed Its head from Its shoulders. A silent prayer, said for the loss. Gable looked up and faced those around him. "Finish the others, we head to the river."

*

The search of the river left more questions than answers. As they looked, night began to fall and Gable called a halt to their progress. They had traveled up and down both sides of the water, the only thing drawing their attention was a patch of earth, scorched and blackened, the wind, holding the smell of char and sulfur. Nothing else remained. The blackness lead up to the river's edge, a slight smell of ash still lingering as the rest was washed away in the evening breeze.

"What does this mean?" Etinnin asked.

"That someone knew we were coming. Whatever was here has already been destroyed. This was probably done no more than a few hours past." Gable turned to search for Etinnin. "Was there anyone new here? Anyone that was not easily identified?"

"No one that brought any attention upon themselves. I am sorry that I cannot offer you more."

"That cannot be helped; however, this is something that you are going to need to keep an eye on. They might still be within the area. They have failed and it will not set well. They may attempt again. I will ensure that extra warriors will be stationed here. I want the ArtimA called. This area needs to be cleansed. Sentinels posted, no one is to be alone at any time. We will proceed forward in the morning."

"Understood." TazaRine spoke up. Etinnin nodding in agreement.

*

They rode back to the Keep at a brisk pace, many possibilities were running through Gable's mind. They had been so close. They might have even unlocked a secret of the plague, but he was not sure yet. They would need to discuss their findings. Was there some clue in the earth, the location, or even in the remaining odor? Frustrated, Gable shook his head.

The ArtimA were made aware of what was needed of them, a blessing done over the area, a cleansing in the morning soon enough for that call. They returned to the Keep, a large cleansing for them all in order now. The ArtimA came and the blessing progressed quickly. Alongside were prayers said for the dead and remembrances. The evening was a solemn affair, though a celebration of their success was also in order. Food and rest, for tomorrow they would search the waterways before returning home. Another long travel to reach home once they could confirm no other darke resided here.

* * * * * * *

Much was done in his absence with CalOwAy and the TA Archers working together to complete the text and begin instructing. Caitrin was nervous, but quickly the magick of the learning swept her up and she took her place with them.

* * * * * * *

Gable's entire absence and return was within four days' time. The sun shined down to announce their victory, something that had not been felt or seen in a long while. He looked out over his Kind, seeing their pride and their thanks. He was able to bring back all of his warriors this time. There would be no grieving families, no sadness here. He smiled to himself. The coming of the Savior had indeed brought luck and hopefully, some prosperity to his Kind. Pulling upon the reins of Batal'Agar, he stopped his battle steed to address them all.

"We defeated the Darke before it had a true chance to take hold at SosallEe. The darke ones had not even had a chance to attack the Stronghold before we arrived. The only ones to fall where those that were discovered to have been infected with the plague, they were destroyed to keep it from spreading. We will celebrate this evening with a feast. Then, I want my warriors to go home to their families and celebrate. This is an evening of honor and thanks to the Creator."

He looked around at the glowing faces. "We shall continue to be victorious." He threw his hands up in the air, their battle cry ripping out through the night, his warriors repeating the cry in the glory of their success.

Pulling on his reins, he headed toward RandelfSon, who offered to take care of his steed.

He slid down. His feet making contact with his own earth and he offered a prayer to the Creator for bringing them all home safely. He ached, everywhere, and his stomach growled out in its need for sustenance. He could feel the grime of his hard riding, as it covered his skin and clothing. *He wanted a warm bath; he wanted hot food and a strong cold drink. What he wanted more . . .* he stopped at his own thoughts, for they were . . . *unusual. The need he felt was to see her. To make sure that she was alright and adjusting well. It . . it was just that so much depended on her.* He thought to himself. He told himself. Shaking off the depth of awareness that passed through him.

He turned to RandelfSon and Batal'Agar, even his horse would need a good washing and rub down after their latest events. He would get his extra share tonight. He offered him praise, giving him a brisk rub behind the ears. His very life could depend on the ability of his steed, this he understood and took in all seriousness.

"I want him given his extra share tonight. A big bucket of carrots, his coat is to be brushed till it shines in beauty. He has done well and deserves the honor." He handed over the reins. RandelfSon nodded in agreement. Turning, he headed toward the Keep. Gable knew that as the evening wore down, he would need to take time to find his own peace. He pushed the thoughts of the girl from his mind. He would go, *eventually.* Soon enough though, he would have to search out CalOwAy and see how things had gone in his absence. His assumption was that all had been well, because he knew that the Elder would have been right at the gate to meet him, if otherwise. Rest was what he longed for. After the celebration, he would make sure he got what his body required.

ɔC

. . . the fire burned like a brand. A languid rush of flames and heat. I felt the burn, the liquid caress. I was flames. It swelled and rushed. Consuming and magnificent. What had once been calm was now a tempest. Every aspect, every atom, burned and longed for more. It grew, it swelled and ruptured. Pleasure, heat, more and more. Growing and smothering me in the fires of passion. Washing away all else. Only flames . . .

Destiny
(6)

The new morning rose as Gable walked steadily toward the practice field. It had been a week since his return. And it had been seven mornings of awaking to dreams of her. The mysterious temptress that called to his soul and made his body burn with need. *He couldn't understand what was happening to him. Why he was being tortured in this way?* His body was suffering as much as his soul and to be honest, he was looking forward to the chance to burn off his tension on the fields today.

Today was to be Caitrin's initiation into the arena of combat, the tiny child following closely behind him. He had to look over his shoulder to make sure that she was still there. For one so young, she was too quiet! This he quickly realized, would be a great advantage in a warrior, but getting her there, he could not see that happening as of yet.

"Gable," a voice shouted out, "could I have a few moments of ye time?"

Looking over, Gable saw ZackaRAy approaching. They had been friends since faeryhood; one would say the "best of friends." They had grown together, worked together and now, as his First-in-Command; they ruled and protected their Kind together. Their only basic difference was ZackaRAy's beautiful mate, and the fact that Gable had none; the one true thing in his life that he could be envious of, but he was not. He only wished the best for his fellow brother.

"All of thee preparations have been finished. Thee new swords were completed yesterday and await ye inspection in thee armory. I had them make a slightly smaller than normal version for thee lass." He added as an afterthought. "Because of her size."

"Excellent, ZackaRAy. The others are already waiting for us. Caitrin," he began as he noticed her small form slipping through the armory door, "is ready. She has had a fair amount of basic instruction from the TA Archers now. She should be ready to begin incorporating the spells into our lessons for her."

"How have her lessons been goin'? I know that she tis thee One, but I still be havin' trouble acknowledgin' it when she tis na taller than ma knees." ZackaRAy said.

"I understand what you mean. I cannot even picture us on the field, hacking away at her with swords, when she is no more than that." Gable said, shaking his head. "I feel like I could break her with my little finger . . . if I tried." The imagery was not pleasant and it settled hard in the pit of his stomach.

ZackaRAy had followed his gaze, the mere slip of a girl disappearing. "She will surprise us, tha tis thee only answer. It tis her destiny; she was made for thee task. We will no be disappointed." Both turned, as they began heading in her direction. Soon enough, they would see exactly how she handled herself.

*

Caitrin walked up to the wooden building. They had called it an armory. It was a funny word. Gable had told her that the warriors were going to meet there, that they were only waiting for one more to show. Now, Gable was busy talking to the other faery. She got closer to the door and decided that she would go ahead and wait for them inside. The wind had picked up and her hair kept blowing into her eyes. *Boy did she hate that!* As she pushed the door open, she noticed that there already was a couple of faery here. They were tall; she had to pull her head all the way back, just to see their faces. She noticed that they all looked tough; she could tell this because of how big they were, just like Gable. But she knew that she had nothing to worry about, she already knew that they would like her.

"Hello." She piped up. "I'm Caitrin. Who are all of you?"

They turned in unison. All startled by the tinkling voice, that held a velvet command. Immediately their heads swung downward. Eyebrows raised and lips quirked at the tiny child in front of them. TazaRine stepped forward, bended down on one knee and offered his hand to Caitrin.

"Good day. I am TazaRine. This," he nodded to the faery behind, "is StarEnen and JAcolene. We are part of the Alphinian Guardians. We are glad to finally meet you, little One."

Caitrin's whole hand circled a single large finger, which she shook. Then, without further thought, she through her arms around his neck and offered him a hug. He was shocked by the sudden, unexplained gesture and caught himself before he tipped backwards. He could hear the others guffawing as they fought back laughter. Quickly he patted her on the back, in an awkward fashion, and set her back on the ground.

She jumped back, at this point the room offering much more than the faery to her curiosity. After a few moments of their curious stares, they too turned back to their own conversation. She quickly became engrossed in the fascinating things that were stored within the building. She did not touch, she knew better. Soon though she came upon a table with wooden swords laid upon it. Looking over her shoulder, she saw that the others were still paying her no attention, so she reached up and traced her hand over a wooden handle.

Checking again, she took hold of the smaller sword and gripped the handle tightly. The wood warmed to her touch and for just a brief moment, she could have sworn that the swirls of the grain moved on their own. But she only shook her head and then gave it a small swipe, careful to keep it close, to keep from drawing attention to herself. Could feel the swish of air across her face as the movement created a breeze, liking how it felt. Smiling and trying again, this time coming in from the opposite direction. She laughed, and then quickly looked behind her to make sure no one had noticed her antics. *"She just had a way of getting into trouble."* As her máthair always said.

She decided that she wanted to do more. Looking over, she saw the large metal swords that the warriors carried. They would know how to use them, they could show her. Walking quickly, but quietly, she approached TazaRine and the others. They were busy in conversation. Speaking, her voice quieter than before, knowing that there was a good possibility that she would get in trouble for having the sword itself.

"Excuse me, TazaRine?" She said.

He did not respond. Her words had been so low. Bracing herself for courage, she spoke up again. "TazaRine?" Still he did not respond. "TazaRine?" She said as a command. This time, a response was met. Quickly StarEnen looked down, as her words reached his ears and he attempted to answer her query. She turned her attention towards him instead, her movements now pulling to the right, the sword in her hands following her motions smoothly. Unfortunately, TazaRine had finally heard her as well. He turned to acknowledge her at the same time that she turned to StarEnen, and a collision began. As TazaRine turned, Caitrin's sword caught him, full force, behind the knees. She could hear him swear as he started going down.

"Bloody Hell!" Came the reply from TazaRine, as his long legs were swept out from under him. He tried to compensate, but the actions were useless. The movement only made the results worse. As he went down, he felt his back come in contact with something solid and knew that StarEnen was quickly on his way down as well. He had no time to react, the collision so quick. In the blink of an eye, there was a flourish of movement. The collision to his chest was like being hit with a small boulder. The air knocked from his lungs as he continued the cycle backwards.

The creaking door announced Gable's entrance into the room, followed closely by ZackaRAy; just as the two falling warriors ended their assault by their two sets of tree stump thick legs, knocking JAcolene's out from under him. JAcolene had watched, had known it was coming, but still the shock of it had been too much. The combined force of the nearly dead weight from the two warriors was too much for him to push back against. As the three fell, a pile of arms, legs and heads were all that were visible. Gable quickly swinging his attention back to Caitrin.

She was the only one left standing, wooden sword gripped tightly in both hands, pointed at the fallen ones. She looked down at the sword, the same time as him. Looking back up quickly, so did he. She pulled the sword behind her back, trying to smile in an innocent fashion, guilt plainly written across her face.

Gable took in the view in front of him. He did not know whether he should laugh or shout. How one little human, with no wings, could have managed to get three of his best warriors, flat on their backs, was an answer he greatly wanted to know. But the look on her face spoke volumes. So he let the laughter some instead. It rolled through his chest, the explosion causing tears to begin to flow. *They would never live it down.* He thought to himself and the laughter became all the harder.

"What thee . . ." Was all he heard, coming behind him from ZackaRAy. A moment later, ZackaRAy broke out in his own riotous laughter. After he got control of himself, he slapped Gable on the shoulder. "And you thought tha we were goin' ta have a problem. At this rate, thee wee one will have thee rest of thee Guardians on their knees in na time. And thee Dark*e*," he was forced to cough, in order to continue speaking, "they will have na idea what hit them! Apparently, na one here did!" He began laughing again, the humorous situation too much to pass up, the warriors on the ground, groaning as they attempted to untangle themselves; debating if it was even worth the effort at this point. Pride could be a truly painful thing, including a couple of bruised backsides! Caitrin finally broke down in laughter as well, knowing that no punishment was on its way.

* * * * * * *

Sleep eluded him, so his trip to the Atrium was a search for answers. Gable knew that he would not receive any. But he thought that sitting there, studying the silent human, maybe something would come to him and it offered him some reprieve. The night was wearing thin. Morning would soon be showing her glorious face to the east.

Since his return two weeks prior, he had taken the time to study the child and she fascinated him. Her training in combat was being handled by himself, ZackaRAy and TazaRine. In truth, they were the three greatest fa*e*ry warriors. She was pushing past any limits set for her. As hard as it was to believe, Gable was actually astonished at Caitrin's ability with the sword. She would be . . . he was not sure of the right word, but "*intimidating*" actually came to the surface of his thoughts, before he pushed it back down again. He would have to wait a little longer, before he came to that consideration for her.

It seemed like once she had picked the sword up, she had not wanted to put it back down. She was a natural. She was moving through the routines quickly; all those watching were astounded at the sight of the small child, holding her own against the towering giants. But this was not what was bothering him. It was her other training that was presenting an issue. CalOwAy had seen to the responsibility of her instruction in magick and its application, using his resources to make the progress easier for the TA Archers to teach her. She was keeping up with their lessons, but she was not excelling. The insight and depth that she should have for the knowledge that she was learning, was lacking. She should have been able to surpass all of them, but she could not. This was a constant strain on all of their carefully planned training.

CalOwAy felt that the setbacks were coming from her missing her máthair. She was now worried about her máthair's absence and fear had started to settle in. It was interfering with her ability to reason. You could see her holding back, holding out. Be it worry or fear. It was causing complications that there was not enough time to deal with. This was all so new to her, the differences between man and faery, that extreme. Fortunately, she had been raised with a very steady background. It appeared at least that her máthair had been unusual, had cared more, been more than the common human. Caitrin was at last, finding that she belonged here. But the fear, it was holding her progress back.

When her day went well and she did well, she would talk to him of herself, of her máthair. She would tell him stories of the máthair that she loved. The woman that he now saw was totally devoted to her daughter. Caitrin, though young, had a mind that was sharp. Her ability to communicate with others was well advanced. She fascinated and she captivated. It was not just the fact that she was a child anymore. Nor was it the fact that she was the Savior. It was the simple fact that good radiated from her. It seemed at times, that it glowed from within her, leightening her features and pose. But still, it was surpassed by the fear and longing for her máthair. She was being held back and that interfered with everything that they were striving for.

He sat in the chair beside Angel's bed. The news from the ArtimA was still unsatisfactory. Her body was making some attempts at healing on its own, but nowhere near what would have been accomplished if she were faery. Her body was now covered in a less dense scar tissue. The skin gone, left behind was a withered flesh that was a dull red and rough. The healing had softened it, somewhat. The damage would have been more severe, but even with what she now had, life for her when she awakened was going to be a struggle. The pain, disfigurement, he was not sure if she would be able to handle it.

Her mind had not yet chosen to return, though she continued to hold on to life. They had told him that so severe was her pain, that it would be a blessing to her, if her life force had simply left her in the healing, that they could guide her essence in that direction. This they could offer her. This he could not allow, if for no other reason than she willed herself to remain alive this long. There had to be a reason for her struggle and he would see it through to the end. Whether it was life or death at that end, he was not sure. Her ability to survive was drawing him in. Was forging a bond between them that was . . . *mystifying!*

Drifting
(7)

Another night was wearing thin as Gable made his way once again to the Atrium. It was crazy, true madness that drew him here every night. *Why? Why was he so obsessed with this woman, with the Chosen One's máthair? Other aspects of his life were much the same as before, but not this. His days with the child were progressing.* He thought of Caitrin. *A child in general was rare here, so her ability to captivate those around her did not really surprise him. The most surprising change had come from RandelfSon.* He thought now of the day that RandelfSon had come to them. He remembered it like yesterday; because it was about the only time he had ever heard the older faery speak . . .

He had been in faeryhood, relaxing his fáthairs study, listening to his fáthairs words of times past, when RandelfSon had entered, explaining his reasons for coming to Ainys'Dai.

"I am not able to offer much anymore . . ." RandelfSon had begun.

"You have been through a terrible ordeal RandelfSon; there is no need to explain. You are welcome here." Jach'niél, Gable's fáthair, had said.

"Much of us have been through a terrible ordeal . . ." He finished with a queer type of laughter. He tried to compose himself, but Jach'niél saw that even this was beyond him now.

"There is more to my story than you understand . . . my . . ." He shook his head. " . . . I lived through it . . . I survived . . ." He began again. But his words were lost. Whatever it was caused agony like Gable had never seen before, to pass across RandelfSon's face. But the words were not to be, so Jach'niél had pushed past the painful moment.

"Say no more. I can see your torment. It comes off of you in great waves. There is no need to add anything else. You are welcome here as long as you have need. You will have the right to remain to yourself. I have been told that you have a way with the animals. You may call the Keep's barn and them, home from now on."

There were tears in his eyes, as RandelfSon had nodded to Jach'niél. Gable had not said a word during the odd exchange.

The words that had needed speaking, would not come, even as hard as RandelfSon had tried to utter them, finally he had turned and left the room, his form . . . *broken.*

*

The old faery had now long lived within the walls of Ainys'Dai, far too many years to count. The death of RandelfSon's remaining family by the Darkness and the fall of his Stronghold had been too much for him to bear.

The torment of the encounter had traumatized him. The ArtimA had done a blessing for him, offering him as much release from the torment of his soul as possible. It allowed him to maintain some semblance of a life, even though he merely existed. However, the ArtimA had let Jach'niél know that RandelfSon's mind was no longer right. It was as damaged as if a physical blow had been made. They had no idea if time could heal the wound, but they were doubtful. "Some things," they had told him, "were just too broken to be repaired."

Even with these many years, he had not recovered. He still avoided others and gatherings. His ability to communicate and relate with others was something he no longer seemed capable of doing, or wanting to do. It seemed that as long as he was left alone, he did well enough on his own. He even chose to rest away from the Keeps chambers. He had retreated into an older section of the Stronghold, taking up residence in a chamber from the Old Temple. Solitude seemed to be all he sought, and he bore his suffering in silence.

But the arrival of Caitrin had changed that. He had taken to her immediately. He had even developed a comfortable relationship with her and it was common for him to be in her company, though in the evenings the large groups of fa*ery* in the Hall always seemed to push him out. Maybe Caitrin would be able to bring RandelfSon back from the seclusion that he had maintained for so many years. Even at Caitrin's young age, she was able to connect with others, bringing out the best in them.

* * * * * * *

Angel's room was not dark upon entering. Candles had been left to burn as well as a lite fire in the fireplace. The room was full of the smell of healing incense, the lavender immediately making Gable feel more peaceful and relaxed. Though her damage was severe to his eyes and heart, the room did not smell of human waste, as was prone in sick rooms. The impure humors having been pushed out of the room by the magick of the ArtimA.

A healing circle had been placed upon the floor, around her bed, the magick contained within it, a slight glow, which was visible to his fa*ery* eyes. He knew that it prevented any contamination from reaching her and causing infection and disease. Her already weakened body was safe, at least from that. She had quickly become a kind of obsession for him, though he could not say why. Her strength was indomitable. This alone, had to be the driving force that was drawing him to her. It had to be!

Ɔ*

. . . The surrounding lights. The mist of bright. Thoughts, imagines, they invaded, pushed at me. Concepts of life and pain. . . . my adopted parents! I

screamed out in my fear, in the horror of their memories. They'd taken so much from me when they'd taken me in after the death of my parents. They'd driven all of the creativity, all of the life from me, purging my "delusions." The abuse, the silent torture that they had forced me to endure had all been in an attempt to create the perfect daughter, the daughter that they had never been able to have themselves. My ability to live in the magickal world of my imagination had infuriated them. Their lives had been steeped in the rational and the "down to earth." As if they'd really known what that'd even meant!

The first memory of my life with them was that of Sherry, my adopted mother. Her face was pressed close to mine, saying "Angel, you were coping. Coping by escaping into your imagination to deal with the death of your parents, living in these worlds that you create in your head, it's not right! You are not healthy!" So it had begun. Their goal in life was to drain me of my obsession, to heal me. They had succeeded. The next memory I had begun months later, after my sessions had ended. What did they care if I could not remember my real parents, it only made them all the happier . . .

. . . happiness? I'd never known happiness until Caitrin . . .

⊃C

Gable gazed around him, he had thought, for a moment, that he had heard something. But apparently his ears played tricks on him. He looked down at her, the sight of her ravaged flesh made his insides shudder. She was all angry flesh now, the red now pinks, replacing the peach of the flesh. A second session with the ArtimA had insured that the tissue that now grew was softer, less severe, and it had been a success. The last couple of weeks had proven that. He feared for her when she awakened. The torment she would go through. It brought him sorrow, the depth of it shocking him.

He could rationalize his emotions for the daughter, but for her? *It made no sense.* And the depth at which he was feeling them? This made no sense at all. This was foreign, *strange.* These could not be his emotions, it was impossible! Though Faery were of the Leight, the depth and range of the emotions they experienced only went truly deep when it was their family that they were encountering. This was a special bond that all Faery had in common. The unexplained feelings confused him. They clouded his thoughts and reasoning's. All that he could do was bring the emotions back to Caitrin. This he grasped on to, as a light appeared to go on in his thoughts.

He grasped at it and held tight. *It was the child of course!* He visibly sighed in relief. *He had developed feelings for the child. These feelings he must have unconsciously related to the máthair.* No matter the reason, he owed it to this woman for bringing the life of the Savior about. For this, he would come and sit and if possible, offer comfort. If she could feel it?

* * * * * * *

His days began to pass much in a similar fashion. During the morning hours, he dedicated his time to running the Stronghold. Going over ledgers, making sure the harvest was completed and ensuring that there would be plenty of necessities should they need it in the winter months. Come afternoon, he would check on the progress of Caitrin and teach her skills that would keep her safe in the battle to come. By the evening, he would have eaten and headed to the Atrium, to the silent listener, she that never complained if he said more than he actually needed too. He found that having someone he could tell anything and everything too and not have to worry about a response, was indeed a respite for his soul. A benefit he had not realized that he had actually needed. He poured out his sorrows, his unspoken fears and finally found a refuge for his years of loneliness. He relaxed as his mind drifted and his voice, like velvet, spoke of that very days passing . . .

ƆC

The assault came again . . .

I no longer felt like a person. I began existing, always responding to them with what they wanted to hear. Never giving them a reason to question or draw unwanted attention to myself. An illusion to the child they wanted. At least

I tried, for a long time. But I couldn't keep it up any longer. So I'd escaped. What did one do at seventeen and on the run? I'd cleaned out my college fund, rightly the money I had been left by my deceased parents. I'd taken it and run. Walking out the door and never looking back. I disappeared without a trace, or so I'd thought. After being away, I'd started to finally live . . .

. . . The pain began fading . . .

. . . "What was the point of this?" I cried out into the nothingness. "What did all of these mean?" And I sighed back into nothingness once more.

⊃C

Gable paused for a brief moment; he had been sure that he had heard the whispering of words this time. But nothing else followed. Shaking his head, he continued on in his litany.

⊃C

Swirling, returning to the time and place . . . I could feel time pass, as if in a loop, again and again and again . . .

It came from around, nudging at my senses. It was like I was in a room with no walls, but boundaries all the same. I could hear, but not fully understand, that someone had begun speaking. Realizing that it seemed to come from nowhere and everywhere at the same time was confusing and though it should have bothered me, it didn't. The voice came from outside. It was strong, but it soothed more than anything. It seemed to me, that it was offering power and peace at the same time. For some reason, this gave me hope.

The lights swept me up, embraced and cradled me.

ↄC

Several days passed, when RandelfSon noticed that Caitrin walked through the courtyard. She was a bit distracted, more so it appeared, a bit frustrated. She was all innocence, so pure and sweet. He could feel himself being pulled toward her, feel the disillusionment of his own soul as it sought out her Leight, her inner beauty. He knew what he had to do . . .

. . . *he heard it.* He felt it more, a scream of rage that echoed throughout his mind and body. It seemed to pierce the night. He jumped up, as if to respond to the anger and fear, when he noticed that no one else seemed to hear it. He shook his head to clear it. It was only his mind playing tricks on him. He knew what he had to do. She was the answer, with her little pixie features turned up toward the warm and fading sunlight. Her Leight would free them all. It would free him.

*

Caitrin stared out at the courtyard around her. It was a bustle of activity as the evening approached and those of them were preparing for the evening meal. She had worked hard today. Her head still ached from the amount of thought that she had put into remembering all she'd been taught. But through it all, she had felt their disappointment. None so much as Gable's though. She wasn't sure what she was doing wrong, but she knew that it was something, for their upset had settled upon her shoulders, and it weighed heavily. She had come to care for them here, especially Gable. Her feelings for him grew, though he hid his well. To know that she was causing them this and to not know why, hurt her. They had taken her in after the accident and she knew that they cared for her máthair who was still too sick for her to see.

Gable had taken her aside when she'd first arrived and explained to her that she was special. He had said that, *"she had a gift, was a gift, to end the long struggles that they had suffered for so long, that they would teach her to discover her power and the ability to use it, to be complete within herself."*

She thought that she was doing well. They were so different here. She could do things now that could only be done by the people in her Máthair's stories. They were magick, real magick all wrapped up in real life. But still, they were not happy. She didn't want to make them sad. She tried very hard and did all that they asked, even if they asked a lot more than her Máthair ever had. They had not let her see it, but she knew. Just like she always did.

"Humph!" she said as she rolled her shoulders and closed her eyes. She dropped down to sit on the step in front of her. Her shoulders lowered in dejection. This was all very frustrating. She didn't like how it felt one bit. Giving up, she watched as the Pixies came out to play.

As the evening light wore down, the Pixies would show up, their tiny bodies all aglow with their inner leight. They resided in the trees within the courtyard. As they took their places amongst the leaves, they showered the pathways in iridescence and made the trees appear as if Christmas time had come. This was her favorite time of the day. They would dance, play and entertain. She started to giggle, until she noticed the shadow fall over her.

"What is wrong with my Moonbeam?" The voice asked in a soothing nature. Gone was the hoarseness it had once held.

Caitrin looked up and smiled. No matter how hard she tried to hide her sorrow, RandelfSon always saw through it. He had become her constant companion, as she knew he was meant to be. He could always make her smile. His nickname for her usually did the trick. It was funny. He had said that she was not Sunshine, for her hair was too white, too silver. So Moonbeam had stuck.

"I'm just having a bad day." She said with a quick smile, it not quite reaching her eyes.

"You cannot fool me. I can see that you are upset. Who has done this to you?"

*

He was not the only one who had noticed her . . .

As he looked out his window, Gable noticed that Caitrin had taken a familiar seat amongst the Pixie Trees in the courtyard and he smiled. A *"place of reflection,"* most called it. To him, it looked like a *"place of escape,"* for her today. Seeing her forlorn, he thought to go and see her . . . to bring a smile to her features, before he turned away at the sight of RandelfSon's arrival. *"Another time."* He thought.

*

Caitrin knew it was better to just tell him, if not, he would pester her for the rest of the evening. "I'm making the TA Archers upset. But I have no idea what I'm doing wrong?"

"Is that all it is? Then you have nothing to worry about. They should be worrying, they that just cannot seem to get it right. There is no need for you worry. You are the answer and that is all there is to it. Everything will work out alright in the end. Just you wait and see."

She smiled at him. This time, some of the sadness in her eyes was for him as well. Sometimes he spoke like this, like there was something that she should know, but didn't. But she was not the only one who thought so. He was different. The others stayed away from him and him from them. But she was unusual, and it drew him to her. She had been reserved in the beginning. His mind was unique, even in ways that the others could not see. She was not sure how she knew this, only that it was something she was able to do. To see truth. But the indecision had only lasted moments.

It was like he wore two masks. The first one she loved, was always kind with an innocence of youth. The second was more intense, as though there was always something hidden within. She liked his long silver hair and the smile that lit up his face when she said something that made him laugh. He was unusual and unlike the other faery here. He wore his age, as none of the others did. Though the others were old, some even older than himself, they all still appeared youthful. Their essence announced their true ages. But he was old. The vibrancy and leight, dimmed. It felt strange, knowing things that the others didn't and understanding things that she knew she shouldn't. She knew that it had made people uncomfortable around her, but here, she was not so different. Not so unusual. Here she belonged more than before.

Inside of RandelfSon was a secret, something that he shared with no one. Quickly though, she had learned that she could trust him, that he would never harm her. On nights like this, he would offer her a tÁle or a sweet treat. She was the only one he shared anything with, him and her and the animals.

"Will you tell me a story tonight? Yours are always the best!" She said with a smile, knowing that he would respond in kind to her request.

"Of course mine are the best!" He said, a smile lighting his features, a quick twinkle in his eyes, some of the sorrow diminishing. "Tonight, I will tell you of the Elf who did not listen to his Elders." He began his tÁle. Caitrin climbing up onto his lap to listen, his arms resting around her comfortably, as if she had always belonged there. Only the Pixies in the trees saw the devotion and the sudden intensity that flared in RandelfSon's eyes as he began to tell his tÁle.

Time
(8)

Time seemed to take on a life of its own as the days sped by and soon, months had passed from the first time Caitrin had crossed the southern gate. The training of Caitrin's magick was going slowly, though she showed that she would have amazing abilities one day. But that was in the far future. Now, her abilities were . . . normal, slow, developing. No amount of manipulation had been able to progress her further than where she was. So they had merely maintained what they had already been doing.

The range of magick that had been involved in the circle that had saved her life was just not present. Gable had gone to speak with the TA Archers of his own findings. They had agreed that her progress was not moving as quickly as they had anticipated, or hoped. But they had also offered him reasons, valid ones. He thought back on their words . . .

AriEsan had come to Caitrin's defense quickly. He had said that, "...in the event of the terror of that night, she might have released the magick unknowingly. This could have caused confusion and setbacks to her development, because she had not been ready for it at the time of its release."

MyInTernin had added that, ". . . she might have stretched the limits of her now limited abilities, in her fight to save her life. At this time, her powers could be depleted and they needed to rebuild, to begin again as she develops them to her greater potential."

On a simpler note, CalOwAy felt that it was probably ". . . a latent sense of guilt over her máthair not escaping unscathed, when she had." Now that Caitrin had been made aware of her máthair's tragic condition. Though they had yet to let her visit. With the fear of a severe regression, they could not offer this to her. Soon. The gist of the situation was that no one really knew, and that no one had "the" answer. Though their answers were plausible, they felt wrong to him. He had this feeling that he had overlooked something. Somehow, they were all missing a vital part of the outcome and he just could not place his finger on it. He would soon discover what brought him this discomfort. He had no other choice.

*** ↄC ***

. . . They were stronger now, the memories. The bits and pieces of my life...escaping the prison of my childhood, my abilities and a sense of self had

returned to me. It was like waking from a nightmare. I'd literally gained the ability to feel, express and live. I suffered greatly with the death of my real parents. But the haze had not lifted in all of my healing. If I truly dug deep, I was able to pull from the recesses of my memory, the sound of my mother's voice. Once she'd said to me, "One day Angel, you will have a destiny to fulfill. It will be grand, you will be grand, never forget that." And apparently, regardless of everything else that had happened, I never had. I held that one memory close, the sound of her voice. The only blanket I'd had against the dark . . .

I drifted, trying to hold on, the pull was heavy, thick and I lost the my will to the swirl of emotions . . .

ↃC

Each day Gable spent with the child, his feelings for her grew. He worked hard, to not let the others see what she had come to mean to him. It was an addiction, one he was fighting twofold. Though he had never had a faeryling, Caitrin was quickly taking the place of one in his soul. In his world, they mated for life. But finding a soulmate could take hundreds of years, which was common. Uncommon for him, was that he was nearly a thousand, and his had never appeared. This turn of events had led to him pouring his passion into his Kinds defense. Not knowing what had become of his mate, or if he was meant to even have one, was something that he had never truly been able to face.

Only once, in all his existence . . . *no, that was not right, not any longer.* Until recently, he corrected, had he thought for a short while that he had found her. She had come in a dream, as real as any spirit could be, only to vanish as if smoke upon awaking. For one moment of his long life, he had found his own salvation and then she was gone again. Now, of the remaining faery, he knew that she did not exist amongst them. Yet he felt her call now, more than ever. She was an illusion. The suffering of his soul was great. Shaking his head, he smiled. This child, she eased some of the pain, the burning torment of his suffering. With her, he felt relief from the longing, for the need of his own family. He felt the need to care for her as a fáthair would.

If he was never to have a mate or faeryling of his own, maybe at least, he could have the love of this child, as if she were his own.

Shaking himself, he sighed. With nothing else left for the evening, Gable prepared for his visit to Angel. Tonight he would tell her of the latest exploits of her daughter, the "Littlest Warrior." He smiled, a small laugh escaping his lips.

⊃C

... Damn it! I was tired. I just wanted all of it to end. All of the pain, the memories and the torment. "Just go away!!!" I screamed into the surrounding, into the nothingness that was my existence ...

... With a blessed tingle it disappeared, all of it. The lights surrounded me, the cocoon of peace, tranquility, filled my soul and being. Washed away was the sorrow and fear, all that remained was the peace ... I allowed the hum to sweep me up, and carry me away ...

Memories
(9)

)C

The weariness continued, the sanctuary of the lights were now my prison. One I could not escape. It seemed like I had been here forever, with its no beginnings and no end. The thoughts and memories of my life, beginning to play in a continuous loop within the confines of my mind, pushing at me. Each stronger than the one before, each wanting to be seen and heard. At first, I thought I understood, but soon, I realized that I was seeing things that I had not expected to see. It allowed me to view memories again and again, washing away the film that had distorted my own view of my life, for longer than I could recall.

It was like my own private DVR. I could rewind and review. Showing me ways in which my life had been shaped, making me realize things that I never had before. Things I had not remembered, twisting and forcing themselves to the forefront. Slowly, everything that I had not remembered became clear, every memory, every wish and every thought. The sanctuary around me shifted, as I fell through the layers of light, falling deep. I felt the world slide backwards, as I tumbled on . . .

My mind took me back. It was like falling into a well, face first, events shifting and shifting again. As I watched, I got younger. I saw my adopted parents and then the courthouse. These were things that I had not remembered before. It rewound even farther, deeper I fell. Soon, my vision cleared. For the first time in nearly fifteen years, I saw my parents, and I remembered. The knowledge crashed down on my shoulders, ripping waves of love and anguish through me. I had been searching a lifetime for this.

We had come from Ireland, my fáthair and máthair and I. Though I'd been born in America, we'd only come occasionally now. Mainly to visit friends, as we no longer had any other family here. Our family had been unique. We had believed in God, though we had practiced the Old Ways as well. We saw, as our ancestors before us, what God had given us, all of us, the magick and the power that all living things were imbued with. That was what my parents had been teaching me, my gift, and my legacy.

I'd always known that I'd had Irish in my blood. I'd just not, until this moment, remembered to what extent. I was Angelwynn McGinnis. My máthair had been an accomplished healer and midwife, while my fáthair had illustrated novels, much the same as myself, though his had been for my máthairs works. All the things that had eluded me, the memories and their importance began to race their way back into my consciousness, they screamed for my attention. Finally, my past was revealed in bold and vivid clarity.

We had been in America because a close friend of my máthair's was ready to deliver, and my máthair was doing the honor. It had been a long awaited and difficult pregnancy. Both of my parents had been gone longer than they'd anticipated, so I'd gone and lain down. I'd awakened suddenly, a scream upon my own lips. In my mind, I watched as their car veered out of their lane, running headlong into an oncoming truck. Allana had been watching me, I'd become inconsolable, then the police arrived, the night having taken everything from me.

When I'd been unable to change the events, a part of me seemed to have shattered, splintered away from the pain. I had locked away that part of myself, my memory, blaming their deaths on myself. After their deaths, members of my máthair's circle had tried to get custody of me, but the courts had denied them. Sherry had already seen me by then, a ward of the state at the time. She had turned everything about my own people around, against them. Making them appear wrong, bad, saying that their life styles were unfit for a child. Then, she and her husband had swooped in for the taking. Amazing people with their generosity, they had saved me from a life of confusion and turmoil. They had worked hard at suppressing my memories and keeping my true nature from me. But no longer, I was now free. Truly free...

Another set of memories crashed down upon me, this time, I was eleven. I remembered a trip we'd taken, a seminar that Sherry had been required to attend for work. It was held in one of those secluded health spas, out in the country. Or as it happened, out in the woods. I'd been told not to wander, but had done so regardless. A rare stubborn moment. I'd left the safety of the retreat behind, searching the trees and forest. Feeling the cool breeze as it blew across my face, feeling a small taste of rare freedom.

It was the cliff face that drew my attention. I understood the idea of danger, I was old enough. But the view was so amazing, so beautiful! It was a sheer drop. I'd run right on up to the edge. Peeking down, seeing what there was to the world below. My breath caught in my throat, it was magnificent! I was over the top of the trees, looking down upon them. I stayed that way for a while, enjoying the freedom, the rush flowing through my veins. It was as I was turning to go back, that I lost my footing and slipped. I felt the rush as the world passed me by, the quick flight to the deep bottom. Seeing a new world as it passed by me, in depth and beauty. Seeing the details and the essence of life and feeling it reawaken me, the craving, the need to escape from my prison. The one I lived within. For one brief moment, I saw freedom as few ever have, and it did not scare me, it drew me in and exhilarated me. Every moment, every thought slowed to a snail's pace, a mere fraction of reality.

As I reached lower, I continued the slow decent, until finally time seemed to stand still, then I realized, no, it was me. I was standing still, no more than a foot off the ground. I let out my pent up breath and ended up on my bottom. Literally.

I'd completely forgotten about this! How? Why? I shuttered. I already knew, with a new understanding. Every time something had pulled to me, had pulled at me, it was washed away in a haze of forgottenness. This I could attribute to Sherry's brainwashing, her hours of sessions and the not so subtle suggestions to forget . . .

The memories cleared, and then they came again, this time it was memories of my adopted parents finding me. My deception discovered. I'd been struggling, had not even been gone a year. Things had just started moving forward when a phone call out of the blue had been placed to the apartment I was living in. From that line, had come the voice of Sherry. I remembered with perfect clarity, the sound of her voice . . .

"We found you. Thank goodness we finally found you. We had to hire a detective. You literally disappeared off the face of the earth Angel. We're so happy. You don't have to worry anymore. You're safe."

As if those words were supposed to comfort me. The ice cold dread I had felt, washing through my senses once more.

"We thought that you'd been kidnapped, we sat by the phone and waited. That's when we found that your account had been drained. Completely cleaned out! We knew, we knew then that someone had taken you and nothing was heard from you or the kidnappers afterward. It was the worst! The police had nothing to go on; you were lost, dead to us. But I did not give up, never. I hired a detective."

"Then this, we find out you're alive . . . and well! You could not believe our shock!" I heard the anger in her voice now. It reverberated through the phone, causing her voice to be washed nearly out. "But we can put all of that behind us now." Her perfectly polished calm, coming to the forefront. "You can come home. We know of the finest hospitals in the country..."

I'd slammed the phone down. I could actually feel the world closing in on me. My mind began spinning and collapsing in on its self. There was an intense tightness in my chest, the air in my lungs evaporating and leaving me gasping, a major panic attack breaking through the surface of my facade. "I would never survive this again." I knew . . .

Then I did something for myself, I closed my eyes and took a deep, steadying breath. "I was beyond this, an adult now. They could not touch me, could not hurt me." Opening my eyes again, I grabbed my coat, my purse and anything else essential and took off. I'd left everything else behind. I had already sold several short stories, so I knew that I could support myself. But this had been my vital mistake; my stories were what had allowed me to be tracked down. I would need a new identity in the future, a way to get my work out, without it coming back to me. That was when my miracle happened.

By mistake, my manuscript had ended up on Catherine's desk. She'd then provided a future for me, a pen name, and an alias. And who would have thought that the allure of a mysterious author that no one ever saw, would have boosted sales to the point of new records in the publishing world? With the simple explanation of a stalker, my life had been cleared and saved.

I felt the sensations coming again, this time as I moved forward in time...

My memories shifted once more, like water passing through fingers. I thought, no I saw for myself how magick had touched my life many times over. More memories came to me now. Caitrin, her life was part of the puzzle . . .

. . . I'd been traveling for several days, on the run, when I'd finally felt safe enough to stop for the night and rest. Almost by accident, I'd come across a small B & B, in this little county in the backwoods. I'd relaxed. It was the first time in so long, that I'd decided to stay for a while. Take some time to try and piece my life back together. To figure out what I was going to do next.

The place was magickal. I'd taken the first two days to just recuperate, mostly staying to myself, sleeping and ordering in. It was on the third day that I'd decided that I needed to get out, to get some fresh air. So dressing comfortably and heading out to explore the countryside, I was only out about twenty minutes when a path in the woods revealed itself, a trail so old, that it was nearly hidden. Slowly revealed to me was a stream, the water flowing in a steady current, not very deep. I traveled along it for some time, tracing the stream backwards, searching for its source, rather than its destination.

Suddenly, I'd fallen upon it. Over a small rise, it had been surrounded by an enclosure of thick trees. A bubbling pool rose up from the earth, its source, a waterfall of close to thirty feet in height. It was fast flowing, muffled by the surrounding trees, the crash of the water on the rocks below a dull roar. It was a breathtaking sight. Walking from one side of the pool to the other, searching for something that even I wasn't sure of. The smell of the tiger lilies surrounding the pool, exotic and enchanting, closing my eyes, breathing in the deep heady scent. I'd become intoxicated listening to the fat bees as they flew past, landing amongst the petals. I'd finally understood the saying of "complete abandon." After watching for a long while, I sat back to relax.

I couldn't remember ever feeling so apart of something, so wrapped up within it that I didn't know where it stopped and I began. Closing my eyes and laying back, the lull of the atmosphere too much for me to resist. The moss was like velvet against my cheek. The large stone I laid down upon covered from one end to the other. Sleep claimed me.

The world that I awakened too was not the one that I'd left behind. As I gazed around, pixies floated upon the air, their wings moving in a slow exaggeration of real movement. The water rippled, as it appeared that jewels shown from deep within its depths, the sunlight casting upon their glitter. The world had become ethereal. I knew then, that I was still sleeping.

That was when he came to me. He was the prince out of any girl's dreams. No, that wasn't right. He was a warrior, strong and dominate, yet gentle. He had offered himself to me, body and soul. And though his body claimed mine, his face had remained elusive. He had stirred within me feelings that I'd never experienced before, a whirl wind of passion that swept me up and above the rising clouds. It was consuming my flesh and resistance. Whispering words that were foreign, then the passion claimed me. I fell as only one who had been truly loved could.

My soul had been altered in a way that I couldn't understand. I'd been ravished and loved. The heat and fire, the passion had seared me to the core. Even remembering it now, it evoked strong reactions within. After the passion, I had awakened, confused but highly satisfied. It had been the most erotic dream. I'd never been with a man before that, never since. The most perfect dream, until three months later, when I'd learned that I was pregnant with no other possible explanation for Caitrin's conception, than a dream, and . . .

. . . and then her birth. The nightmare, the intense fear of loss! The pain seizing me once more. The fear had been there, the terror cursing through my veins. The fear of losing her, before I'd even known her. An emergency C-section had been required to save her life, her vital signs gone . . .

. . . then to hold her. To cradle a child so small, so tiny, so . . . perfect! Even the doctors had stared in wonder at her utter perfection . . .

. . . The memories swirled, and then they cleared. I felt myself falling forward, but upwards. My life's memories flashing before my eyes, until the accident came upon me again. I watched as if an observer, as the trolls attacked and my car was tossed. This time, I saw another car involved, damaged. I had not seen it before. It was further past the bridge, the side we'd never made it too. There was blood; I could see the crimson of it as it reflected in the full moon's light. I pulled myself back, shying away from the suffering, from the loss of a once beautiful life.

As I continued to watch, I saw the horror of the explosion of light, totally entranced, the circle it cast in miles, each way, and then I was thrust forward, totally. Back to the pulsing lights and sounds. I screamed in my secluded prison. I knew that I needed to escape from the confines of this bodiless state. The only thing that I hadn't done yet was confront the dark, the turbulent colors that only offered fear. They sat off to the side, within their own "space." I braced myself, because I knew there was going to be pain. Knew that I had to face whatever was required to breech the confines of nothingness.

I was no coward, but the pain was excruciating. I steeled myself; if I could just get the strength to push through, but then, I had no clue what was on the other side. I was weighing my options, the mindless droning or the intense pain, when the voice came back to me. As he had come and gone before, the voice *had become more focused. He had offered me hope and reassurance.*

I grasped on to him, using him as a lifeline to the other side. He spoke of my daughter and my life, offering me more to remember, to feel. Now I could hear him clearly and I strained to reach out to him. To find the connection that held us together. For the first time, I was able to hear him in visual detail. I realized that there was no choice; I had to get through the dark and the pain, because this was where he was coming from.

☽C

Gable entered the room and took his usual seat to the left of Angel's prone figure. He no longer looked at her through his own eyes, when he saw her, he saw her through the eyes of Caitrin. The girl had filled his mind with the images of the way Angel had been, beautiful and carefree, a dedicated máthair that had loved her daughter above all else. Caitrin told him of the stories that Angel would weave for her, the magickal realm which her máthair had created. In it, he saw the strong similarities to his own world and it fascinated him. She would also bake "goodies" as Caitrin called them, picnicking and playing outside with her under the trees "forever," as she had recalled. All the things that a máthair should do, this was how he chose to see her. He laid his strong and warm hand down upon her scarred and wrinkled one and he began to speak, this new vision of her, washing away the unease from before.

"I feel like you are the only one that I can speak truthfully to these days. I have fears and reservations. It seems that you are the only one I can trust them with . . . you see, when you and your daughter were brought to us, the entire Keep rejoiced in the fact that our salvation had come at last. I could not even describe to you the relief that passed through me, for this battle has raged so long, that it seems that it is all that even I can remember." At this, he released her hand and stood up. He began to pace the length of the room, stopping by the window, open to allow the evening breeze a few more moments to blow into the warm room. Though the sight was peaceful, it offered him none, he all but shook in his frustration.

"I have doubts now!" He said, as he turned back to face her sleeping form. "It has been nearly four months, and though her training progresses, there is no evidence in her of the great faery magick that we should see. All that I can see is a faeryling! One that is going through the normal bumps and bruises of learning her place in the faery world. But I do not understand how this is possible?" He threw his hands up in frustration, words of anger, clouding his thoughts and judgment. At the moment, kicking something was more to his liking, but he refrained. Struggling to clear is mind. His handsome features were pulled taunt as he grimaced at his own thoughts.

Falling back to reasoning, to the faery way of being. "There is no way that a faeryling could have been born in the Realm of Man. You are her máthair. You are human!" He shouted at her as an accusation. He wanted answers and he was tired of the prone woman who could not offer him any. He felt like he knew her, like she had always been a part of his life, yet he did not even know what she looked like. He threw his hands up in the air again, this time in disgust. *What was wrong with him? Why were his thoughts taking this path?*

"Damn it! Could you not just open your eyes and offer me some answers?" He yelled one last time. The surprise of seeing her do just that unsettled him so badly that he almost fell to his knees. What followed next put him there.

Her eyes were the color of violets. He thought to himself, a moment before...

Awakening
(10)

ͻC

It was sudden, blinding, terrifying! The swirl of color turned black as violent ravaging pain rippled through every fiber of my body and consciousness, a consuming fire of torment. Every fiber, flayed alive and ripped back in upon itself, the flesh pulled back and recoiled as new took its place. The pain so severe that for the space of a single heartbeat, for an eternity of a second, I believed that I'd died and gone to Hell, then leight, it emerged from within me. Encompassing all that I was, it shot out of me like a ribbon of the sun, so potent was its Source. It swallowed up all that was me and not. There was only leight. The fear, the burning and excruciating pain, all disappeared in the brilliant beauty of it. I floated for a moment, every fiber of my body floating free, a collision of cool and satin, the bliss more beautiful than anything I'd ever known. Ribbons of pleasure that fluttered by me. Then it began to recede.

ͻC

I could sense my vision returning . . . *everything* . . . fuzzy at first. Blurred vision as my other senses returned. Sound, a strong, deep beating heart and an intake of breath. Smell, the aroma of musk, wrapped up in the deep, dark aroma of tiger lilies . . . *a man*. And finally, the blurred edges became solid . . . across from me was the most beautiful pair of aqua colored eyes, the very eyes that had haunted me for a lifetime. This time, there was a man attached to them. *No, that was not right.* He was definitely male, but he was not quite human. He was raw male beauty. His hair was black; dark as a raven's wing, with inner silver glinting only were the flames light reached. It was worn long, reaching nearly to his waist. It was set in thick locks, some with golden rings as adornments. It sat over features so beautiful that they appeared to have been carved of a god; deep eyes, a strong nose and full lips; they would make any woman dream. His eyes were his softest feature, while the scar that ran the length of his temple, to disappear into the neckline of his shirt, was the fiercest. His ears I noticed, were pointed, much like Caitrin's. On a man, no male, it had a very different effect. Then it struck me.

I actually felt myself blanch. It was the wings. A male of such carefree beauty, such power, and he had wings. They appeared as if they had been created of wild abandon. No rhythm or reason and yet, perfect, all in one breath. They were a combination of green and silver, crystal and gossamer threads. Burning with an intensity all their own. Suddenly, I felt overwhelmed. It pulsed through me in great waves. I thought that I was ready for just about anything, apparently, I was wrong. I felt the wave as it washed over me again. Only this time, I understood what it was, a reprieve. Then there was only blissful darkness again, as I followed it down. This time willingly, my mind shifting to give me time to adjust. *Only the darkness remained . . . and I sighed for it.*

*

He watched as the leight had started slowly, as it had pulsated under her damaged flesh. First it had appeared orange, then blue and then white. Then the leight had ruptured through the skin. It ripped through the scar tissue, replacing it all with a strong glow. It was blinding, devastating, so bright. It obliterated everything; all he could see was the leight. Then, just as quickly, for it could not have lasted more than a few seconds, all he saw was the woman. Whole and beautiful, staring back at him as she had finished healing herself. The leight gone, but Grace remained.

Of all the things he had ever seen, never had he been prepared for something of this magnitude. No ArtimA could have healed her, to the extent she just had. He took his chair for the moment continuing to stare at the now sleeping woman. Her beauty was beyond exquisite. She was all curves. Ample was the only word to describe her. She was short of stature, with hair that lay to her waist. Within its folds was every shade of gold and brown that one could imagine. It pulled to him, wanting him to sink his hands into the silky locks. Her eyes had been violet, a dark and turbulent violet. *The heat of lightning in the midst of the storm.*

To him, she was simply perfect. He felt the pull then, the all-consuming need to be. The impact to his gut and heart left him without words, struggling to breathe. He felt layers of himself, ones that he had never known existed. Like an entire part of himself that had been hidden until this very moment. A new existence bared to the core, an essence of creation that swept him away. *She was the one.* The female who had haunted him in his dreams for several years. He had torn his Kingdom apart in search of her. Yet here she was now, a human. *It was not possible, or was it?* She was here. He closed his eyes and said a quiet prayer to the Creator. Life was suddenly a new concept, a new beginning.

*

He heard the footsteps first, before the pounding began on the door. He knew from the noise that at least several of his Kind stood outside the entrance. *The leight had been so intense, it must of escaped the confines of the room to alert the faery nearby.* Faery that would be looking for answers, answers that he was not ready to give.

Getting up, he walked to the door, opening it only enough that he could let himself out, and that the others would not see in. There were things he needed to do first, before the entire tÁle of what had happened could be explained. Squaring his shoulders, he faced them with an aura of strength, of calmness, that he did not feel.

"Gable, what happened here?" It was the unison of several voices that asked. All appeared confused, but excited at what they had beheld.

"Was what we saw possible? The depth of the magick, it was so strong!"

"I know that you have questions, but I am not able to give you all the answers yet. There are a lot of things happening right now that need to be addressed before I can explain to everyone." He turned to the young healer SeldWynn, speaking to him above the others. "I need you to go and get CalOwAy for me. At this time, he will be in his chambers. It is very important that he comes quickly and that you do not tell anyone what you have seen. Soon enough, you will all understand."

SeldWynn nodded to Gable, already heading to the Elder ArtimA's chamber. Gable turned to look at those remaining. "You know what I ask. The same applies as well. Please, I want you to return to your chambers for the evening. Soon, you will have the explanations you seek."

Their respect for Gable was a powerful thing and they held back the questions they longed to ask. Even with their curiosity, they knew better than to question their Leader.

*

SeldWynn quickly moved to find CalOwAy. He told the Elder what Gable had said, saying no more. After his message was delivered, he headed back to his own chamber for the night. Sitting on his bed, he thought again about what he had seen. He wondered, dreamt of the possibilities for a few moments more before bowing his head to pray.

*

After all left, Gable reentered the chamber and closed the door behind him. He knew that CalOwAy would come to him shortly. His curiosity spiked by the rushed summons, the need for secrecy. He had to explain to him what he had seen as confidently as possible. The endless possibilities to phantom. His nerves were on edge. He felt like he had live wires, deep thrumming electricity running through his skin.

What he had witnessed should not have been possible? But happen it did. It was a miracle, a miracle from the Creator. For so long the Darkeness had held such a strong hold. Miracles and acts of the Creator's Will had been missing from their lands, from their memories. Suddenly, strength of awareness filled him; it had his body rocking from the depth of its knowledge. His legs gave way underneath him.

*

CalOwAy entered into the room alone. He stared in shock at the sight of Gable on his knees, bare to the ground, his hands in submission at his side, the look of utter amazement on his face. Turning his gaze to the bed, CalOwAy felt the impact straight to his gut. She was whole . . .

*

All of the questions, all of the doubts were gone. The pieces suddenly fell into place. In simple wonder and absolute truth, Gable looked up to him and said. "She is the One. She is our Savior."

The One
(11)

We are in trouble. The refrain kept playing over and over again in his mind. So many other things fought their way to the forefront of his thoughts as he headed back to his study, but this was the most solid. At least she was alive and here. *She was human!* The very thought was astonishing. He slid into a chair and quickly stood up again, the pacing starting on its own accord. Everything was different. Things could finally change. Suddenly, he stopped, the color draining from his thoughtful face. *Caitrin? How was it...was it even...?* He could not finish the thought. *There had to be an explanation. But how was it even possible?* He stopped mid-stride...*Was it really that simple?* He felt a sudden peace, an understanding, a rare gift of the Creator.

He felt the massive rush. The emotions beginning to swirl within him, taking control. It was a maelstrom, his mind, his heart, his gut. He was spinning, everything at once calling out to him. Wanting to be felt, to be answered and accounted for. He pulled his hands upward, bracing his head in them. The world was spinning, he was out of control and he needed some semblance of balance. He closed his eyes and took a deep breath. And he focused on her face, on the beauty that he had waited a lifetime to find. The thoughts, assumptions and unanswered questions raced through his mind. He needed the answers this time. He had to have them.

As much as he needed to know though, he knew that she would not be ready yet for all of the things that were waiting for her, that he was going to say to her. He felt the control, as it began to return. Not entirely, but no longer was he sinking in the storm of emotions, emotions that he had no idea how to control. He would need time, the same as she. He acknowledged this. He threw his hands up in the air, this time, his wings mimicking his hands. *This was becoming a habit, this impatience!* Suddenly, he burst out in laughter at his own thoughts, a final release of the boiling emotions and thoughts. *An impatient faery! There apparently had to be a first for everything! The irony of it!* He realized he would have to deal with one problem at a time. He brought himself back to center, to focus. *Time,* he decided, *was definitely not on his side.*

* * * * * * *

The knock on his door roused him. He had fallen into a deep, dream filled sleep, propped up in his chair. Turning his head to gaze out the window, he realized that his neck muscles were sore. The light in the sky showed that it was still early, yet morning was on its way.

"Come in."

"Gable, she has started to awaken. She is restless though it is clear that she does not suffer anymore." CalOwAy said.

"She is fully recovered then?" He asked.

"Better than fully recovered. She is healthier than any human could be. What is going on here Gable? None of this really makes any sense." CalOwAy asked as he slide into a nearby chair, for once the look of his age was present.

Gable watched him. He was definitely out of sorts, much the way that Gable had felt himself. "Actually, things are finally making sense." He walked over and rested his hand on the shoulder of the Elder faery. "I am going to talk to Angel now that she is waking up. I want to speak with her privately at first, then, I will have you come in to hear what else needs to be said. There is much more going on here, more than any of us realized."

"As long as we have answers soon, I do not like the feeling of being left in the dark." CalOwAy said with a slight shutter moving through him.

Neither did I. Gable thought to himself.

They walked together in silence. Gable thought back to the past and how CalOwAy had come to mean so much to him. Gable's fáthair had fallen in battle several centuries ago. Suffering a mortal wound, CalOwAy had brought his fáthair back to the Keep safely, at peril to his own life, so that Jach'niél could spend the last of his time in the presence of his mate and son. His fáthair had passed into the Leight after two days. CalOwAy had been able to keep his fáthairs pain to a minimum, allowing his parents those last few moments together. But still, Gable's máthair had gone soon after. With the loss of the other half her soul, her heart had merely stopped trying. Their love had been amazingly deep. Together, they had traveled on to the Creator's Heaven. With their loss, CalOwAy, friend and adviser to his fáthair, had maintained his position with Gable. Now Gable acknowledged him more as family than friend. The trust he felt for the Elder had been greatly deepened with the devotion that CalOwAy had shown to his fáthair, all the way through, to the end.

They walked through the main living quarters of the Keep where activity was beginning to show as faery awoke for the morning. The fresh scents of breads and fruit rolls were wafting their way through the halls. Gable's stomach growled in answer to the sweet aroma and he realized that he had not eaten in a long while. Soon he would need to remedy that, but first things first. They took the main staircase down into the entrance way and exited the front doors, taking the covered breezeways and admiring the open courtyard as they walked to their final destination, the Atrium.

In the open courtyard, the rising sun gave the illusion of golden mist dusted upon the realm. Even to his own mind, Gable thought that this was indeed the vision of a faerytale. He was going to see to it that it remained that way. So much had been lost to the consuming Darkeness. He knew that soon enough, it would be knocking upon their walls and doors. He would be ready when it arrived!

The beauty of the morning stayed with him as he entered the Atrium. It offered him some tranquility that his rapidly changing world had displaced. CalOwAy stepped behind him as they climbed the worn and narrow staircase to Angel's chamber, a sense of mystery invading their thoughts and notions. New steps, they were preparing to make, into a future that was still unknown, undetermined.

"You need to remember to take it slow Gable. She has been through an amazing ordeal. She is probably going to need time to adjust."

"I will give her all that is within my power. But we have no idea how much longer that we will be given. We have already lost much time in the mistake that we have made with her daughter. I feel that we are running out of time." Gable said.

"It is not time lost. We could have done no more, for it was she who needed to awaken. Just remember to be gentle." He paused for a moment, searching for the right words. "Try to not be too…*intimidating.*"

Gable raised his eyebrows, disbelief upon his face. *Intimidating?* He thought to himself. He coughed abruptly, swallowing the initial words that rose.

"I . . . will try. Too much depends upon her now." He said quietly. Gable offered him a slight smile as he knocked and opened the door, then with more force. "I will call for you as soon as possible." As he entered the chamber, Angel's gaze looked upon him.

*

As I lay amongst the pillows on the bed, I ran my hands over my body. Looking down, I saw no visible wounds or scars, yet my body felt exhausted. To me, it seemed that I had been the boxing bag and someone had taken liberty with the gloves. I was not sure I understood how I could feel so bad and have no evidence of injury, for there was none that my eyes could find.

As door began to open, my eyes immediately raced to see who would enter. Through it he came, the warrior of my dreams and the eyes of my past. My heart accelerated and I could feel the swirls of pleasure as they moved through me in a languid fashion. *He was beautiful, in a wild sort of way. It was easy to say that he was a giant, because he had to be nearly seven feet tall. Power emanating from him, all muscle.* That was my next thought. At such a height, he should have looked disproportional, like those tall basketball players, but no. No, he was perfect. If I had to guess his age, I'd say somewhere in his late twenty's. But his eyes gave him away. They looked older than time itself. So much was etched within them. *Then there was the question of those wings?* I felt a turning in my stomach, an unease that washed through me. I was certain that everything I thought I knew, was about to be turned upside down.

"It is good to see that you have awakened. My name is Gable and I am the Ruler of My Kind. You have been with us for a while now. Four months to be exact."

Four months! I couldn't imagine that much time passing!

I listened to his voice. The timbre was familiar. His words were accented. He had a similar lilt to his voice. *Irish.* It was similar to my own, but in a more musical kind of way. My own voice still carried the melodically ring, though it had faded over the years in America. I liked how it sounded, so inviting. *I felt it wrapping itself around me, almost like a blanket of comfort.*

It hit me then like a brick wall, I felt myself tied, an unbreakable rope of titanium, bound from him to me. *I knew him.* I could feel the pull on my very soul, claiming that I had always known him. But he was a stranger to me. I was intimidated. There was no question about it. That was the only way to put it. Well over my head in swirling and sinking waters. I knew I wanted to drown, I realized it with utter clarity. I had never wanted anything so badly. I wanted to drown in him. I shook my head, trying to clear it and my racing heart. Shoving aside the intense emotions suddenly spawned within me, the confusion making my thoughts muddled and unattainable.

"I . . ." Stuttering, it felt like the words did not want to form on my lips, I attempted another approach, my throat parched . . . "four months . . . ? How is that possible, it felt like only yesterday . . . what's happened?" Sudden flashes of Caitrin passed through my mind's eye. "Where is Caitrin, my daughter? All that I can remember is the dark and an . . . an explosion of light!" Suddenly the words tumbling over themselves to be free. My fear of the unknown consuming me.

"First, Caitrin is safe." Walking to the stand, he poured her a glass of water. Passing it to her, she drank deeply. "You and she were brought to us the night of your accident. You were attacked, but you both survived. Unfortunately, your wounds were quite severe. You have remained here since you were brought to us." He informed me, his hands sweeping out in an unconscious gesture to encompass the room.

I looked at him and then looked away. I was trying to remember. It was there, but hazy. I knew that I needed to face it, all of it. "We were attacked? It's all very . . . *confusing.* It was late; we were racing to stay ahead of the fire. It had started to gain on us with unbelievable speed. We were attacked . . . it was dark . . . I was trying so hard to escape . . ." The force of the memory pushed me back, pinning my chest to the bed. I could feel the tightness as the memory gripped my chest and throat. "I was so scared for us! We had reached the bridge . . . oh my God. . ." I shot up in the bed, "we were thrown over the bridge. Caitrin was crying for me . . . I couldn't get to her . . .

then there was only . . . light?" I leaned back into the pillows, my eyes feeling heavy, closed in remembrance.

I blinked. "There had been creatures of some sort, trolls if I had to give them names. There was no other explanation for what I saw, for what they were." I looked up into his eyes. "There was light after that, light and nothing more." I challenged him with my mind, on a level deeper than he had ever experienced. "What happened? Where are we?" My voice rose as I struggled to put the pieces together on my own. He walked to the bed. Sitting down next to me and placing his strong hand upon my shoulder. I took it to be a show of comfort. But it did so much more to me. The contact sent silver sparks from his hand to me. I gasped in surprise. The rush of heat following it was unexpected, and yet thrilling.

Gable fought to hold his reaction in silence. Not expecting the extent of the attraction to begin so quickly, to move through them so completely. He would have to move more slowly with her. She was not ready yet. He pulled his hand back to himself. "You need to remain calm. I know that it is probably asking a lot, but I promise that you will have all of the answers that I have to offer. As soon as we are done, I will have Caitrin brought to you. She has asked for you every day since you were brought here to us. With your injuries as serious as they were, it was not advisable for her to see you in such a dramatic condition. She has done well though, been strong. She is a brave, beautiful child."

I smiled. "Yes, that is one way to describe her." In my mind, flashes of Caitrin moved through me, her stubborn nature at the forefront. "Was she hurt at all?"

"Not even a scratch." He said.

I wasn't sure how that could be possible, but relief coursed through me, a smile touching my lips.

He saw her confusion warring with her relief. "You protected her, you *shielded* her."

I just nodded, not really understanding yet.

It offered him some relief to see her smile. What it did to his insides, the impact of it was devastating. Pushing the sensations away took effort, but he would think on it later. "I will start at the beginning and we will work our way through from there."

I nodded to him once again, it felt like the only thing I could do. Words were at a loss for me, my thoughts running rampant with possibilities. "Am I in Heaven?" I suddenly wondered out loud. I could feel the blush, caressing my cheeks.

"As close to it as you could get, before Hell came along." He gave me a condensed version of the story of my accident, starting with *"trolls were a pretty accurate description,"* before moving on to my wounds and the long road to recovery. I felt that he was leaving something out, but I was not sure why he would do that. So I continued to listen.

Gable was careful to not explain yet about the miraculous healing. He wanted her to keep as open a mind as possible, for as long as possible. After he finished, he spoke of Caitrin.

*

His words were a balm to my soul. He let me know that Caitrin had been well taken care of and that she had quickly adapted and come to feel that she belonged. That she actually enjoyed her time with them and being here. After he finished, he sat back and allowed me time to think things through on my own.

*

He watched her features. She went through a myriad of expressions. But he understood that the most change was yet to come. *How would she hold up?* He was about to find out.

*

I heard all he said, but still it felt like my questions were not being answered. "I know that you have told me what has occurred to Caitrin and myself, but you still have not filled me in as to where we are, why we are here and how in the world do you have wings? What's really going on?" I asked again, this time raising my voice, the frustration within me flaring.

Gable smiled. *Her courage and curiosity were remarkable.* Just facing him, she was facing the physical proof of another reality entirely...she would be a force to be reckoned with, when he was done helping her.

"I understand that were you come from, the world is an entirely different place. What I have to tell you, it might scare you, it might not." He paused here to gauge her reaction. She looked at him for a moment, like she was ready to defy anything to get her answers, so he continued. A sudden flare of...pride in her, flashing within him. "You are in the Keep of Ainys'Dai, one of our Strongholds. We reside within the Realm of Magick, or the World of the Faery, whichever you prefer."

"Magick?" I asked. My emotions were shifting from wonder, to disbelief and finally to the need to believe, a yearning as old as time began pulling through me, wanting it to be true, knowing that it had to be.

He felt his insides warm, his reaction quick and acute to her distress and then wonder. This attraction was going to be harder to fight than he had imagined. "You were brought to the Faery, to the Leight, for healing. Your wounds were quite severe; you could not have survived in the Realm of Man. You see, you have a very special destiny, and your survival, it will mean the survival of a lot more Beings." He finished confidently.

"A very special destiny . . .?" I could feel the inkling of familiarity tugging at my memory. "I have heard that before. My máthair said something similar to me when I was a child."

"You have heard of this before? How much do you know?"

I could hear the excitement that entered his voice. "Not much. Both of my parents were killed when I was young. But I know that they were teaching me about the past and the future, about magick, before they died. I wish that I'd had more time with them. They were never able to really explain. None of this is offering me any understanding...but I know that something about it feels like truth." I shook my head then I looked at him again. "Let me get this straight, you are saying that you are Faery, so explains the wings, and that I am smack dab in the middle of the "real" Faery Kingdom?"

He laughed first; he could see the humor in her understanding. "I am not quite sure of some of your language. But yes, everything you said is true. Our realm is quite large, even though we are not that far from your own. We are actually side by side, though that will take some explaining as well. I will try to explain as best as possible." His expression shifted, his thoughts obviously having done so as well. "Though I know you are going to have to explain some things to me as well." He finished, thoughts of Caitrin flitting through his mind.

"Thank you, I need that very much right now. I'm not sure what you need from me, but I'll try to help." I started to relax again. I knew now that I had always believed, somewhere inside myself, that magick had to be real. Even if it had only been on some minutely small scale, it had to have existed somewhere. I could now remembered the stories from my máthair in my youth. I had believed back then, when I was a child. In adulthood, I had been searching for some truth of my own, offering the world some evidence of an unseen world in my stories, through the lives in my books.

"I will tell you a tÁle." Gable began again. "It is a long one, but it is very important that you know it. You see, I believe that you play a large role in how it will end." He sighed for a moment. "Before I begin, I would like to introduce you to someone that has been a constant companion in helping your daughter adjust to her life here. His name is CalOwAy. He is an Elder and he is the ArtimA or *Healer*, who has been with you from nearly the beginning."

"That would please me a lot. I would like to thank him for all of his care."

Gable walked over to the door and signaled for CalOwAy to enter. "CalOwAy, I would like to introduce you to Angel. I have explained to her who you are."

"Good day Angel." CalOwAy bowed to me in the bed.

I studied him for a moment. And it struck me as odd. He appeared to be much older than Gable. His hair flowed as liquid silver and unlike Gable's, it slide down his back in a full thick stream. His body was lean; he was very athletic in build and his smile . . . that was genuine. It put me at ease immediately. The oddity was the fact that his face, his very structure, appeared as youthful as Gable himself. But it was not so. The charisma of age was drenched through his being. I really did not understand, but I hoped to soon. *Faery?* I sighed. *I guess "anything" really was possible!*

"Hello CalOwAy. Gable has explained to me that my injuries were quite severe. I would like to thank you for getting me well again." I smiled up at him.

CalOwAy returned her smile and nodded. He had worked hard at keeping her alive, but it had not been him that had accomplished her healing.

"I know that CalOwAy did everything in his power to heal you. But in fact, it was not him that was able to finally heal your wounds Angel, it was you, yourself." Gable finished.

I looked from one faery to the other. "I'm not sure that I understand what you mean?"

"I am going to explain everything that we know. I wanted CalOwAy to sit in on this so that I would not need to repeat the information. If you need to ask questions, please feel free to ask. I will try to give any answers that I have. I want to make sure that you understand everything that I have to tell you."

I merely nodded in response.

"The tÁle begins when you were brought here. You see, I told you that your wounds were severe. In fact, your entire body had been burned; there was nothing left untouched by the flames. You held on when there was no possible way that you should." He could see the disbelief on her face, but she asked no questions. "CalOwAy and the others did all that they could to help you. But you are human, so your body was only able to heal so much, even with magick. Humans carry pollution within them, on a deep level. It has a resistance to magick. They were able to create a softer scar tissue, one that would protect you. It helped with the healing and it was better than what would have formed from the destruction itself. They created as clean an environment as possible. We had no idea what was going to happen. We were not sure if you would ever awaken." He paused a moment to look at me. She was listening intently. Focused, trying to understand.

He could see that she was trying to see herself as they had seen her, her concentration severe. "Several weeks passed as you lay in this very bed. Fighting with a tenacity to stay alive that awed even the best of us. But after that, your recovery was minimal. We watched day in and out as you suffered. Then yesterday, something amazing happened." He paused here, the effect still astonishing him.

"Last night I came here to sit with you, as I have done every night for a little over three months. But you opened your eyes this time. It was the first response that we had received from you the entire time of your stay." He turned and walked to look out the window. He chose his next words carefully, because he did not want to frighten her. "I was amazed and relieved to finally see this response from you. In all honesty, I was not sure myself, if life was something that you would have wished to return too. Life for you would have been extremely difficult at best."

I spoke then. "I remembered the sudden burst of pain. I had followed your voice through the darkness. Your voice was like a beacon, it offered hope, but yesterday, it was different. You were upset, in pain. I followed it to find you. The pain I felt was excruciating. Then I saw your eyes. All my life, I have known their sight." I quickly looked up, then down, the blush creeping across my face as I realized how this information could be perceived. I did not have an answer for it, and I did not expect him to have one either.

Gable seemed to take the response as fact, CalOwAy on the other hand seemed startled by the remark, contemplating her words for their meaning. Gable turned back around from the window. The sight of the fields aglow with the rise of the sun was always a breathtaking view. He drew strength from it. They were all going to need as much strength as they could muster, in the days to come.

"I know that the events that have led up to this moment are probably confusing to you, but it all serves a purpose. I will finish with my recollection of yesterday, and then we will move on." He paused. "After you opened your eyes, something amazing happened. You see, the Leight of the Creator, the very heart of faery magick, began to pulse out from your body. You were nothing more than raw and ravaged scars, your burns so bad that all identity to your person was gone. Then in a matter of moments, you erupted in the leight of healing and emerged whole and beautiful."

I looked up as he spoke those words. In all my life, I had never been called beautiful by a man. I liked how it sounded, coming from his lips. I had always been on the plump side. Beautiful was a word never used to describe me. To hear him of all . . . *beings* say it, it made my insides warm and flow like molten gold. A memory came unbidden to me then, and within a mere moment, was lost once more. No answers offered. Unconsciously, I pressed my hand to my fluttering stomach, as I tried to keep up with his tAle. I was having a hard time fighting the sudden attraction that I felt for him. After my intensely erotic dream, after it all, there had just never been an attraction to another man. It had seemed that my imagination had ruined my reality. Later there would be time to figure this attraction out, right now I needed answers. Forcing myself, I questioned him. "Are you saying that I just miraculously healed?"

"Yes, that is literally what I am saying. Here, magick is as commonplace as breathing. Yet what I saw yesterday was magick unlike anything before. You are human, and the power that you unleashed yesterday to heal yourself, was more powerful than any Faery magick known." He continued. "We live for thousands of years. In all that time, I have never witnessed what I saw in the mere blink of an eye. You seem to have an ability that can only be attributed to one individual." He spoke carefully. He knew that he had to deliver the information just right.

"Thousands of years ago, a great Evil stalked across our land. It devoured all within its path. The Creator was forced to purge the Earth of this evil. When Hé was finished, only a score of humankind remained. But Hé warned that the evil would eventually return. The Creator spoke to Faery and Man alike. Hé told us that when the time came, Hé would send us a Savior. We believe that this Chosen One is you." He finished.

CalOwAy understood, from Gables words the night before, that this was how they were to precede. But it left so many other questions unanswered.

I on the other hand, looked at him like he'd just lost his mind. *What in the hell was I supposed to say to that? There was no reasoning in that assumption. What, just because I was here, I was the One? Didn't they know who I was? I was going to have to explain to them.* "I'm not, not . . ." This was new. *Having to prove my sins? To prove that my soul was not . . . perfect. Spotless. Deserving of such.* "I'm not some great Saint. I am flesh and bone woman. With all the same wants, cravings." *I could feel myself blushing.* "With all the same mistakes and . . . and sins." *I may not have made many of my own, but I had done enough in this life to warrant some mistakes.*

"I know that this is probably going to sound crazy, but at the moment, everything seems to have gone crazy." I broke for a moment. I felt myself becoming overwhelmed and worked hard at holding it at bay. Planning my next thoughts and words, I took a deep breath and began. "Deep down inside, I have always known that I've believed in magick. But what you're speaking of...what you're saying...you just need to stop right now! Even if I believe what's right in front of me, do you really expect me to believe, that me, an author of young adult books, is the Salvation of all Mankind?" My voice was rising in my disbelief. "Some foretold Savior?"

"Faerykind, as well." CalOwAy added.

I stared at them like they were both insane! Forget it, I knew that they were. *It just wasn't possible! I would know? Wouldn't I?*

"Please tell me that this is all just some delusion! That I'm still asleep, laying in a hospital bed somewhere? Please !?! I . . ."

"I'm sorry, but too many depend on you for that luxury," Gable said, "your responsibility is too great!"

"My responsibility . . . ?" For a moment, anger took hold of me in dangerous amounts. *Didn't they understand what I had already been through, the extent of the damage that I had suffered? But then again perhaps they did, maybe even better than I understood myself.*

"That is right, they probably do." I looked up at the voice, but it was only my self. My inner guidance. My anger deflated quicker than I thought possible. Gable and CalOwAy continued on, almost like I wasn't there. But soon enough, I was brought back into the conversation.

"There is so much that we need to discuss and go over. You have been through much, but we need to start preparing. We need to make sure that you have enough time for instruction and training. I know that you feel that you are not capable of this, but you are. It is a woman, this time, who has enough inside for what needs done. You are the Creator's Messenger. You are the twin of the initial soul, an ending to His beginning."

I felt like I was being swept up in a torrent of emotions. Thoughts, suggestions, all took me to the extreme and I could not put them into words.

"Just believe in yourself." Came the unbidden reply.

Suddenly, feeling a shift, words started coming from me, finally unlocked from somewhere deep within me. "I had training, as a child." I blinked in surprise at my own words. It was like a recorder had suddenly been switched on inside of me. Shaking my head at my own confusion, I continued on. "But it in no way prepared me for anything like this! No one said anything like this. My parents were of the Old Ways. I remember the things that they taught me now. About nature and the essentials of magick that God gave us. They were people that studied the natural earth. They revered nature and worked to keep their lives in balance with it. They studied the magick that was imbued within all living things and worked with it. My máthair, she knew that I would have a great destiny, but even she did not know what it would be, only that it was so." I could feel the fear filling me now. "I know this seems to fit in with what you are saying, but I cannot make myself understand this. This is so crazy!"

"No it is not! You are just scared!" I wished my conscious would just shut up.

"At least it is more of a start than we thought we had. It should help our TA Archers to know that you have had some basic knowledge. This is good." Gable replied, a smile lighting his features.

My stomach fluttered again. I decided that I liked the feeling; though I was not sure that I really understood it. I had never felt an attraction like this before. There had just never been a man to spark my interest. I realized that my mind was wondering and I tried to focus back on the conversation. *What was with these strong, uncontrollable emotions? I was never one to be like this before...*

"We need to start going over the rest of the information. However, I want for you to get some rest as well. I will allow Caitrin to come to you, as well as food brought to begin nourishing your magick back. Afterward, if you are able, we will talk more. If not, we will continue on the morrow." Gable said, as he and CalOwAy rose and headed out together.

*

In the hallway, they turned to look at each other.

"I have a request? CalOwAy, could you please go and recover the Book of Prophecy from the Hall of Knowledge. I plan on going over it with her after she eats."

"I know that she appears to have been prepared for some of this. It seems that we have more luck on our side than we originally realized. The problem is that she is not ready for this. Perhaps if her parents had been able to prepare her more properly, as it seems they were destined too, she would have been more open to all of this. But that is not the case."

"I understand that." Gable said, frowning. "As it stands, she was supposed to come to us as a child, which was our mistake in the identification of her in the first place. If nothing else, we now know why she is an adult and not a child. Apparently, her parent's death played a large role in this. Unfortunately, this only leads me to the conclusion that we were supposed to have more time to prepare her, which means . . ."

". . . that you do not think we have even as much time as we believed before!" CalOwAy said with sudden understanding.

"Exactly! I have a feeling that our time is running out."

Origins
(12)

RandelfSon had left the stables and was heading to get his noontime meal, when he noticed across the way that Caitrin was following MadaREn into the Keep. It had been whispered that her máthair had awakened, though he was not sure. That was fine though, it would not interfere with his plans.

He felt a nagging buzz; it began to build at the nap of his neck and moved forward. Like a tingling crawl. He rubbed his temple, trying to push it away. It became louder. As the sensation continued, a feeling like his mind was falling from grasp controlled him. He slid down onto one of the many benches in the courtyard. He sat there, when suddenly his thoughts became very old, but very lucid . . .

. . . *his memories drifted back, until he could see her. He could feel the heart in his chest accelerate, his breathing becoming heavier and more insistent. So beautiful, she had always been so beautiful. They had been seven, racing in flight across the river and back, the hum of their wings drowning out the bees along the banks, stealing pollen for their honey. The hum growing as the two of them flew faster and faster...*

. . . *then they were twelve, going to the Solstice celebration. The night was magickal even to them, under the full blue moon. Smoke drifted in the air from the bonfires, causing the lite snow that flew, to glimmer in the night air. They had stolen a flask of Swéetberry wine, laughing at the unfamiliar taste and tingle that had followed it going down, going for a walk in the moonlight, the glow cast off of her pale, silken hair. He had stolen a kiss from her then. A sweet token of the love they shared, of their souls . . .*

. . . *then there was darkness and despair, pain raging . . . his soul ripping apart as she lay broken upon the ground. Her beautiful features torn, blank and frozen, her leight gone, ripped from her still form. The unbelievable accident taking her life, her soul. The damage done so sever, so irreparable, that the very essence of his life was torn asunder . . .*

His soul was shredded that day. He had lived through it, only the Creator knew why. The loss of his mate, of his leight, but he only survived, his family, his only comfort from the intense pain. It seared him through, then and now, pain rolling through him in great consuming waves. Then it, all of it, simply . . . disappeared . . .

. . . A blank wall suddenly engulfed RandelfSon's mind, a blissfulness of nothingness quickly washing over him. Shaking his head at his own forgetfulness, RandelfSon stood up and continued heading into the Keep to eat his noontime meal. Perhaps, Caitrin would join him later for the evening meal?

*

Soon after, Caitrin arrived with a female faery to my door.

*

She raced to my side, throwing all caution into the wind; she jumped on top of the bed, throwing her arms around me, relief and love surging throughout me. I could feel myself relax a little bit more, as I truly knew that she was safe. Her fat tear drops falling from her eyes, Caitrin sniffled from the flow, my own tears wanting to follow suit.

"Máthair, I've missed you so much! Everyone kept telling me that you were so sick, that I couldn't visit you, but I was so worried. I was so afraid that...!" She suddenly caught herself. Saying that she thought her máthair might have died out loud, was suddenly much worse than thinking and fearing it in her head had been.

"Caitrin, it's OK! I'm OK! I'm so sorry to have put you through all this! You mean everything to me. I never would of wanted to hurt or scare you like that." Tears were glistening in my own eyes, no attempt at blocking them now, my vision a glaze of pain. "But I've heard that you've been brave. Every day you kept waiting until I could finally see you again. I'm so proud of you!" I said as I hugged her close to me. Though time had passed differently for me, Caitrin had been acutely aware of my absence. With Caitrin in my arms again, it did indeed feel like it had been forever since she'd been there.

"Máthair, I can't breathe!" Caitrin cried out in exaggeration. I burst out in laughter, as well as the faery who'd accompanied her. Loosening my grip, I looked closer at the faery. I decided then, that I had been right earlier about my conclusions. She was indeed older, but not. She was slim, with white hair that cascaded down her back to reach her waist. She wore it pulled back, in an attractive fashion, with silver combs. Her eyes were a brilliant, glowing crystal blue and her lips were creased with lines turned upward. I gathered from this that she smiled often. The comparison of a faery godmáthair came to me first. But once again, the oddity of youthfulness was very apparent. Even with age, they seemed to maintain a vibrancy of youth, a deep sparkle to the eyes. They glowed, apparently, age only lending to it. The idea that this faery had taken care of Caitrin during my illness, gave me comfort and I felt a deep sense of gratitude.

"Knowing that you took care of her, makes all of this more bearable."

"I can understand." She smiled with a nod. "My name is MadaREn. I must say, being able to care for her was a pleasure and honor that I will not soon forget. She is precious and it was an experience that I will treasure always."

Though her expression did not change, I could sense sorrow was beneath the surface of her demeanor. I realized that the thought of losing Caitrin apparently cut MadaREn as deeply as it would myself. Quickly I made up my mind as to what I could do to ease her fear. *What I could offer her in return.*

"I was wondering? Caitrin will still need care while I recover. I have a feeling that it is going to be awhile before I'm fully in command again." *Be it physically, mentally, or my life in general.* I thought to myself. "Would you mind terribly staying with her longer? I feel that she is safe and is well cared for with you. She has never known the love of a grándmáthair and I can see that you have given her this. The two of you together is a good thing."

MadaREn's appearance drastically changed. It was like she had been offered the moon and stars. The smile that lit her face was pure radiance. She was unable to speak for a moment, her emotions strong, but in the end, no words were needed because Caitrin piped up with the perfect response . . .

"You mean I get to have my very own faery godmáthair?"

*

Speaking with Gable to gain permission, MadaREn had arranged to have the noontime meal prepared for the three of us. We ate a dish that was similar to tomato soup. It was accompanied by small toasted tomato with cilantro and cheese sandwiches. We sat together, getting acquainted and enjoying each others company. Quickly the time began to pass as Caitrin tried to explain to me, all of the magickal things that she had been learning over the past months, her words running together and over themselves. It must have been obvious that I was having trouble following her explanations, because Caitrin rolled her eyes at me. She then decided to just show me instead.

"This is very important Máthair. I learned how to do this weeks ago. Maybe you can start doing this stuff too." She said proudly. She held her hand out, palm upward. As we watched, Caitrin whispered under her breath, *"firenz Uh liva,"* and a small spark of light began to dance upon her hand. It glowed, and then with more power, it took shape, the glistening of it, rotating and pulsating. The glow flared, orange and red, and then gold. It appeared to hold life all its own. Soon, within her hand, sat a perfect sphere, contained within its bubble-like depths was a flame. Fire sat upon her open palm, beautiful and bright, the flame perfect, yet burning not. I watched as the pleasure cursed through her. *She was brilliant.* Then she tossed the golden orb at the now burned out fireplace. Quickly, the flames spread and consumed. In no time, the room warmed from the heat of the embers.

I felt amazement flare within me. The magick, the power and Caitrin was at the control. My small, beautiful and highly inquisitive daughter was whipping up magick with the flick of her wrist. *It floored me! I couldn't find the words!* "It was unbelievable . . . !" My amazed reply, and probably highly comical expression, brought another round of laughter. All other words, lost in the feminine madness and delight.

*

Time passed quickly at our reunion. Soon after, CalOwAy and Gable returned. Caitrin wasn't happy about having to leave me so quickly, but MadaREn's promise of a mousse dessert from the ChAEfen, *the chef,* and a faerytale from RandelfSon after dinner, offered her a pleasant alternative that put her smile back in place.

I couldn't believe that it was evening already!

"You will still be here tomorrow, right Máthair?" Caitrin asked me. Her face was one of sudden fear. I could feel my heart wrenching in my chest, my face flushing.

"I'll never leave you again Caitrin. I promise you that." I pulled her close for another strong hug. I never wanted to see that look on my daughter's face again. After quickly returning my hug, she jumped down from the bed and headed for the door, MadaREn quickly following on her heels. *"How well she already knew her."* I thought to myself.

MadaREn promised to return to me later, offering to take me down to the healing baths of the hot springs. Before leaving, she paused for a moment, walking back over to me, and bending down close, she whispered in my ear. "The very first time I saw Caitrin, I felt a sudden unexplainable attraction to her. There is no one whom would be able to separate us. It is just that simple. Our lives have become interwoven. She is as safe with me, as if she were my own." She stood up and smiled, and then she was excusing the both of them for the evening meal. I felt more comfort at that moment, than I'd known in a long while. Looking to the window, hiding the tears, the sky was already darkening in the distance.

"She is quite a handful," CalOwAy said with a smile, "but an enjoyable one at that." Both Gable and I agreed with a silent, barely acknowledged nod.

Knowing that such time had passed since her noontime meal, Gable brought with them a thick stew for dinner with stiff-crusted, buttered bread. I decided that I'd never seen or tasted anything better. A spiced, red wine was used to wash it down. As I drank, I noticed that the wine swirled on its own and the bubbles exploded like mini-fireworks. *I was in awe of their beauty.* I didn't know if I'd ever adjust. This was definitely a world that was going to take time to get accustomed too. After the filling dinner, I was tired, more than I'd realized. I could feel the weariness as it weighed down upon me. But my curiosity for more answers won out over the need for sleep.

*

CalOwAy observed her as they sat. She was masking well, but not well enough. "Will you be able to continue tonight? You do appear weary." He asked, the kindness in his eyes, extending to wash over me.

"As long as my eyes are still open, I want to know what's going on." I answered with a yawn and smile of my own.

CalOwAy nodded, but he smothered a smile of humor at her stubbornness. *Apparently*, he thought, *like máthair, like daughter.*

*

Gable began to read the TÁle from the book:

"God created many levels of life and intelligence. Between Angel and Man, there was Faery. Even man had many varieties. They lived together, some even reproducing and blending. A great many of these varieties died out though. Their lineage destroyed by the wars of men themselves. It was mankind that was the last of God's intelligent creations. They were the most unique, those with the ability of complete freewill of character."

"God created them in Hís image. However, Hé soon learned that the Darke played upon their temptations, causing them to often follow a much darker path. Their free will was a hindrance as much as a blessing."

"Thousands of years passed as the rule of Faery and Mankind alike covered the face of the Earth. The Faery lived in great cities, called Strongholds; their culture blessed with the magick of the Creator. Faery cunning and strength far surpassed that of other Beings as time went on. Their knowledge and abilities grew as the years fell away. But their hearts remained pure and faithful. Then a great unrest began. The source unknown, it spread amongst them like the diseases of man. It twisted the hearts of the individual, spreading evil as a plague across the land. So the call of war was answered."

"It came to pass, that the forces of Darke became so potent, that it attempted to cross over the boundaries of the Land of Magick and enter the Land of Men. The Faery knew that the faith of mankind was far weaker than those of Faery. If the Darkeness was able to cross the boundary, the hearts of men would fall to the evil and the battle would be lost. The numbers of Darke Faery far outreached the number of Leight. Wars raged as the Faery fought, but the Darkeness broke free and fell upon the Land of Men. Knowing that we were lost, the Leight called upon the force of nature far greater than themselves, they sought out God."

"It was with blinding intensity that the Lands of Magick and Man were scourged that day. Leight rained down from the heavens and rain of a ferocious appetite fell down upon the world. The Cleansing had begun. In order to keep those faithful to Hím alive, God set a boundary unlike one never seen before. Hé introduced the Shimmer. With it, Hé cleaved the Realm of Faery and Man apart, permanently separating our two very different existences."

"The earth shook, the water levels rose and the shimmer took hold. At the center of the Earth, it drew power. A new energy, the fusion of the tamed hydrogen atoms bonding and spreading, the wall of iridescent leight multiplying and spreading, pulled from deep within the core. A twinkling glitter, the Creators own touch of magick joined it. It shot out in a cascading effect, out through the cracks of the crust and mantle. When it was done, the Earth was forever changed. Those faithful; Noah and his son's and his son's families, they of different colors but the same faith, took flight upon a mighty barge. Safe they were for now from the evil that had raged."

"It would come to pass, that the knowledge and the truth of the Faery would nearly disappear from the small remaining groups of Mankind that reproduced and prospered. So, the Faery fell into myth and legend, amongst the groups of Man."

"Many among our Kind had remained loyal, heart and soul, to the Great Lord of Creation. So, with Hís love, Hé removed from our lands the evil that plagued it. Hé reached deep and removed as much as could be pulled from the ragged wound. The threat was brought to a minimum. The Creator spoke to one and all, Hé spoke of the many, many years to come. Of the Great Blessing Hé would send and of the Great Curse that would eventually follow to plague the world, for Hé knew that evil was a festering sore. Eventually, it would spread once again."

*

Gable described how it had begun as a slow trickle and as its numbers grew, it began to swallow whole Strongholds in its destruction. Soon afterward, even the survivors became rare, until, even they did not surface any longer.

"What is the Darkeness exactly? I need something that I can put a face to." I asked. I could feel the dread building inside of me, fear struck sharp and deep for this unknown enemy.

"Evil, pure and simple evil. It finds its way in to you, be it temptation or need. Once it gets in, it is a disease that spreads. You are quickly taken over, from the inside out. Inside, your leight is drained as it feeds off of it like a parasite. From the outside, physical changes occur in the body. You will actually darken. The eyes and hair all darken to a shade of brown or black. The skin takes on a mallow appearance, much like wax. The wings begin to shrink. They develop an appearance that is brittle and broken. But do not let that confuse you. They are quick! The evil that is eating them up is used to defend them till their last drop of leight is gone and they are consumed."

Here, CalOwAy picked up on the break in the discussion. His expertise on the body and healing was apparently able to give him more insight. "The disease actually does consume you. From what we have learned over the years, it burns up the body. It literally feeds off of your energy. Starting with the leight of the soul, it moves on to the muscle, bone and flesh. It is a complete corruption of the mental abilities, the physical and the leight. By the very end, you simply waste away until there is nothing left. It is a horrible way to die. But more importantly, it is a horrible way to live."

He continued on. "It is not quick; it can take centuries, or longer. When it first happens, the faery maintain their looks, their beauty. It becomes a twisted dark*e* beauty. But as the centuries carry on, they change. Their appearances becoming grotesque, dark*er*, evil. They truly become the monsters they are, before they are done. Eventually, all fall prey to the Dark*e's* hunger." He shuddered as he finished. In his mind, he could recall all of those that had been close to him and had fallen, the dark*e* versions of them that had followed. "We have tried to save the infected, but there has been no way." He felt the sorrow of it, but looking at her face, at her reason for being, he suddenly felt hope for the first time.

"When one has changed, the only way to stop them is by removing their head, to severe the heart from the mind, a slicing of the soul. This ends the cycle of feeding and it frees them from this living death, frees the soul." Gable added.

"What happens after it affects someone? How is it able to spread so quickly to others? Wouldn't someone notice?" I felt at a loss, asking all the questions, but I needed to know, to catch up.

"There is actually a second stage. Once several fa*e*ry are infected. This alerts the dark*e* ones, those that have already been turned, their appearances complete. In the confusion of the outbreak, the dark*e* ones come as an invasion force. They come in the hundreds, sometimes the thousands. What usually happens is that no one is yet aware of the infection before the others arrive. It is a battle, because the Dark*e* is literally let in the front doors from those infected."

"We have had to make many changes to our defenses in order to fight this type of evil. Over the years, we have become more successful, though we still loose way too many of our Kind. Our numbers have taken too many blows. We are losing. We need hope, and you are that." Gable finished.

I looked at the both of them. I realized now, what was at stake. Life itself was near the brink of extinction. "If you fall, what happens to the Realm of Man?"

"It would be a slaughter. The souls of men are not nearly as virtuous as the souls of fa*e*ry. They would fall quickly and the world would be cast into eternal dark*e*ness."

"You cannot allow this to happen!" The words, a command, ricocheted throughout me. *But I was only one person. What could I do? If this disease, this evil was so potent, what could possibly stand in its way? What could end this torture?* "How does it end? In your book, in reality, how does this end?" I asked, looking from one to the other. Waiting desperately, hoping that all the answers were written in their book for me.

Gable finished the TÁle:

"So the Creator set forth a Prophecy. For when evil shall rise again, Salvation would come from among the Realm of Man. Through the blood of woman, a child of fa*e*ry magick would be born. She would have a choice; embrace the L*e*ight, or surrender to the Dark*e*ness. Through her magick, would the world be recreated into its original image. The Shimmer would fall and the Union of Faery and Man be complete. Through her failure, the Earth would be destroyed, as evil reigned supreme throughout the land."

Believing
(13)

I leaned back in my chair. Weariness seemed to be etched into every muscle of my being. As promised, MadaREn had returned and had taken me to the healing springs to relax my worn body. I'd felt absolutely wonderful afterward, but returning to the room had once again allowed my mind to wander over the troubles that faced me. So much, so many depended on me to have this ability and to be the one that everyone was searching for.

"You are the One." I shook my head at the thought, the sudden swell of fear.

Looking in the mirror, I only saw myself. The me that I had always been. Although changes had taken place. My features were more perfect, more refined. It was like the flaws had been removed. My body was by far a fair cry from the thin beauty that human women envied for. But to me, the voluptuous curves were far more beautiful. For the first time in my life, I realized that my outside matched the way I felt about myself on the inside. There really had been a beautiful person inside of me all along. *But a strong force, a fighter, a leader?* I didn't know.

I looked away from the mirror. The reality of the situation was simple. The entire future depended upon my ability to find in myself, where I had locked away the magick. Facing myself in the mirror, seeing what I had already been capable of, helped to cement the idea that I could be powerful, that I could fight with these faery and make a difference. Finding the ability was going to be something else. I had no idea where to start. *Tomorrow,* I decided, *I would see what they had been teaching my daughter. Maybe, I just needed to start at the beginning. Maybe that was all there was to it.* I was afraid, I felt fear at the unknowing. It washed through me in waves, making me terrified. *I was only human, after all.*

And what was with this attraction? These crazy emotions and sensations that Gable was awakening within me. I had always been more of the...*bookworm*, I guess. Boys had never been an important part of my life, even in my teenage years. There had never really been an attraction there. Yeah, they were handsome and even exciting in their antics, but an actual blood boiling attraction to one of them had never been there. I'd thought something was wrong with me. But now? No. I definitely felt attraction, and it was...*explosive, deep.* To say the least. *I now had this to face as well?*

Moving slowly, I walked over to the darkened window. From here, I could see the countryside. The moon was nearly full as it followed its path among the clouds in the sky. The teaming Keep life within the walls had slowed and I felt the weariness of the day upon me. I stretched my legs. I still felt weak, but the feeling was less than it had been before. I guessed that this was a normal reaction from the intense magick and healing I'd gone through. Moving over to the bed, running my hand over the thick cotton coverlet that lay on top. Morning I knew, would come sooner than I was ready for. At this point, it was bringing to me a whole new world. One that I understood was going to be full of strife and suffering, before a better life could be achieved. I feared some, my fear guiding me, but soon, my weary mind began to fall into sleep, a pair of green eyes lulling me there. I thought I felt, for the briefest of moments, a hand caress my cheek as I drifted off.

*

I awoke late the next afternoon, only to learn that my plans for the day were not going to happen. It appeared that the ordeal of yesterday had left me more exhausted than I'd realized, though now I felt rested and relaxed. A knock sounded on the door not long after awakening.

"Come in." My voice sounded rough, unused.

"Good day to you Angel. I am SeldWynn. I am an ArtimA *en* Learning, here at the Atrium. It is good to see that you have finally woken."

"Oh, well...could you please tell me the time?"

"It is nearly two in the afternoon."

"Two in the afternoon?" I felt the shock of it pass through me. "Why has no one woken me sooner? The day is getting away from me."

"Actually, CalOwAy asked us not to awaken you. He was pretty certain that you would be exhausted after yesterday and he wanted to make sure that you were recovered enough before moving about. However, if you feel well rested, we have a surprise for you."

"A surprise? I've had too many of those lately. Is this one, at least, a good one?" I asked in trepidation. Not really wanting to face anything more at the moment. *Maybe after a filling breakfast . . .*

He laughed at the expression on my face. "I think so. Gable has provided a chamber for you within the Keep. We wanted to make sure that you felt ready to leave, before moving you. What do you say?"

I felt the relief rush through me. "I think I'd like that."

"Good. It will not take long. Once we get there, you have been instructed to take this last day to get acquainted with your chambers and surroundings. Let the others know of anything else that you will require."

"I see. Well, you might as well get me started." I said with a laugh.

"Very well. I have some clothing here for you. Go ahead and get dressed. Then I will show you the way to your chamber."

*

I looked down at the dress I'd been given. It was beautiful. Woven from silk, it was a pale cream color. It hung as a simple sheath, down my body to my ankles. It had thin straps, as well as slits up both sides that ended above mid-thigh. A covering of shimmering material that hung from waist to foot, covering it. It was not something that I normally would have chosen for myself. It was form fitting without being snug; my curvy shape was well accentuated. *I loved it!*

Over this, I put on a long vest of the same color and fabric. The sleeves reached only to forearm, leaving my wrists and hands exposed. The vest glittered in the light, as it appeared that thousands of tiny crystals had been woven into the silk. The light silk felt cool against my flesh, giving me a momentary shiver as I adjusted. A pair of soft leather slippers, these with crystals as well, finished off the ensemble. I felt like royalty. *I fit the part now.* I suddenly thought as I gazed in the mirror. The time to see if I could accomplish it was coming.

SeldWynn came in and together we left the Atrium. The Keep, what I could see of it, was beyond beautiful. None of my dreams or creations could have prepared me for the real thing. It was a quick walk, but it was enough for me to realize that the weather was changing. Doing the math, I realized that it was probably around mid-October. At home, the leaves would already have begun falling. While here, only a faint trace of color was beginning to show in the trees of the courtyard. It seemed that even the seasons had their own ways here.

We walked a little longer, following a covered breezeway that ran along the side of the Keep. Cobblestones were our pathway, beyond ageless, they had been rubbed smooth along the way. As the sunlight caught off the wall to my left, a glitter of light caught my attention. Walking over to the wall, I noticed that the cobblestone walls had patches, in and out, where instead of stone, were what appeared to be clusters of crystals. It appeared that they were growing from the stone itself, a nearly seamless union of the two.

"They are quartz, with an occasional amethyst." SeldWynn said before I could ask. "They offer a sense of well being to the faery within these walls. As well as providing another line of defense against the Darke. "

"They're beautiful. I have never seen anything like this before."

"Beauty is one of the many things that you will see here; we have a large variety of artistic expression. As well as our beauty, we have many lines of defense here as well. Soon, I am sure; you will begin learning of them."

I realized that Gable must have spoken to his Kind of me, if they were already aware of whom I was. Turning back, I followed him as he led the way into the Keep through a smaller side door. It attached to the main entrance and hall, but we went around, taking several staircases to reach a destination on what I assumed was the fourth floor, though I was not sure. We stopped in front of a large wooden door. The face of the door was intricately carved. The designs of what appeared Celtic knots ran deep and old, the brass door handle continued the design, though the knob itself was smooth. He opened the door for me and I preceded him in. It appeared that everything about the faery spoke of art and history, their influence appeared to be in just about everything

I saw on my way. Looking around me as he began talking, words were beyond me at the wealth and beauty I saw here, my thoughts and words, frozen in wonder.

"This is one of the larger chambers. You will have a bed chamber, study and washroom. Caitrin said that you preferred purples, so your preference was taken into account. We hope that you are pleased and take the rest of the afternoon to enjoy yourself, getting acquainted with your surroundings."

I merely nodded my head at him, words still beyond me at the moment, walking in circles around the room. Everywhere I looked was art of fantasy, brought to life. The walls were covered in mythical scenes; maidens and unicorns, a hunter and a centaur, even a view of the moon, full and bright with a nymph gliding sensuously. There were brass carvings along with wooden. Both rubbed smooth by age. On the table by the bed, sat a mermaid, her smile and tail both raised in a silent, come hither appeal. Thick plush carpets and tapestries, everything was straight out of any girl's imagination, out in real life and able for me to touch. "It's beyond perfect." I whispered to him.

SeldWynn nodded and left, a smile lighting his features as he closed the door quietly behind himself.

*

Quickly, I became lost. The room was a treasure trove. Like a child in a wonderland, I explored everything. The bed to the side caught my attention. Draped from the ceiling, in all four corners were silken sheets that served as screens. Upon the bed lay velvet and silk coverings along with pillows, all done in various shades of amethyst. It was striking. The furniture of the room was wooden and solid. Again, evidence of their carving abilities was evident in the deep swirls of the grain. Sitting on the bed, I sank deeply into the luxurious bedding, a side table full of bottles and jars, perfumes and lotions. And a set of wide double doors leading out to a balcony. The view only slightly distorted by partially pulled curtains. Jumping up, I ran over to the door, pulling back the curtain just slightly more and looked outside. It was carved of white marble, solid, durable. I could see a chair and table, both metal and beautifully entwined and blended. Flowers of brilliant shades still blooming.

From there, I searched the study. It turned out to be more of a library. Wide open windows and a large stone fireplace all provided ample light into the room. A desk provided a place for me to write, if I wished, as well as a settee and ottoman. It was truly breathtaking. Next came the books themselves, they were a trove of information. Row after row of leather bound books sat upon the shelves. I soon discovered that most were written in a script I could not identify, but it was beautiful, fluid and flowing. There was also a large portion that contained an older English script that I could read, with a little work, the delicate artwork on every page taking my breath away.

I drifted back to the chamber; my gaze caught on some type of...*something*. Crystals, they were spheres or orbs, suspended from the ceiling. They ranged in size, and moved freely of each other, beautiful jewels and another addition to the magick around me. *I wondered what kind of purpose they served, other than just being beautiful?* Curiously, I walked over, rubbing my finger tip over a smooth, glistening surface. It was with much surprise that I realized it had its own warmth...

. . . The orb shifted, not much, but enough to make contact with the next one. It rippled out, the contact and . . . and music began as a steady hum, a lovely cry of the violin, then the pipes and harp. It was transfixing . . . *music*. It was the most beautiful music maker I had ever seen. My inquisitive wanderings ended, when I suddenly realized I was no longer alone . . .

"Simply exquisite." He said with a smile upon his lips as he looked at her.

"Yes, it's beyond anything that I could have imagined." I remarked in awe.

He laughed at her misunderstanding, but said nothing to the contrary. "I was wondering if you might like to sit and talk."

"I would love that." I said with a smile of my own.

"I am having lunch brought to us. I was informed that you have not eaten yet. It should be here shortly."

My stomach growled. "Thank you. I had not realized how hungry I was until you'd just mentioned it." A slight blush to my features was warming my face.

He led the way to the study. His clothing was different today. They appeared more "relaxed." Dark leather boots sat to just under his knees with darker leather pants. More leather criss-crossed as threading, running up the side were tucked into his boots. His pants were snug. I noticed that they displayed his muscular thighs and calves. A slight tremor of heat, passing through my stomach. I sucked in air. His shirt was a shade of light. It fell to right about mid-thigh, open at the neck, revealing more thick muscle and hair. I could see that his scar continued down and disappeared into the rest of the shirt over his chest. The sleeves rolled up to his elbows, displaying strong, attractive, tan hands.

His wings as usual, where tucked down, but they were glorious all the same. Being this close to him, I noticed that his hair was unlike anything I'd seen. He wore it long, nearly to his waist. At first, from a distance, I had thought that it had been in a type of lock, similar to the dread locks worn back home. But closer now, I could see that every "lock" was an intricate braid, so many layers and a solid thickness that it appeared as if a rope of solid satin, random golden beads, woven into the layers. The in-depth beauty that they displayed, in even the smallest detail, made me feel slightly off cord. *How could I compare?*

As I followed him into the study, my hand brushed against his bare forearm. It was fire spreading. It started at the small contact, and before it was broken, it surged through my veins, consuming my being and heating my blood. I stopped breathing, exquisite pain and absolute pleasure. My heart crashed into my ribs. Heat flooded my lower half. I stifled my groan of longing, just barely, before it had time to leave my lips. Feeling my face flush, but I also felt embarrassment that he might notice my reaction. *"How could he not be affected?"* But it was there, for a brief moment passion, a flare of familiarity was present in his eyes. A sudden lifetime of wanting, and then, it was gone. Replaced with their friendly glance instead.

I shook my head. It had seemed so real, but I had to have imagined it, there was no other explanation. He gave nothing away. Working hard at getting my breathing back to normal, the struggle, hard. I'd never had so much trouble in my life. He on the other hand, seemed perfectly unaffected.

Gable smiled at the reaction that she tried to keep hidden. He pulled his arm back from its position, allowing the contact to be broken, the hairs on his arms, still standing from the pleasure. It amazed even him, the strength of these feelings with the slightest of contact. He could not resist, he wanted so much, but for now, he would take all that he could have, even in the smallest amount of pleasures. Rather than nothing at all. Taking a seat upon the settee, realizing that there was much for the both of them to face, in the coming days.

Only a few moments of uncomfortable silence passed. "I cannot thank you enough, for the chambers . . . oh, and the dress. They're both beyond beautiful!"

"I am glad that you think so. This really is not an area that I am familiar with, but I am glad that you were pleased."

His smile was devastating as it graced his lips. I really needed to get this under control. The emotions in themselves were distracting, how was I to deal with their effects to my system?

Smiling in return, he continued. "Once, long ago, artistic pursuit was our staple in life. But since the Dark*e*, well, we have had to specialize in areas that have become more important..."

"Art is important. It marks the success of one's culture. If you forget that, then you begin to forget what all you are fighting for."

He smiled at her, a bit abashed. "I did not mean to make it sound the way it came out. I should have finished with . . . *more important out of necessity.*"

"I can understand that. But reminding ourselves always keeps our souls on . . . on course." I said with a slight hitch in my breathing.

He smiled at her fresh perspective. *This is what he needed, they all needed.*

"Caitrin's room is directly down the hall to the right. If you travel down, two more doors, you then reach my chambers. This is actually the family wing of the Keep."

"Oh? I had not realized. Surely we are putting others out?" I wondered out loud.

"No. I have had no other family for a while now. Our families are much smaller than those of humans . . ." He said the words with ease.

. . . But I could sense, no, feel so much more in them. There was an uncomfortable strain to his voice. "I'm sorry for your loss. I imagine that with your limited abilities to care, it must be felt much deeper for the ones that you are capable of feeling for." I could relate to the loss, and my heart went out to him.

He stared at her a moment, her insight quite unique. "Yes, you are right. Our emotions for our families are quite deeper than those felt by humans. It is odd that you should know that." *Maybe there was something more to her understanding? Something deeper.*

"I . . . I meant no offense . . ." I was shocked at myself. I did just seem to know that. *How?*

"There was none taken." He said, his expression becoming more serious. "It just astounds me, the insight that you seem to naturally have."

We were interrupted by a knock at the door. A faery that I did not recognize delivered our meal, a large salad with tiny slices of hearty beef. "I'm glad that you are not vegetarians. I must admit that I love a filling meal." I said ruefully.

He surprised me by breaking out in a deep, rolling laugh. It took him a moment to get it under control. "I think that I will like having you here. You say things that others would not. Sometimes they are really amusing things."

I could feel my face turning red at his backwards type of compliment. "I only meant that at my home, it seems that faery in stories and movies are almost always vegetarians. Excluding mine, that is. They never eat meat." I finished explaining.

"I did not wish to embarrass you, that was not my intention. It is good to know that you are capable and comfortable enough to say what you actually think or feel. From your words it is obvious that the "people" of your realm, do not really understand anything about real faery. We enjoy the bounty of the Creator's Harvest. We are indeed a heartier breed than that."

We finished the rest of our meal in silence, both enjoying the delicious food, trying to replace the sudden unique silence that had developed. I really just didn't know what to say or do. I'd never been good at this sort of thing.

*

I sat back, satisfied. The food here was beyond magnificent. There was so much flavor that one could almost see it, and then my earlier thoughts started intruding and my curiosity was once again unleashed. "When you mentioned art earlier, I've seen the richness of your world, of the things that you surround yourselves with, but I don't really see any technology? Though it appears that you lack no comforts, how is that possible?" I asked. "I want to understand. I'm somewhat overwhelmed at the things that I've seen so far."

"There is far more wealth here than even you could imagine. We are surrounded by riches, but everything we do, everything we are, revolves around one single thought, *"and we do no harm to the Earth"*."

"I've seen that much already. Though I cannot imagine how much more there is. The intricate clothing and jewelry you wear. The bookmaking skills from the books here, in this very study," I said, sweeping my hands out to the bookcases surrounding us, "the interesting language you speak and the test of its written form. Then the decadent foods you have, the modern living, but no electricity and appliances. Even the use of the Celtic stylization and traditions, all of it speaks volumes in the area of tradition and yet, modernization."

He nodded to her. "It is, and always has been about nature. We have all that your Kind has ever striven for. Yet, we have never taken it at the expense of the Earth. There is so much in the magick of the Creator, so much that Hé has given us. But man, he has drifted away from the simple truths, thinking that things, for some reason, need to be more complex, more "scientific"." He said the word with a grimace. "Life is about believing, about being. The earth was a gift from the Creator. From beginning to end, Shé will be kept safe."

"You say that like she has a soul."

He looked at me in a funny way, and then shook his head. I suddenly felt like the little girl, caught in the midst of doing something wrong.

"Perhaps, Shé has the greatest. For Shé has borne the brunt of your world for thousands of years now and still Shé spins, only the Creator knows the truth. But if we all took more time to care; perhaps Shé would give us more time as well."

I thought about what he said. On the strange events in weather that had been occurring before I had ended up here. *Was it possible that "Mother Nature" was finally tired enough of Man to start setting the record straight?* This time, I shook my head. If it had been me, I didn't think I would have been able to wait this long. "God help us all." I said with a shake of my head. Then I listened to his simple words.

"The sad truth is that it is all there, everything everyone ever wanted to know about the Creator and Hís Love. Every religion has a piece of it. It was always meant to be a unifying force, to celebrate differences and bring unity to humanity. A learning experience, through understanding, through truth. Instead, humans turned it into a bloodbath over who was more superior than the other. Who's visions, interpretations and words were truth. There never was truth in them, it is the Creator that is Truth. They never got the idea right, even in its simplest form. We are all equal. Sometimes, it appears that simple, is the most complex."

My thoughts come back to me after a moment of contemplating his words. *It should be so simple.* I agreed. Watching him, he was . . . *unsettled.* I could tell that, so I switched topics, back to what we had started talking about before.

"I know that your Kind used to be dedicated to the Arts. But it seems like it has been so long for you. It's hard to believe that a race that has had to change so much, could go back so easily to the before?" I questioned.

"We have become a warrior race. We have not had much of a choice, with the Darkeness and the war. It was something that was thrust upon us. There is much of our way of life that has been interrupted, but not forgotten. Our hopes are to begin again, when the danger has passed. It might not be easy, setting all that we have become aside. However, to give up war is more our dream than anything."

"I see." I thought for a moment, weighing my thoughts and questions. "So, in essence, you are like the Warriors of God? Like Hís right hand?"

It startled him, such a simple revelation, a simple truth, but he had never himself, truly thought of it that way. "Here on Earth we are." Was his thoughtful reply.

I watched the look on his face, puzzled by his shock. "So what about Angels?"

"They do not come to Earth as much. Those that are here are mostly the Fallôn, hiding in the crevices of the Darke." He straightened himself up in his seat. "You have to understand. There is so much out there, so many places that the children of the Creator reside. Many years ago, before any of us were here, the Creator used to walk these lands. This was Hís place, Hís sanctuary. After a while, Hé decided that Hé wanted to share it and not be alone. This place is the Beginning, where all life came into existence. The Creator, Hé created us, the Faery. We took our place here, among the woods and mountains. Faery, are the Creators' Earthen Angels."

"This may be hard to understand, but the Angels were needed elsewhere. The Creator has a large Kingdom. It spreads out over many places, many existences. We, the Faery, are unique to Earth. The Creator, Hé is brilliant, Hís ability to create and Hís need for it. Afterward, Hé brought

Humanity into existence; we became the protectors of Earth and Humanity for the Creator."

"If Hé had Angels and then Faery, why did Hé bother with humans? It seems that we are nothing but trouble." I couldn't imagine that we were offering much in the way of optimism, for the world in general.

"I cannot tell you of His mind, for that I am not privileged too, but I can tell you . . . what I understand it to be. Even though we are all each unique in our own right, we are also all the same. We each have different levels of allegiance and freedom from the ones before us. The Angels have complete obedience and allegiance to Him. The Faery has complete allegiance, but the ability to interpret with understanding for change. Humans have complete free will, to do and think as they so choose. Their choices are their own. Freedom is their Right."

"It is my belief, that Hé was looking to see the extent of what one's faith was, when they were given more of a choice in their own destiny. Hé was looking for the best in all of us. With you, humans, Hé was searching for the greatest power. I do not know if Hé ever found it though."

"Hé is so close." The words came again. I thought about that. *How freedom was our Right and about how, in my own realm, we had to fight for every inch we had!* It only made me sadder. "I never thought of life on such a large scope before. It really makes all of us seem so small, insignificant. We're almost like specks of dust on the wind."

"No Angel. It should make you feel loved and cherished. We are each His children and we are all in the palm of His hand. The Creator remembers and believes in us all."

"No simpler truth could be spoken."

Knowledge
(14)

My first complete view of the Keep was breathtaking. The cobblestone and crystal clusters continued throughout the rest of the Keep and walls. Larger than anything I'd ever seen, there were floors upon floors, with great towers and walkways. It put the castles in the movies to shame. It was wondrous and overflowing with life. Pennants, actual pennants, flared from the tops of the tower gates, bearing the arms of the Keep of Ainys'Dai. Above, clouds were fluffy and marshmallow like, while the courtyard was still full of green life; trees, shrubs and grasses. In all my life, it was a sight that I could not imagine, could not believe, and it was to be my new home.

There was no poverty here, no suffering. Even with all that had happened around them, each was cared and provided for. Even the inner wall, as it spread out past the inner courtyards, did not distract from the beauty of the Keep. It was pure magick and romance rolled up into one. Here, seeing all of it like this, made me believe in the faerytale.

* * * * * * *

I quickly learned that training was going to be a lot more complex than I'd originally imagined. Even though I knew it was true, I could not believe how true it really was. Seeing what I now saw, I knew that I was way, way out of my element. Breathing deeply, I focused my thoughts on the situation. Pulling on my imaginative abilities to try and see something that could help. Suddenly, a dawning of understanding came to me.

"You have always had the answer." I bristled a little, at my own insolence.

As I opened my eyes, I realized that the answer was indeed something that I had always had, my stories. I could be the heroine of one of my own stories. I could place myself, in my own mind, in the stories of my imagination, replacing my lead with myself. It was not entirely the same thing, but with my vision, I could give myself the focus I needed to see this through. I could let the story take its lead and put me in the right direction. Not simple, but something I understood. Turning my head, I looked at Gable as he began to speak:

"We are going to follow the same basic structure that we were using with Caitrin. You'll have lessons in the morning with the TA Archers, on magick. We will give you a week to prepare with the lessons, to get a firm start. Then you will join us. In the afternoons, you will begin basic combat with my warriors and myself. I am not going to lie to you; we are going to push you as far as we possibly can."

"I would expect nothing different Gable. I only pray that I am able to be ready when the time comes."

"You will be."

I followed his lead as he led the way to the Hall of Knowledge. This was where my instruction would begin. It was much like a library and a school room in one. It was enormous, with its high vaulted ceilings and generous stained glass windows, to say the least. As I looked around me, I noticed that several faery were already in attendance. I understood them to be my teachers as I walked over to them to be introduced. I was nervous, realizing that this was it, the beginning. I took a deep breath and made myself relax.

Gable turned to address the closest faery. "Good day AriEsan, I would like to introduce you to Angel." The faery bowed slightly to me, a sign of respect. Gable turned slightly to his right, his attention shifting to the remaining teacher. "This is EelfWen. MyInTernin will continue teaching Caitrin at this time." Gable addressed the last, directly to me.

"It is the humblest of respect we feel, as being those chosen to be here to guide you on the great quest that the Creator has set for you." EelfWen said as he bowed his head to me.

"I can think of no greater honor, than to receive training from two such highly recognized TA Archers. It's I that feels the greatest respect for your assistance." I bowed in their honor. A look of disbelief was displayed on the faces of the two faery. They were greatly honored by my heartfelt response.

From here, my instruction began with an aura of comfort. Gable left me in their care, promising to see me when we were finished for the day.

*

They brought out books, multiples of books. I was literally in heaven. I could not believe the depth and extent of the beauty that was laid before me. The books were ancient, their beauty and magick very much apparent. The texts were of all sizes, some containing only a few pages, some with hundreds. All of the texts were illuminated manuscripts, in rich vibrant colors and hues. They spoke of the TÀle's and explained the use of spells, some of them written in their ancient writings, some in the older form of English that I'd noticed before. *I wasn't sure where to start.* But apparently they were. They separated them out, the texts, and placed those before me that were of Humanity. I knew that the shock must have shown on my face, because of the amusement on EelfWen's own.

"We are going to take a different approach this time. We are offering you all of the mistakes of your forefáthairs, in the hopes that you can do what they have been unable to succeed in. We thought them the blueprints of destruction; perhaps, they are the blueprints of Peace." EelfWen said.

"We will work on history, more so, once we feel that you are gaining well in this approach, we will start the practical application of magick. We will work on the language with you, the correct pronunciations and the actual application of it." AriEsan finished.

The idea was to start here, at the beginning. Read, or be read too, and see the sequences as they were intended for use. All of their knowledge was contained within these texts and I was going to have a lot of catching up to do. The first books in my course were six large texts. Some appeared to be very old, the last two, not so much in comparison.

When I looked at the words, at their meanings, I saw . . . *the truth*. They were a fierce contradiction, the Faery, beauty, caught up in war. The world had been through much, it had nearly been torn apart countless times by the force of man and his need for continued power. According to the text, according to all of them, all six, these were the accounts of Earth that none alive knew of, except the faery themselves. The TÀles of the Epochs, the Faery were the Keepers of the Texts; they were the very Archives of Humanity. I could only imagine the drooling of any scholar, able to get their hands on even one of these texts. It would be beyond a dream come true. They explained so much, filled in the gaps in our history that had caused confusion and so many misunderstandings.

Each text was highly detailed in its description of the way man progressed and moved on. In each, they ended with near genocide and destruction, only a small few remaining to populate the earth over again. Each time, the Faery played their role of Provider and Nurturer. The final chapter, the sixth, was the story of Noah, of the Great Flood. Here was the difference. The Faery were kept back from Man, to be lost in the shrouds of mist, the forgotten memories of old. Only to be remembered as vague myths and concepts.

One pulled my attention more than the others. It spoke of earth in terms of tens of thousands of years ago. "The world was a thriving entity," I read to myself out loud, "Man had progressed further than ever, even the earth, untouched by pollution in their wake." It was the fifth book. It spoke of humanity in terms that far outreached what we had even now. Their society was advanced, similar to that of the Faery. They had progressed well, working within the confines of the Leight. "Cities in the clouds and modern wings of flight," was a simple description given of their society. "Thousands of years of near peace and prosperity, their end had come as a flaw."

A flaw in human nature, it came about in their thought to create the ultimate power source. Though they had all and lacked for nothing, they sought more. Their brilliant strategy, ended in the death of nearly every human on earth, as a raging inferno in the earth's atmosphere, cast down raining fire. Obliterating and erasing their existence. The beauty of the earth destroyed, only a handful of small children the survivors. So much hope had been placed in them.

They had been so close. I could feel the tears falling down my cheek, before I even realized that I was crying. So much suffering, so much pain, and for what? More power, more greed? Was there no end? I could feel it within me. I knew that we were on our last chance, here and now. We were living book seven, and it was coming to a close. I realized more in that moment than I thought possible. *It was not even our end that we were fighting for; it was for the very end. The ending to the TÀle, the end to God's TÀle, it made me wonder, were we even worth saving?*

"Until your very last breath." The words whispered throughout me.

*

I worked hard with them; no one watching could deny my dedication and stamina. I learned of ancient Faery history. They taught me the core of Faery magick, its basic rules and responsibilities. I learned that magick truly was their gift. It was used for spiritual growth and protection. They were able to control the four elements, to call upon them when needed; they could also set magickal circles of protection. These were their basic skills, the first one learned and accomplish in youth. Because of these basic outlines, magick for them, was not able to be used in warfare or battle. That was why the warrior class was forced to develop. Why they needed and depended upon me so much. I was not faery and I could use my magick as it was needed. I had the ability to make up my own mind, humanity was my strength. *Such a flawed contradiction!* I was not governed by the same laws of magick that they were. I was indeed unique, could be their Savior. Soon they brought me to the heart, or perhaps I should say the soul, of Faery Magick.

"Our magick, all magick, springs forth from our soul. It is our very essence; it is the Leight of the Creator that gives us our powers. When the ability to control it is present, it is merely an extension of us, an extension of a word or thought. Everything that the Creator created holds a piece of life within it, something to be tapped into. Magick comes from air, earth, fire and water, the four elements. The fifth is the soul. All magick is deeply ingrained. This is what we wish to teach you." AriEsan instructed.

"The power that the Creator has given you is immense. It has the ability to blend all aspects of the circle, to end the trial and suffering that has been upon us so very long. Even we, in all our learning, will not be able to offer you much. But we will give you all that will be the basis for your journey, your foundation. We are going to start your journey now . . ."

* * * * * * *

As the end of my first week arrived, the TA Archers decided that it was time to tap into my potential; to put me in contact with the Source of my powers in an attempt to get them flowing. *To help wash away some of the restrictions placed upon my mind by being human.* I relaxed back on the reclining settee. Deep meditation, they instructed me, was the quickest and most reliable way to get things started.

"I want you to close your eyes. Then breathe in and breathe out. Deep from within your abdomen pull in the relaxing light and release the tension and anxiety. Relaxation is what you feel."

Listening to their words, I followed their directions, falling deeper and deeper under their spell. I could feel my feet and legs relax, warmth spreading outward and up, my hips and waist following in the same manner. The creeping lethargy flowed into my chest, arms and neck. My eyes became heavy. My head feeling weighed down, though my mind was clear. I felt safe, loved even.

"You are reaching the deepest level of relaxation now. Your entire body is relaxed and heavy. Your mind free of the constraints placed upon it. Reaching deep, I want your mind to search within itself. Search for the Leight and the Source. You are seeking to communicate with yourself on the most basic level. Deep within your subconscious are all your answers. The subconscious is a direct connection to the Creator."

I could feel my body as it drifted in a state of nothingness, then . . . a happy hum of vibrancy. My body was tingling, the sensations deep rooted, feeling thick, heavy and disconnected. After a while, I began to feel my consciousness disconnecting from my body entirely. *I was searching . . .*

"You have reached complete relaxation. I want you to focus around yourself now. Notice the dark and the leight. Hear the sounds of your soul and feel it. Around you, see the Source of your magick. Seek it out, call to it. Listen for its answer." He said.

I felt myself moving, though my physical body remained motionless. All around me were lights. The flow was serene, washing over me. But then it washed through me, sensations piercing the skin in a deluge of rare ecstasy, feelings based entirely on the sensations of my mind. Changing again, I could see the lights, ebbing and flowing, a rippling effect, such as a pebble cast on water. Curiously, I followed their movements inward.

Before I could hear, I could sense sound from in front of me. It was similar to the beat of a heart, but it appeared as if played on a harp, a poignant sound. I continued on, reaching closer and closer, until I came upon my core. *Here was beauty . . .*

Before my eyes appeared to be an orb of molten gold, it stood as tall as myself, glistening and rotating, pulsating out the rhythm of my life. Within its depths, it appeared as if a looking glass; for it reflected myself back at me. I realized it reflected scenes of my life. The music from before radiated from it. Beautiful and sorrowful, the harp song made me feel things on a deeper level. I recognized it now; it was the song of my soul, a litany to my pain and passion. My very thoughts and feelings being reflected back at me. The constant struggle I faced came from my very core.

"Move closer." One of the TA Archers instructed me. I did so, the orb only getting larger. "You must make contact. You must free that which is inside of you."

"I already know." I found myself saying to no one in particular. I crept closer; raising my hand I took the final step to the orbs presence. Heat radiated from it, making it welcoming and safe. Breathing deep, I placed my hand upon my essence. The touch was like lightning, the strength of the explosion rushing through my body. It was static and heat, frightening and beautiful. I could feel the extension of myself. Feel the magick as it arced and curled around my fingers. I could feel the surge of power as it went deep. Then . . . I jerked awake . . . confusion lashing through my senses. Searching within my own heart . . . I could hear my soul's response, *"A heart not met. I was not ready yet."*

*

I heard the knock on the door and I glanced up in surprise. No one, save Caitrin, ever visited me here, especially this late. Standing, I put the robe back on that I'd discarded earlier. I pulled back the door, even more surprised to see Gable on the other side.

"I did not mean to bother you, but I noticed the light on and needed to speak with you." In his hands . . . was a large package? "Our training will start in the morning, so I am bringing you your clothing. Inside the main package is your "*gilden sul* dá," your jerkin. It will provide near impenetrable protection from neck to wrist and ankle. In the second package, is your actual "uniform."" He looked me in the eye, but quickly looked away.

A bit abashed, or uncomfortable, I realized. This was unusual, something was going on.

"I am somewhat aware of modern human clothing, what our females wear might be something new for you. But it is comfortable and nonrestrictive."

"That's fine; I'll just have to adjust if necessary." *I seemed to be all about making adjustments these days.* I thought to myself.

He nodded. "Our "*gilden sul* dá" are permanent. You will only ever need the one. It might take a little bit of . . . getting used to."

His behavior was definitely odd. "OK." I wasn't really sure what he meant, but weariness had me in its grasp and falling asleep on my feet.

"I will see you in the morning, try to sleep well."

"I can manage that." I said with a smile on my lips. "Goodnight." I closed the door, throwing the packages and my robe in the chair next to the bed. Tomorrow morning was soon enough to look them over. Falling asleep, I dreamt of myself, immersed in full length chain mail…

Guardians
(15)

Move faster! I yelled at myself, trying to hurry! I'd overslept. I still wasn't used to having no alarm clock. Yet no one had bothered to come and find me either. I looked for my clothes and suddenly remembered the package from the night before. I sprinted back to the chair, picked up the package and pulled the thin string. Paper fell one way while the slinky material, the other. I reached down and picked up the cloth.

It was flesh colored, and sparkled like diamonds. It was extremely thin and stretchy. I could not imagine how this would offer me much protection. Soon I realized, it was entirely one piece and had to be pulled and tugged upward from the feet first. It was work, but not hard. I readjusted several times, until it was comfortably on. I glanced in the mirror, thinking that I looked naked, grimacing. Suddenly, I was seized. It was an intense tingle, covering the length of the *gilden sul dá*, then quickly, a flash of burn and a thick tightness. For a moment, I was brought to my knees. Then the tingling returned and the squeezing pressure released its grip on me. I stood up slowly, afraid that it might happen again, but I was fine. Looking in the mirror, I reacted in sudden shock and horror.

I was naked, completely naked, the *gilden sul dá* gone, as if it had never been! I ran my hand over my waist, my thighs. It was me, nothing but normal, peachy colored flesh. Nothing felt wrong, still soft, and still pliant. Then, Gable's words came back to me. *"Our jerkins are permanent."*

"Damn!" I said out loud. No wonder he had looked so uncomfortable, he knew that I would have never of put it on, if I'd been aware of what it really was. *He was sneaky. I couldn't believe it! He was going to regret this. Oh yes, he was definitely going to regret this indeed!*
*

My training with Gable. I laughed to myself. *He had better be ready, because this was going to be an interesting matter, definitely.* After being closed up with the learning portion of magick, I was filled with longing for the out of doors. But still bracing for the idea of combat. *And now, I owed him one for that damn jerkin! And apparently, the uniform as well! He was going to pay! I approached the field hesitantly, but with anger seeping through the edges.* My thoughts were full of trepidation. *You would have thought that having to learn to fight would have put me in this state, but on the contrary, it was the state of my attire that was giving me heart palpitations.*

Last night, when Gable had given me the clothing, I'd never thought that I should have taken the time to look them over, I knew better now. *Yeah, my gilden sul dá, or now my skin, if you wanted to get technical, was as indestructible as titanium, being blessed with a massive spell of protection.*

But the clothing that followed was the real problem. Or should I say lack of clothing. I had almost passed out from the shock of skin, visible skin, after putting them on. Inappropriate, no one at my weight should wear this. *I was plump. No amount of imagination could change that. Sure, I'd had dreams of being someone exotic, mysterious even, what young girl hadn't? But I wasn't that girl anymore!*

The outfit was golden and cream. A golden torque, held the cream fabric in place over my breasts, almost like a bikini top, my waist bare. Then a golden belt, inlaid in jewels, held a long flowing cream drape in place over the bottoms. Much like a skirt, with a slit up the sides for movement. The actual bottoms no more than a bikini strip of cloth. I could see how it was good for battle; lite weight, nonrestrictive and comfortable. This outfit would have worked perfectly, but not on *me* . . .

I grimaced, looking down at myself again. *Forget fear, I was mortified!* There was no way I could wear this in public. I could see Gable and the other warriors as they came into view. If I acted quickly, I could still turn around and go back before they noticed me. *What to do?*

"Damn!" I could feel the heat flooding my face as they turned this way. My chance of escaping had disappeared.

I could feel all of their eyes on me, a huge group of gorgeous male flesh, because they all seemed to be perfect specimens. Their wings only accentuated their muscular forms. I could see that their clothing was perfect for them. Some wore leather leggings of sorts, while some even had a wrap, similar to my own, but covering much more. *But dear God, it was so wrong on me!* I shook my head and continued closer. *I knew that faery females were mostly slim, though they could be short or tall. I imagined this outfit would probably be fitting for them. But come to think of it, I wasn't sure how the whole female warrior thing went? I had never actually seen one, and none appeared here.* I shook my head, it didn't matter. On me, this was trouble.

*

Gable had to fight past the lump in his throat in order to breath. It felt like someone had punched him in the gut and attempted to knock his knees out from under him at the same time. *Bloody Hell, she was gorgeous!* She had pulled her hair back to keep it out of her way. Her neck accentuated by the sweeping of her satiny mane. It was the neck down that set him on fire. The clothing only accentuated her curves. The top fitting her like a glove. *One hell of a lucky glove!* Supple silk caressed and glued to her skin, her breasts and hips fairly bursting out of the attire, her exposed waist, a trove of curves. Her long legs were bare and they ended nice and snug in a pair of calf high leather boots. Flesh, she was all beautiful exposed flesh. He really should have demanded to see how she looked before she had come out in front of him and his warriors.

His warriors! He quickly turned to see his rows of warriors, most with admiration showing in their eyes. Though they were faery, beauty was deeply ingrained in their society, they would have to of been dead, to not appreciate the blatant female beauty in front of them. No strong attraction would be there, but they could still appreciate it. Apparently, they were. He felt heat flare within him. He wasn't sure if it was completely desire, or a sense of rage. He really needed to march her back to the safety of the Keep. He was sure he was going to kill her himself. The power of the passion he felt, raging through him, corrupting his balance.

He swung back around to face her as she approached. A good healthy dose of pleasure flared within him again, causing annoyance and anger to suddenly stab at him. *This was not going to be easy.* He quickly realized. "I see that you finally made it." He said, biting off his words at the end, appearing the sudden, intimidating warrior.

I felt myself flinch. "Yes." I replied, my eyebrows lifted at his abrupt attitude. I felt the sudden jolt to my insides, his manner startling me. Then I realized that he appeared more agitated than angry. I looked back and forth between him and the admiring looks of the warriors. Maybe this wasn't such a bad thing after all. "You know what they say. A real woman takes her time." I winked at him as I walked past, hips swaying side to side, to join the other warriors on the practice field. The laughter of the others, was more admiration, than humor. My blazing face kept hidden from his view. The courage of such a move usually beyond me, but that should have put us at just about even, for now.

He only stared at her in amazement, before a thundering laugh erupted from within him. *Annoyed or not, this was definitely going to be interesting.* He decided, his sudden anger melting away, his passion, holding firm. *Definitely interesting!*

The field they used to practice on was off to the east side of the inner courtyard. It was surrounded by a wooden post fence with two out-buildings, used to store weapons and supplies. There were a total of thirty-one warriors in attendance, with the addition of Angel.

"Angel, I would like to introduce you to the Alphinian Guardians. They are the first line of defense for Ainys'Dai and the best warriors to be found. It has been determined that your training will come from the best. By watching us and training with us, you will be able to see the multiple skills and styles each warrior displays. You can adjust and adapt to what works best for you." Next, he introduced them all by name.

I looked them over, the Alphinian Guardians. They were all different, though similar. There was no mistaking the air of warrior. *Definitely no faery wisecracks here!* All stood to nearly seven foot tall, maybe one or two over.

Each was thickly muscled and their power undeniable. They were giants, but beautiful ones. Like all before, they had vibrant hair, radiating hues of color. Their appearances ranged from short cropped auburn hair, which glowed like flames, to several warriors who wore their hair long, like Gable's. Only one had locks similar to his, but his hair had a golden hue. They were all muscular of build, well defined and handsome. It seemed that bright, lively eyes were a strong characteristic of the Faery as well. The colors and depths, so brilliant, that they could be compared to gemstones. *Vibrancy and richness, it was part of everything they were, and lived.* I glanced back, as Gable's voice spoke up louder.

"Now, they are going to break off into smaller groups. For an introduction Angel, you will watch as they demonstrate a single battle scenario. Some of them will be on the ground; some of them will be airborne. I want you to pay careful attention to their skills. Our goals are to develop your own, in a similar fashion, to make you unstoppable, so that your chances of success are concrete. I understand that this is all going to be new to you, so I do not expect you to understand at first. But together, we should be able to see you through." He said.

I felt awareness at his words, like he was speaking into me, reassuring my soul as much as my fear. I held strong to his words. They were one of the few things that were indeed, going to see me through. As I watched, the Guardians broke off into groups. Some composed of two, three and four faery. Almost in unison, the intricate dance began. They moved as if they followed a very tight choreography. Like a dance of high energy and passion. Forward and back, thrust and deflect. Suddenly, they broke into flight, wings a mere blur.

I felt the impact, the devastating power that they welded. The power they displayed, breathtaking and dazzling. Nothing would ever compare to the rapid expansion of wings, as they were thrown wide and beautiful. Their wingspan encompassing the area around them, I could feel myself shrink in comparison to their size and glory. Seeing them open, fully extended, was a truly life changing event. Mesmerized, I forgot to watch for the moment. I was lost in the Grace...the yelling snapped me back into reality. I watched as one warrior was able to mirror the other. A depth and intimacy, were one would never expect to find it. *My life had changed; I realized that it was as concrete as cement.*

They fought in a way foreign to me. Like nothing I had seen on any show. They had moves, skills that went beyond the ordinary. *How was it possible for men so large, so magnificent, to move with such grace and elegance? Feline could be one word used to describe them, stealth, another.* I knew that no human would be capable of what I was seeing. *So, where did that leave me?*

"It's beautiful!" I breathed, at a loss to the splendor.

"Beautiful and deadly, what you are seeing is at half pace. I let them know that we were going to have to move slowly at first. We are nearly invisible at our full potential. But you need to see to understand and learn." He explained.

"Half pace? How will I ever keep up with you? My abilities, my defenses, they're not nearly as advanced as yours." I commented. *I could not see myself doing this in a million years, let alone, in as little as a few weeks.*

"I do not have all the answers; I will not lie to you. It is our belief that your magick, your skills, will play a larger part in your defense and protection, in your attack strategy."

"I hope you're right there." I said.

"I am not proven wrong often." He said as he turned back to face the training field.

"Of course you aren't." I said quietly under my breath. *Oh to be so certain in one's own mind, it must feel nice.*

"It does. You will be there soon." The words drifting through my consciousness.

We continued to watch for a while, before the groups slowed down and finished. Their stamina was amazing, at the very least, an hour had passed, maybe even closer to two. Gable nodded to them as they passed, each on his way to get water. "We will begin again in about thirty minutes. Everyone back then." They each nodded in turn as they passed.

As the last one walked away, I watched as Gable turned back towards me. I figured that now was as good a time as any to get some answers. "A little while ago, I was speaking with SeldWynn at the Keep. He was telling me that the land itself has defenses against the Darkeness. What other defenses do we have to work with?"

"The actual Stronghold has several natural defenses. The first, and simplest, are the crystal clusters of the walls. They are dispersed within the inner and outer walls. They are composed of clear quartz and amethyst. Quartz is a massive conductor of energy; it can store, process and relay information. Amethyst is similar, but not quite as strong. If the presence of evil passes from the shimmer and makes contact with our soil, the crystals will recognize the evil essence and glow. They are a warning signal, announcing the arrival of the darke ones. Unfortunately, they are not able to detect the plague that comes in the first wave."

"Second, at the farthest reaches of the Stronghold, located in the four corners and dead center, are enormous lodestones. They are nearly four tons each. With the five of them in the locations that they reside, they create a huge magnetic field. It provides healthful benefits to us, those of the Leight, to the Darke, it has the opposite effect. When they come in the presence of the highly condensed magnetic field, it actually causes their skin to burn, much like an acidic reaction or sensation. It is purely on the emotional and sensory level, as the damage is not physical, but it provides a great deterrent in battle. Most become occupied with the pain and they are not able to fight it very long. This allows us to have more of an advantage."

"Our third defense are diamond outcrops located in strategic points around the Stronghold. Thousands of years ago, the Dwarfs from the mountains, brought to us the diamonds. The stones stood between seven and nine feet tall. In the Dwarfs fires, deep in the mountains belly, they heated the diamonds in the flames. Their strength, their durability is beyond anything that has ever been seen. We placed them in groups of two's and three's. They were buried at their base by twenty-four inches deep."

"Diamonds are nearly pure, more so than anything else on Earth. They heighten and release Leight out in sound waves. The pitch of its frequency is nearly deafening to the darke ones. They are not able to penetrate through the frequency because of the darke that has tainted their essence. Their extra advantage is that it creates protective circles around each base, in a solid diameter, a solid wall of protection for our fighters to fall back to."

"It looks like we have some strong defenses in our favor. Why then have so many Strongholds fallen?" I asked confusion evident in my words. *It seemed a given that we would have more of an advantage than what we have had.*

"Not all of the Strongholds have the same defenses. Some of them have lodestones; others have diamonds, all have the clusters. The problem is that there is not enough of all three to go around. It was determined that, as the largest Stronghold, Ainys'Dai would have to have the strongest defenses. If the time comes, all forces will fall back to these gates. We will make our stand here."

"What if faery want to come before that? What if they fear for themselves now?"

"They are always welcome. At times now, faery arrive at the gates. No one is ever turned away. This is a way of life that we have lived for a long time now. All know that this is the real sanctuary of Our Kind. It always has been."

I nodded at his response. So many leaders in my realm could have learned from his simple understanding and acceptance.

Gable left my side, heading off to one of the wooden outbuildings. He disappeared inside for several moments, before heading back with something in his hands. I waited, knowing that the Guardians were not due back for a while yet. As Gable got closer, I saw that he carried a sword. Upon closer inspection, it appeared to be wooden. "So, am I to learn much as a child would?" I asked curiously.

"Yes and no. We will work quickly with you, moving through the routines, working you with multiple partners to ensure that your physical abilities match those of the mental. We want to ensure that you can be put directly into combat."

I thought about that. *The idea of it blatantly terrified me.* I understood, to some extent, what was coming. But I really had no idea until the time actually arrived what it would be like. "What about the wooden sword?"

Here he smiled at me. "All warriors receive wooden swords as they begin their training. We work with magick and this is no different. A sword is finely crafted. The sword comes from the wood of a tree, which comes from the earth. Therefore, it contains magick. It is as unique as its warrior. You will begin training with this sword. As you learn, as your skill increases, the sword gathers knowledge about you. When the time is right, we take this sword to the Smythe, or *smith*. There, he will take the knowledge from the sword and combine it with his own to create for you, your sword. After you receive it, you will have become Learned, a Warrior. It is a great honor."

"It is an honor that I plan on living up too." I nodded at him. "While we're discussing training, I have a few more things that I'm curious about."

"Good, a curious mind is an brilliant one. What do you want to know?" He asked.

"I don't see any females among your ranks. Are there any female warriors here or am I the only one?"

"Very observant of you, actually we do have a couple of female warriors, though none are currently at Ainys'Dai. It is not as common for a female to join as it is for the males, though it does happen. In our society, the females are looked at as the nurturers. They are mates and máthairs. Some do hold higher positions in our society, like TA Archers and ArtimA. They are not limited; they are able to do as they are called. Occasionally, great warriors do rise up from amongst them, much like your Joan of Árc. They follow the call of their soul from the Creator and take their place were they belong."

I shook my head, trying to understand. "How do you know so much about our world if you are so separated from us now?"

"Just because we are separate, does not mean that we cannot see. We were placed here to watch and protect. We can see into your realm, even if you cannot see into ours." He nodded his head to the side. "There is much that we still have to talk about, but the Guardians are returning and we need to begin your training. Are you ready?" His smile was evident.

"As ready as I'll ever be." I responded in kind.

Allies
(16)

I quickly got caught up in the routine. I watched as Gable had a mock battle with the faery TazaRine. Though it was only routine, the energy they expended became very apparent to me. Afterward, they had me take a turn with the both of them, allowing me to get a feel for the different styles that they used. I was definitely out of shape, no surprise there, and it was going to take hard work to get me to where I needed to be. But I was not expecting the passion either; it moved me, moved through me. Like dancing was seductive, so was the intense battle movements. I felt the pull and the attraction. It was seduction in a dark way. A deep burn in the middle and a punch of adrenaline. I was blown away at myself, at my own dark craving. *This was going to take a lot more than I had realized. Would be a lot more of me given in the conquest, than I had understood until now. I suddenly felt all to human . . .*

After I finished, they continued the scenario in the air. I was amazed. Though I had no wings myself, I would be taught to defend myself in case of attack from above. I was glad that they were covering all the bases, but it was only in theory. I honestly could not see myself doing half of the things they were showing me. *And I had a pretty avid imagination!*

Time began to pass more quickly as the end of the mock battles came and my hand to hand training began. Like before, I was walked through the same routine with the Guardians. I watched what each did; they did indeed have their own unique style and form. It was all basic, but to me, new and intimidating. There was much more to learn than I'd anticipated. The idea of it excited me. Had me craving more. *I couldn't believe this was me. I was changing, but was there time for so much change? The depth of understanding for just what I was in for, left me wondering if it was even possible for me to learn it all in a lifetime?*

"You will have many lifetimes." I shuddered, the words cursing through me. *How many lifetimes would it take to accomplish this?* I thought.

After my basic introduction of hand to hand combat was completed, they finally brought forward the swords. I grimaced in trepidation. The idea of swinging the blade actually scared me. Though I did not let it show, hopefully. Not even as a child, had I ever felt the need to play with the plastic ones, and this one, or at least, the one I would eventually have, would kill. I was nervous, but I would do it. *There was no longer a choice.*

They instructed me in unsheathing and sheathing my sword in a quick fashion, drawing it for optimal deliverance and the best form of arc for my form and size. Explaining that I needed to keep it well controlled, even one mistake, and it would cost me my life. With surprising ease, I got it under my belt. From now until completion, it would be my job to learn new routines, learn all of the variations of it, and practice. Memorization and practice, day in and day out.

Even to myself, I could feel that I was changing. I was becoming someone different. Someone the old me probably never would of identified with. *I wasn't sure if that was a good thing, or a bad one. Time would tell. That was all I was sure of.* But I would not give in, would not surrender. I was touching a new depth within myself that I'd never confronted before and I was . . . *afraid.* Or ashamed? Was I supposed to feel things in such a dark manner, to feel the thrill of it? *How was I to even get an answer to such a question?*

* * * * * * *

I worked hard, nonstop, for several days straight on all that I was given. I had not believed that there could be so many different ways to fight, to defend. Each new routine, each subtle change, was something more to add into the now growing library of my mind, added into that, the magickal learning and instruction. Trying to place the two together, to create a middle ground that I could feed my power off of, was exhausting. There was no way for them to help me with this, they were as new to it as I was and I was having trouble; there was no doubt about it. There was just so much, so much knowledge and application. I did not know how anyone could remember so many things. They had to trust me as much as I had to trust them.

* * * * * * *

But I did not let any of that stop me. After several weeks of constant work and exhaustion, I could feel myself becoming drained. But I fought against the strain. *How could I have so much inside, so much to give, if the very basic of it was such a difficulty for me? Was such an issue that the TA Archers were becoming frustrated?* I gave myself an unsatisfied laugh. *It was something to see, an unsatisfied faery. I would probably be shaking in my boots, if it wasn't for the fact that I was too tired to care right now. The sad truth was that I was following in my daughters footsteps in this case. Only, I really had no reason for my issues. I just seemed to be the problem.* Focus, I had to keep focused!

As the evening wore down, I could feel the tension and soreness throughout my body. I was weary, beyond belief, when I joined Gable on his way back to the Keep, another day of tackling magick and exhausting exercises. "I'm not sure if I will be able to get out of bed tomorrow. I don't think that there's anything left in my body that doesn't hurt." I said with a grimace of discomfort.

He laughed, a purely masculine sound that sent my stomach fluttering.

"That is to be expected. We are going to have much work to do, to completely get your body battle ready. But the more you do, the better you will become. Maybe you should go to the healing springs, it would be good for you..." He paused, his body moving in a sensuous fashion, before finishing "...it will make it easier for you to face tomorrow." His manner more normal now.

For just a second, I thought that he was thinking of me. I meant *really* thinking of me, but then I realized that, of course, the training was what mattered to him. "I think that I would like that. The Springs." I clarified.

"Will you need anyone to assist you . . . ?" His voice trailed off again.

But this time, I could see the sudden flare in his eyes. *I was not mistaken.* The bright intensity suddenly flamed, before disappearing quickly. Without a trace. *I wish I knew what it meant? What he was coming to mean to me?*

" . . . I could send MadaREn in to help." He offered after his exaggerated pause.

He had to be doing it on purpose, making me think that he was going to offer himself. But why? Why would he be doing this? I could feel the heat rush into my cheeks. I turned my head away, hoping that he hadn't noticed. "No, that's alright. I think I . . . I would like some time to myself." *I actually stuttered!* "I have a lot to go over. Caitrin will come and see me before she goes to rest this evening as well." I attempted to smile, but another grimace crossed my face. "It should not be possible. Even the muscles that I use to smile, seem to be sore!"

This time he broke out in a roar of laughter. It shook his chest and rumbled out. He smiled at the feeling it gave him. At the feelings she gave him. It was wonderful.

"Good to know I can make you laugh." I said in disgust, embarrassed that he was able to bring out such reactions in me. Baiting me so easily!

"Yes, it is good to know." He said, quite seriously. Then he smiled again. We walked a ways in quite.

We were getting close to the doors, when I realized that I didn't want him to go yet. I needed a reason for him to stay, if even for only a few moments longer. I wanted the time with him, alone. Moments spent with him always seemed to pass to quickly, and never accomplished much for me in my attempt to know him better. *OK, back to basics.* I thought. *If he could do it, then so could I.* "I was wondering about something? Do you fight alone? It appears that the Darke has Allies. At least, I saw other things that fell into my realm that appeared darke. Do you not have Allies in this as well?"

"Yes, we do. There are many magickal creatures, though not like there has been in the past. Some of them are passive; they do not take part in war and its ravages. By nature, the Darke invokes violence and destruction, while the Leight is peace and prosperity. When the time comes for aide, as it has in the past, the Centaurs and Dwarfs come. They fight alongside us. While our greatest Allies, they would be the Dragons."

"Dragons!?!" I fairly screamed in my honest excitement. "You have dragons?"

"Yes, Dragons are real. They live mostly amongst themselves. Their knowledge is great and war is the last call that they wish to answer. But, if they are needed, they come."

I thought about that, the magnificence of seeing such a larger and splendorous being, it quickly evoked another question. "If Dragons exist, how do they get around? They must be huge. It would seem to me that they would be well seen, if not their shadows alone, with their size. How are they able to travel without being seen?"

"The Dragons travel within the shimmer to get from place to place, the same as ourselves. But yes, you are right about their size, but also, because of the enormous amount of magick they project. They leave shadows as they pass from magickal realm to magickal realm. That is why they try to travel at night only, though it is not always convenient."

His words pulled from my memory, an image and thought that I had once experienced as a child, and I wondered out loud. "I've been outside, when a sudden shadow would come up out of nowhere. It would pass over quickly and when you looked up, there would be nothing there. My máthair always said that it was the Angels flying by. I always told her it was the dragons!"

"It is truly amazing, the way that you hit on topics that most would never consider, much less ask. Some humans are more sensitive and they have sensed our presence over the centuries. You are not the first to notice, but yes, it could possibly have been a Dragon. You see, we, magick, have never truly been that far away, only hidden."

"This world, all that I have seen so far and have yet to see, it truly amazes me. I am not more than a little humbled by the power that God has brought into our existence." I said the words, believed them, but my doubts in myself found their way in, crossing my heart and, my face.

"Angel, what is it? What are you not telling me . . . us?" He quickly amended his words.

I couldn't look him in the eye. I had done all they asked, I gave more than I'd even known I had, but did it makeup for my shortcomings, for the truth.

"There are things you don't know, things about me that you cannot understand!"

"I will never understand if you don't trust them with me in the first place." He reached his hand out, doing something he'd never done; he pulled me up and into his arms. Just holding, just offering the support I'd needed, a lifetime of needing.

I felt the tears come; they were quiet at first, warm and flowing. Then as the truth about me raced through my head, through my memories, they came in a torrent. They ran hot and heavy. Not once did he push me away as I cried out my torment, my shame and embarrassment for the life I'd lived, been forced to live. *I was not strong . . .*

"Don't you see? I am not some force to be reckoned with. I was submissive. Trapped in a situation I couldn't escape until the only other option was death. I was weak." The words tumbled out of me, each more cleansing than the previous. The truth, in all its ugliness, was revealed to him, all of it, and all my shame. I rubbed at my eyes, to clear them from their watery state.

He smiled down at me. I could feel the honesty behind his gaze. "The people that should have loved you most offered nothing but abuse, fear. You escaped. You bore your daughter and built a life for yourself. When they caged you, you found a way to escape, even when it took you years of suffering torment and abuse to succeed. Have I missed anything yet?"

I sniffled, shaking my head "no" in response.

"You were courageous and strong. You faced fears that would have backed many into a corner, and you never gave up. This is what I see, when I look at you, a hidden strength, a bruised soul and a loving heart. Qualities that others seize to possess, you live; you have more than most people can acquire in a lifetime, yet you fear. Open your eyes as you have opened your heart." He spoke with a burning hunger, strength of truth that burned me through.

"Why can you not see what I see? What is within you! You are a survivor all right, but you are also a fighter. You never gave up. You have walked through hell and returned. Instead of letting it destroy you, you made yourself better and carved out a new life for yourself, and Caitrin. You are one of the strongest and most brave people that I know. Now let go of the shame and let yourself live."

His words blew me away. He was honest, so strong in his honesty, every word. When he looked at me, he saw the strength and not the weakness, the wounded. *"Could I do that? Accept that I was stronger than I thought?"* I offered a little, not sure of myself yet. "Caitrin and I are the only "people" you know."

"Exactly, I could not imagine any better."

This time, I really laughed, great lung fulls of air and laughter. It felt wonderful, like a cleansing rain had washed away a part of me that had been too stubborn to be forced out before. As I finished, I looked back into his face, into his eyes. What I saw there seared me. Realization took over and I felt his arms around me. The flush of heat as it raced through me, my body responding to his gentle embrace. I froze as his lips descended onto mine.

My response was immediate, the gentle pressure, the strength that he gave. I felt my heart stop as his kiss awoke within me, an intense flame that I was not prepared for. My heartbeat returned with a fierceness, an assault that left me reeling and dazed. The blooding surging throughout me, his heart beating strong and true under my palm. I could swear that its beat matched my own. He held on for several moments more, offering so much, before gently letting me slip from his grasp.

"Sleep well Angel, and think about what I said. The truth always comes out in the end."

I watched as he walked away. Perhaps, a little differently for all that had passed between us. For all that my heart bleed at the sudden awareness of who we were. Soon enough tomorrow would arrive, and with it, the future was one day closer.

Epoch
(17)

Snuggling deeper into the warmth of my quilt, I didn't want to let go of the last remaining moments of sleep, of the amazing dreams that plagued me. If only I could find such comfort in other aspects of my life right now. It had been several weeks since my unexplained, inability at releasing my magick had occurred and several days since Gable's unexplained kiss. Day in and out, I studied hard with the TA Archers and I'd been . . . unable, to excel. In whole, I had let them down with every word I uttered and with every weak spell. It seemed like the harder I tried to find a release, the more it just slipped through my fingers. I tried to understand the message I'd been given, "*a heart not met...*" To unlock its secrets, but I'd been unsuccessful.

They seemed far more patient than I, but I knew that even they were mystified. As it stood, Caitrin could out do me in magick, hands down. My daughter was now flourishing under their guidance. Secretly, I was beginning to wonder if Gable had not had it right the first place. *Maybe I just wasn't the One? But I knew better!* I had seen for myself, the magick within me. I had felt the power that had radiated from my Source and knew that it was there. It was simply that "*I*" was the problem. I needed to discover what it was that would release our salvation within me.

I thought back over the previous few weeks. When it had become abundantly clear that I wasn't ready, the TA Archers had advanced their tactics with me. Beginning from scratch, they offered me a different way of learning. I had success in Humanities beginnings, so they carried on. They started at their beginnings, teaching me their tÁles, trying to give me more insight into their world. I sighed, my world. This was my world, just as much as the previous one never had been. I was learning history, when I should be whipping out magick as if it was as easy as breathing!

I knew that I was blocked. *Magically blocked!* It was the first time I laughed in days. Now here was a good joke. Writer's block be damned, this was on a much deeper level. I needed something, but I had no idea what and no idea where to start. Closing my eyes, I began to breathe in deeply and breathe out. What I needed was to relax. I was under too much stress and I was afraid that if I didn't get some relief soon, I was going to snap. After taking a few moments for myself, I opened my eyes and gazed at the view around me. The balcony doors were thrown wide. It was still dark, but I could see the basic lighting to the sky that would announce morning shortly. It was still early, but I needed to get up and get ready.

I hummed as I rose, searching for something comfortable to wear. I'd learned much about the fa*e*ry in my short stay here, they were a complex and yet simple Being. From their beginnings, they were the essence of peace. They watched over the world at large. Their role was that of Protector. But it was different, at the start. When man was new and unlearned, they had worked with them at creating a livelihood, teaching them the basics of life and nature. But as man developed, their darker urges began to set, to come out. Temptation, greed, these things began to shape their day to day. Not all were like them, but it was sad that the majority fell away from the teachings of love and faith.

There had come a time, when the faery had pulled away from them, falling back to their Lands and their Strongholds. They prospered, as Man began to bicker and war amongst themselves. The faery watched as the earth turned red with the blood of the innocent and guilty alike. They stepped in, finally. Pulling those that were weak, yet faithful, away from the destruction and loss. When the warring finally stopped, Mankind had taken a massive blow. Those faithful were returned to the lands, where they began again. This had been the continuous pattern. It emerged over and over again, as the Earth was nearly destroyed by man several times over. Each time, the faery had stepped in, seeking to preserve the best of the Creator's creations.

It was actually the force of the Darkness itself that had required the Creator to step in, and cleanse the world of its evils. After so many attempts, the Faery had not been strong enough. God stepping in had been the breaking point. Now I realized it was a combination of both, that we fought. We had no breaking point, it was all or nothing! The World of Man had reached new heights in their technology and their disillusionment of what power really was; as well as the Darkness having taken a staggering hold in the Faery Realm. We were greatly in trouble and I had to figure out a way to save us all. This was my destiny and it was a burden that I could not carry lightly.

Let me try this again. I took a deep breath and relaxed. *I needed to relax!* Looking down at myself, I smiled, humor coming to the forefront. As far as I could tell, this was the only outfit I now owned that actually covered me. I almost laughed, I had gotten so used to the scantly there clothing, that I actually felt overdressed! But I looked good and I was really excited about going out.

With my heart racing, I thought back to last evening . . .

Gable had stopped me on the way to my chamber. "Just a moment, Angel, before I forget, I have arranged a surprise for you tomorrow. I would have you meet me at the stables around sunup."

A surprise? It was so unlike him. He never seemed to do anything spontaneously. "I look forward to it." I offered. Now, my curiosity was piped and it left me imagining what it could possibly be.

"One more thing, dress comfortably." He finished as he walked away, this time, a smile on his features.

Were things finally changing . . .?

*

Well, I'd managed that. I wore loose fitting leggings, reminding me of my gaucho pants that I wore back home. Over them, I wore a spaghetti strap shirt that fell gracefully to my hips, both were made of a cotton that was as smooth as butter, and the color of pale mauve. They were pulled snug at my waist, an intricate golden belt, set with large amethyst gemstones my clincher. My cashmere woven jacket a shade darker was the finishing piece. The outfit emblazoned my eyes, making them brighter, more alive. I thought I looked beautiful, I only hoped that Gable noticed. *Desperately, I wanted his attention, his affection to be directed in my direction.*

I started out, heading toward the stables. Already, the smell of the horses could be detected by my nose. I loved the heady aroma. It reminded me of the horses I'd ridden in my youth. My mind continued to wander over the things I now remembered and all of the new things that I was learning, as I walked at a steady pace. The more that I had discovered about the faery, the more fascinated I'd become. Being drawn deeper and deeper into their society and culture.

Caitrin was thriving here as well. I couldn't remember ever seeing her so happy. She fit in here as if she had been born into it, her skills increasing at an exponential rate, her fear no longer playing a role in keeping her abilities back. I wondered if it was the simple innocence of childhood that let her venture forth, while I seemed to be continually reined back in with my own jaded views. *Was it a loss of my own innocence that was creating such an obstacle for me? I wished I knew.*

Caitrin was already able to do so much. She could shift things with her mind now; just yesterday she'd created a magnificent show with her powers. I closed my eyes, and replayed the scene in my mind...

"Máthair, you have to look at these." Caitrin was yelling.

She had come barreling towards me, her arm outstretched, something grasped tightly within her palm and fingers.

"What do you have there?" I'd asked in curiosity.

"We went out in the fields today and you will never guess what we saw?"

"Who went out in the fields?" I'd asked.

"You're missing the point! MadaREn and I went out into the fields! Now guess what we saw!" She was jumping up and down, her excitement in no way contained.

"Well, let me think about it." I said, putting my finger on my chin and scrunching up my face. I knew that it would drive her crazy, it always did.

"You're taking too long, Máthair!"

I could see that she was ready to burst, so I let her off easily. "Well, I'm never going to guess right with all of this crazy jumping up and down you're doing. You're distracting me. You might as well just tell me."

"Fine, fine. But you should have guessed." She said as she rolled her eyes. "We actually saw a rainbow. But that wasn't even the best part. The best part was what we found at the end of it! Rainbows really do have ends Máthair, just like you said they did. But you know what?"

"No, what?" I asked in amazement as she seemed to get even more excited.

"They don't have pots of gold under them, nor do they have leprechauns. They have these." And she held out her hand to show me what she'd brought with her.

I startled. "No Leprechauns? What do you mean there are no Leprechauns?"

She rolled her eyes at me again. "Of course there are Leprechauns, Máthair! But they don't just sit around under rainbows all day! They have better things to do. MadaREn said that they only have to sit under them once a year, because they are their *Fountains of You!*"

I was stumped me for a moment. I'd admit. Then it dawned on me, quite easily. *"Their Fountains of Youth."* I corrected for her.

"Yep, that's what I said" Her smile blossoming, "Now look Máthair!"

They were crystals of all different sizes, each a brilliant blazing clear, like a diamond. But within their depths, there was so much more. It appeared that gas was trapped within each and every one. The gas swirled and moved within them, as if alive. Within the depths of each, were . . . *rainbows*. The colors numerous and thriving. Flowing as if suspended, then moving and twisting, the colors blending then separating again. A bubbling champagne of diamonds, of life, the smallest about two inches, the largest about five. "They're beautiful! What are they?"

"MadaREn said that they were called "true diamonds," that the light in them is not broken, so it remains whole." Caitrin said with pride, glad that she had remembered everything MadaREn had said to her. "Do you want to see what I can do with them? It's really neat!"

"Absolutely!"

Carefully, she laid them out, side by side, on her palm, all in order. I could hear her whispering under her breath, words that I was unable to make out. Suddenly, one by one, the stones began to rise on their own accord. Upwards in the air, about two feet above us, they stopped, arranged in a circular pattern. From here, they began to spin. They whistled as they moved, giving off a pleasant sound. But that was not the amazing thing. As I continued to watch, Caitrin convinced the sun to shine down one of its many rays in our direction.

As the ray hit the spinning stones, a perfect rainbow emerged. It fell from the stones and down to the earth at our feet. I gasped. The magnificent kaleidoscope of colors dropped down more rainbow stones at our feet. I picked them up, some for myself. I looked at Caitrin's face, at the joy radiating from her.

"See Máthair, now you can take a rainbow with you anywhere you go too." Her laughter was ringing in the air around us.

I joined in, still as amazed at her as I was with the rainbows. I thought over her words, over MadaREn's. *Pure diamonds . . . uninterrupted leight? Pure leight?* I could feel the wheels turning in my own head. *Pure leight!* A straight shot of adrenaline rushed through my heart.

"Caitrin, start collecting as many of them as you can get your hands on."

My mind jumping ahead, thinking of possibilities not heard of. Caitrin's ability to manipulate the sun, giving me an idea I had not thought of before. That no one had thought of before.

*

The abilities that Caitrin had now were making her stronger and bringing out serenity in her that made her nearly glow. The only thing that she lacked from the rest of the Faery Kind was a pair of wings. I smiled at that, remembering Caitrin's most demanding request of last night, quite clearly . . .

"Máthair, when can I have my wings?" She had finally asked me. I had actually been dreading the question that I'd known was coming.

"You have to have been born with them, the same as the faery were." I'd replied. A small smile trying to form on my lips, anything to lighten the moment for her, her certain disappointment was surely forth coming.

"But I wasn't born with magick and I have that now!" She had said mournfully, her face falling with her upset.

Gable had stepped in, his expertise making him appear all proper and knowledgeable. "Magick is an extension of one's soul. It is bestowed by the Creator. You have always had it. It just took you finding the ability to use it, to set it free." Here, Gable had turned his attention to me. This was where the playfulness left the moment. *I just wished that it could have lasted longer.*

*

Was it me? Everyone was just so certain. Why wasn't I? What was the right way? I didn't know. But damn it, I was tired of the struggle. Didn't I get any credit for all of the effort I'd already put into it? I did envy Caitrin her sense of belonging. I wanted to feel that way. Wanted to feel that utter acceptance and know that I finally belonged somewhere after a lifetime of searching. Caitrin had that now and I would ensure till my dying breath that she always felt it. To belong was a gift, and I wanted to feel it drenched within me as well.

My thoughts drifted to Gable, Caitrin absolutely adored the rough warrior. His tall height and scarred face held no fear for her. It was true that he felt the same way about her. One only had to look to see. Every night he would put aside time for her, either before or after the evening meal. Occasionally, he would pick her up and swing her around. Caitrin had later said that it was like she could fly. As close as she would ever come to being able too. They would have time to talk, laugh or just joke. RandelfSon was the only one that Caitrin spent more time with, than either of us. But Gable was changing as much as the rest of us were. Even the others had noticed the regard that had developed between Caitrin and himself. He treated her as if she were his own child. Something that I now knew was a rare delight to the Faery. His feelings for Caitrin were a surprise that warmed my heart.

It was the feelings that Gable provoked within me, that warmed me up everywhere else as well. We'd been working together for several weeks now. Finally, I'd found something that I loved and served as a purpose for helping those around me, my calling. It was hard for me to believe that it was the fighting, the skill with the sword that I excelled at. I guess that I should have expected it. *Obviously, I would have to be good at it to make all of this work out in the end.*

I knew that it was the same with Caitrin. Once we'd picked up the sword, it had felt like there was no need to put it down again. To me, it felt like magick in my hands, a true extension of myself. This was something that I was good at, really good at. Gable was an excellent instructor. His battle techniques were exquisite and deadly. He was teaching me to fight, while teaching me as many spells to try to use for defense as he could offer. Here I could say, I was excelling and I knew that he was proud of me.

The more time I spent with him, the more that I found myself fighting my feelings for him. *With each choice, with every step away from him, it felt like I was falling farther away from my goal, and I could not understand why?* But he had made no other moves towards me since the kiss. I wanted desperately to feel him put his arms around me in an embrace, one that held fire and passion. My nights were offering me no comfort either. I dreamt of him often, waking up in heated sweats, sad and frustrated. And longing, intense longing that washed its way through my veins and burned its way through my very soul.

These feelings, they filled me with just the thought of his face, or his wide expanse of chest. But it wasn't only that. I was attracted to everything about him, especially his heart, the one that he tried to keep hidden. I knew, I understood that we were different, but it didn't matter. I wanted to be with him. I needed to feel a release from all of these staggering emotions he evoked within me. The greatest frustration came from not knowing for sure if we could be. I saw the passion flare in his eyes, knew that possibility of the passion that had been in our kiss. *If he could feel for me, even a small amount of the passion that flared within me for him, I did not know how he could keep it hidden so well?* I didn't even know if a relationship between faery and human were possible? Nothing that I'd read, had ever hinted to a possibility of it having happened before. But that also meant that it wasn't impossible. *But who could I possibly ask?* As I continued to think it over, my blood began to rush and I felt my face flush, a blush gracing it. My confusion flaring, my anger and frustration following closely behind. *I desperately wanted to throttle something.* Proper or not!

*

Gable thought about the arrangements that he had made. The past several weeks had been nothing but torture. There was no other possible description for it. Angel was doing immensely well in the hand to hand combat. Her skills with the sword were already outdoing Caitrin's, outdoing most. But the TA Archers were growing weary with her inability to unleash her magick. They had felt it, the inkling of power that was right below the surface of her skin. The ability to unlock it seemed to be the final piece in her training. He had felt her frustration, felt it getting worse over the past few days. But he had no idea if it was anywhere near what he himself, was feeling. Working with her, day in and out, putting his hands on her in acts of violence and war, when all he wanted was to rub and caress. His feelings for her were growing. His craving and need to claim her as his own, nearly killing him.

She was the One. He was suffering as he had kept to himself, his feelings for her. He had believed that anything on his part would be a distraction from her work, her duty. But he could not fight it any longer; his soul was screaming for release and today was that day. *His obsession with her was more intense . . . it was a lifeline, and he was sinking without her.* He knew it and it was time to make sure that there was no more suffering, no more doubt. *Whatever their results may bring.*

He had arranged to have MadaREn take Caitrin on an outing today. It was something that she was readily up too. Though MadaREn had a mate, the two of them had never been able to have a faeryling. She was not yet an Elder, but her age was so progressed that faerybirth was now beyond her. He had known when he had assigned her to the child, that she would protect Caitrin with her own life. They were a family now, much the same as they had all become. Today, he was taking Angel away and he would finally bring his family together in the end.

Though horses were not a necessity for the Faery Kind, they still bred the majestic beasts for pleasure. Today, he selected a mare for Angel. It was the purest of white, like fresh snow, except for its glitter. He knew that the rare beauty would spark Angel's curiosity. Gable's own steed was a great Grey giant. It was his height that gave him that impression. He truly was a majestic beast. He stood tall, his head just over seven feet, only a couple of inches higher than Gable himself. They made an intimating pair, on the field and off. The faery had come to depend on their steeds in battle. When the wings of a faery were damaged, their very survival depended on their steed's ability to return them to safety. Gable straightened himself up in the saddle, the reins to Whisp eR Har in his hands. *Soon, Angel would be his.* This is what his soul screamed in its need.

*

Halfway to the stable, TorinA intercepted me. He was young, near to my age at least. Often, he would assist in the stables when needed. He redirected my course, as I was now told to wait outside the inner gates for Gable. I could feel my excitement begin to flare. *We were leaving the Keep. I couldn't wait!* This was the first time that I'd been allowed to set foot outside of the wall.

The view was absolutely magnificent! Until now, I had only been able to look through the high tower windows. Now, I was right there. I imagined that this was what my realm had looked like, once upon a time ago. Before man had corrupted through modernized and had polluted the many faces of Earth. I walked far enough out that when I turned around, I could really see the Keep. My breath caught in my throat. In all its entirety, with nearly everything visible, the high towers rose into the sky, each capped with perfectly proportioned cones. As they came lower, there was outside walks, they continued down more to the large archway entrance over the hall. On each side of the arch were more covered walkways that circled the Keep. Off to the left and right I could see the tops of the other buildings that were housed within the inner wall. All constructed of the same stone and crystals.

The sky to the east was a periwinkle, dusky blue with dark still covering the other three-fourths of it. I could see the stars as they twinkled, great groups of them that you wouldn't see in the cities back home. To the east, a golden rose hue announcing the coming of morning. Looking back to the horizon, I truly looked at what surrounded me. It was flat fields and grasslands. Small cottage homes made of cobblestone were set at various locations. I could see fog as it lay upon the fields, swirling in wisps, some reaching nearly three feet off the ground. The farm fields harvested for the year. The farms I knew, fed the inhabitants of Ainys'Dai. The grass itself was a shade of green that I was pretty sure had no name. The earth was a dark and moisten brown. As I walked along, the aroma of it blended with the freshness of the air. My eyes adjusted as I looked out further, past the fields and flatland.

I knew that the mountains were behind me, those spread out to the east and west. In front of me, away off in the distance, the flat lands turned into forests, the trees standing tall and proud. The leaves, even from here, held a fiery blaze as fall had finally taken hold. *It was all that I could see in the distance . . . what was beyond them, I didn't know?*

I closed my eyes and breathed in deep. I would never forget this feeling...

Traditions
(18)

From behind me the sound of horse hooves, clattered as they made their way across the stone walk, and to my side. Turning, I watched as Gable drew near. He sat high upon a Grey horse with unusual silver markings that seemed to glow. The beast was a giant. It had to be to hold Gable's weight. He alone probably weighed well over 350 pounds, his height and muscle contributing to the fact. My heart collided with my lungs, the very air leaving my body. I came alive. The blood surged as it came upon me like a crushing intensity to my middle. *He was beautiful. They made a handsome pair, horse and rider.* The power that they eluded was truly catastrophic to one's system.

Gable's dark flowing locks, his wide shoulders and powerful, muscular thighs were all well displayed in his soft leather jacket and pants. I knew that the leather would be butter soft; like everything the faery made, it was made to be beautiful, comfortable and nearly indestructible. I could see myself, running my hands over his wide chest, the muscles, the furls of heat once more attempting to reign over me. I took a deep breath, forcing the flutters in my stomach back down. The hot spurt of passion as it flared. I was tired of having to do so, but this was something that I would have to face later. Right now, I just wanted to be able to breathe. And speak.

"Take the chance!" The words roared through me. My passion spiked. I pushed back at the words . . . and the heat.

*

He noticed her beauty, her appeal. She was all soft and . . . *feminine.* Her angelic Grace called to him and made him shudder. Her body had changed, she had become leaner, more toned from the exertion of her routines, but she was still as curvy as ever. She was so unlike faery females, but his reaction to her, he had never felt for one of them. He needed to keep his mind on his goal. He had to keep moving and not allow his strong feelings to frighten her. She had no idea what he was capable of, the extent of the passion that flared within his veins.

When he spoke, his voice was rough, "I have decided to show you our Stronghold. To show you the many things that are contained within the outer walls. There is so much that you have yet to see. I thought it might help you to see what you will be fighting for."

I smiled up at him, a little nervous. It appeared that today would be another lesson as well. I could feel the disappointment replacing the desire in my belly. But I could not let it get to me. At least we would be together, maybe, just maybe, something more would come of it. "From what I see, your realm is pretty endless. There is so much here."

"Endless it is, but I do not just rule over Ainys'Dai. As you know, there are multiple Strongholds that are within the Faery Realm and the entirety of the Realm is under my responsibility. They are all separated by their own walls and shimmer. Each has a ruling family, of sort. All answer back to us here. Travel is required between each and every one. Although a great number of our magickal Strongholds have fallen, we still have a few that display the kind of beauty that you see here. Today I will show you what I can of my majestic realm." He swept his arms wide, encompassing all within. "One day, I would like to take you out and truly show you all of the wonders of our world. There are things here that you could only imagine in your wildest dreams, things that no human has ever seen or known of."

Though he spoke with pride, I could still see the hint of sadness in his eyes. He took every loss as his own and seeing him with such sorrow, gave me more insight into this raging war than the actual storÀtelling did. I wanted to take away the pain. I wanted to wrap my arms around him, to find solace in his arms as much as what I could offer. But I knew that it was not my place to do so.

Paying attention to the following mare, I stared in wonder. My breathing hitched. *She was magnificent!* I'd never seen anything like her before. The purity and the golden glow. Walking forward slowly, I offered my hand, palm up to the mare. The mare sniffed at it a moment, before she whinnied in assent. Reaching up, rubbing her behind her ears, the horse's pleasure was readily apparent. "So, if you want me to go with you, why don't you introduce me to your friends here?" I said, the cheerful being forced on my part. *I would make it through.* I vowed.

"This mighty stallion," he said as he ran his hands over the horse's neck, "is Batal'Agar. He is my companion, in war and peace. It is his job to ensure that should I fall in battle that I am not left behind." He rubbed the stallion's neck once more. The horse threw back his head and shifted from the attention. "As for this fair beauty, this is Whisp eR Har. She has a mighty lineage of her own."

"She is a beauty indeed. How do I settle myself on her, does she prefer left or right?" I asked, the old knowledge of riding from childhood, coming to the forefront.

Gable nodded to her. He truly hoped that the attraction between them would ignite their passion before the night was out. "She prefers to be mounted from the left." He offered.

I grasped the pommel, pulling my weight up and into the saddle, my feet finding the stirrups with ease. Sitting high, this new view I was offered was impressive. *I felt like I belonged here. In that moment, something shifted, the world shifted, sliding into a fit that I'd never experienced before. I belonged and it gave me such a rush.* I felt heady and powerful. "So . . tell me of this mighty lineage." I said, as he set the pace with me following along beside him. Breathless from the power.

"Whisp eR Har is the descendant of a unicorn. Each mare born from this line has inherited great magickal beauty from him. She gets her pure white coat and the gold fringes of her mane and tail from her forefáthair."

"Do you mean that the gold is real?" Wondrously surprised.

"Absolutely! That is why it is only the tips that are golden. It would be too heavy a load for her to bear, if all of the hair was gold."

"That's amazing!" I breathed, unable to imagine having actual gold for hair.

"Thank You!"

The voice appeared out of nowhere. I jumped, startled, then shifted in my saddle, looking to see if another faery had arrived to join us. The voice had been feminine, I was absolutely certain of it. But no one was there. There was no one at all as I gazed further out around us. "Did you hear . . ?" I started to ask, swinging back forward. Finally I answered myself with a "never mind." To Gable, I started shaking my head, as if clearing my ears would help. *What was wrong with me?*

He only smiled at me, a mischievous grin on his face . . .

He was up to something, but I had no idea what. I shoved the thought aside and continued to follow him as he started moving forward along the path again. That suspicious smile was still firmly in place.

We traveled through the open fields, passing more buildings of stone and earth along the way. We waved as faery began emerging for the day. Always welcoming in their manner, a smile and wave in passing. It was as I was getting truly settled into the saddle, that I noticed something that took me by complete surprise, a smile of wonder lighting my face. There, playing in the field was a faeryling. He was young; probably no more than five or six. He was watched closely by two older faery that I assumed would be his parents, and a little further away, two warriors. He was sprinting across the field, his wings stretched as he went into flight, laughing in happiness; he did a somersault in midair. Both of his parents were clapping at his show. As I watched, the young one noticed us coming and raised his small hand in a wave. Waving back at him, my enthusiasm suddenly reignited from the childish display of pleasure.

Gable watched her reaction to the young one. The look of pleasure on her face warmed his heart. Seeing her this way, he wanted more of it. The unguarded version of herself said far more than any words she could have spoken. He turned to her as she watched. "He and his family traveled a long way to reach us."

"Has he been here long?"

"No. As a matter of fact, they only arrived a couple of days ago. I was going to see to it that he and Caitrin were introduced. It would be nice for her to have someone her own age around. It would give RandelfSon a break." He laughed at the thought.

"I think that Caitrin will love you even more after this." I said in a whisper, turning back to watch the faerylings play.

Gable could feel the swelling within his chest. Caitrin's love was something he had wanted very much. Knowing now that he really had, made him feel like he could do anything. Today was the day, he knew it now. He was possibly being greedy, but he did not care, his time had finally come and he would seize the opportunity that he had been given.

*

We continued forward, moving at a comfortable pace. "Why is it that Faery only ever has one faeryling? What is the reason exactly?" It seemed sad to me, with the beauty of these Beings, why were they not granted the privilege of raising more young ones.

"The answer goes back to the very beginning. We never had a need for the high level of reproduction that you humans had. Long ago, your people lived for several centuries. They would have their children in their first century, while they would live out their last few remaining, enjoying their lives and their future. Man became more aggressive. That is when the change came to your Kind. The change decreased your ability to live longer and it dwindled down to a mere century. Our Kind however, we live for thousands of years. Our long life spans and tendency for peace allowed us to move forward in life. We just did not need to reproduce like you. Faerylings were a gift to be cherished. They replaced a soul when one was eventually taken for old life. With our intense emotions for family, our faerylings live a life of ultimate love. But you must also remember that if there is need, there can always be an exception to any rule."

Exceptions, I had seen so many exceptions since I had come here. "But if soulmates tend to die together, or in a shorter time frame, why then, when they are born again, are they so spaced out?" I wondered, it made no sense to me.

"Ah! I think I see that there has been a misunderstanding for you. It would make it appear to be confusing with your understanding. They are not the same souls reborn. Those that pass, pass on to the Creator's Heaven. It is new souls, new lives that are awaiting their chance at creation from the Great Nebula of Souls."

How beautiful. I thought. "Is it like the *Well of Souls* then? It is similar to the Jewish belief. A resting place, until it is their turn to begin their circle of life. While the *Well* is full, life will continue on."

"Yes, that would be a good way to describe it. If humans would only *see,* they would know that each of their religions holds a piece of truth to the understanding of the Creator. The problem is that with the Darkeness, we began losing faery too early. They never reached their peaks. Their conversion, their loss to the Darke, does not allow for faerylings to be born and our numbers have dwindled down. Now our numbers are nearly barren, from what they were before."

"Are there any exceptions?" I asked curiously.

"Indeed, there are." He said, somewhat distractedly.

*

I could see the conflict in him. "I'm so sorry for all of this." The words wrenched from within my soul. "The death, the destruction, I know that I'm not responsible for it, but I'm letting it continue with my ignorance and inability! I need to end this!"

"And you will." He said to me with complete conviction, the burn of it seared me to the core.

*

As we traveled on, he introduced more of his world to me. "All that is beyond contains the creatures of the Leight. The WÁ Táren lives amongst the lakes. They live deeply below, but are often seen above land as they enjoy the suns light, like the rest of us."

"WÁ Táren?" I asked.

"What you would call the mermaid." He answered.

"Mermaid . . . what are they like? Are they similar to us, or are they more . . ." *I was not sure how to proceed. I did not want to say "fishy" and be insulting.* He only let me hang for a moment.

"They are similar in appearance to us, their skin a pale shade of green, like a sea-foam or mist. It actually has a pearl like quality. The females are beautiful and the males would be handsome. From the waist down, they have fins and scales. While their hair is billowy, it is thick and hangs in long locks, the color varying in shades of greens and blues, sometimes even in violets as well. They are beauty. There kind have developed into a variety of races, as they would say in the human world. Many varieties."

"Do they ever..." It took me a moment to figure out how to ask. "...do they ever take on human form?"

"Actually, they take on human form when it is time for females to have their young. When they are first born, they are complete air breathers. They go back to the water after a few weeks or so. They could remain longer, but the call of the water is strong. Shifting is an ability that they can control."

It made me want to see them all the more. I could learn so much from them, from all of the Beings here.

After remaining quiet, he continued on in his original explanations. "The Pixies and Sprites are more often woodland dwellers though, like those at the Keep, they will move at will. From the fields, you will often see Brownies. They love the soil and the richness of the earth."

"Now those are something that I understand. In Ireland, they still speak of Brownies. Little helpers, or troublemakers they are!"

"Then you might as well know that they are no different here." He said with a laugh before continuing on. "In the mountains there are still Dwarfs, as I mentioned before, along with the Dragons of course." He said with a smile. "Also, in the higher regions we have Unicorns and Merryflyers."

"Merryflyers? What are those?" I asked with interest.

"They are a smaller variety of horse. They stand no more than two feet tall at full growth, but they are agile and strong. They were graced with wings and the ability of flight." He finished.

Flying horses. I could feel the wonder fill me. Feel the exhilaration at a childhood favorite come to life. "A Pegasus! They're really real!" I turned to him in my absolute delight and exuberance. *Magick truly was a wondrous thing!*

"Oh yes, they are quite real, though the numbers of their herds have gotten smaller over the years. Once, long ago, even before my time, there were larger ones. So large, that the faery themselves could have ridden them, if given the honor. But they are no more. One more casualty to the Darkeness' wrath. Those that remain, the smaller ones, used to roam the hilly plains but much of their territory has been lost. So they have sought refuge in the plains areas of the mountains here, the open valleys of the mountain floors. Their coats are a thick, curly type and it allows them to dwell in the cooler regions of higher altitudes. It is safer for them. You see, when the Darkeness takes over the faery, it also takes over the land and all of its inhabitants. It will consume all within the protection of the walls if they are not able to escape." His eyes became deep, seeing something that I could not. *Old memories.*

I let it go for a while. Not liking the sorrow it evoked, but soon, my curiosity won out and I was back to questioning him. "Where do the darke creatures live? The goblins and the trolls, those that were falling into my realm before I came here, where is it that they exist?"

"The answer is not easy to explain. When the Darkeness was originally purged from our realms, the darke creatures were still here, but hidden. Like their own space. With so much of our realm now lost, it gives them ample places to hide, including our own realm. Not all dark creatures are actually "darke," those that were not, did not have as much restrictions as the Darke ones did. Even though they are not good, neither are they typically evil on their own, only trouble. The Darkeness brings out the worst in them as well." He continued. "Since the cracks in the shimmer have begun, we have been attempting to monitor them as much as possible. The darke creatures have been falling into your realm, the same as they have been reappearing into ours. It was not until your attack, that we were even able to cross over into your realm ourselves."

I wondered. "But what of the people there who are hurt or killed by them? Is there nothing that we can do for them? Could we not enlist them in their own aide?"

"Only fight! Fight until the very end. We have battled long, now the battle will once again start to reach into the Realm of Man. Eventually, our entire realm will be opened up to them. Its means the end is near. Men fight with weapons of destruction. They fight out of fear, rather than faith. They would destroy the Earth along with themselves. So, it is us who decides how the end will be this time."

I sat back in silence, my mind going over his words. *Nothing would end until I could get control. But I was having such a hard time! Every day there was some reminder of what my failure was costing the Earth.*

We continued on in our silence. The guilt filled thoughts of my mind were absorbing my concentration as the scenery began to change around us, however, my thoughts began shifting with it. *Here,* I thought, *everything was provided by the Creator and the Faery shared it all. They worked together to create and maintain this way of life, none lacked. Each was as rich as the next. It made me mad that humankind had been given the same and they'd thrown it away in their greed, in their senseless pursuit of the riches that they'd actually already owned. To stupid and ignorant to even be aware of it.*

The flat fields gave way to the grasslands. Here, dew clung to the long blades, creating small prisms that reflected in the rays of the afternoon sun. The fog continued to creep in front of us, getting thicker as the tree line came into view, the abnormally warm day owning to its continued presence. As the trees began to close in around us, I could sense it, the lichen and moss, the life that ebbed and flowed around me, around us.

Gable picked up his speech, as if he had never left off. "Here is where the Elves roam."

"Elves. The little people?" I asked.

"Actually, yes. Another thing that the humans seem to remember clearly." He laughed. "The Elves roam the woods. They make their homes in the world above," he pointed to the high tree tops, "or they make homes deep in the roots below. They stand no more than eighteen inches tall and live for hundreds of years. They create, often using the offered wood of the trees to make their specialties. You have seen evidence of their work in the wooden goblets we use at home."

I looked at him. Saying *"home"* moved me and offered me hope. Within me, a thought took hold; I could feel my youth returning. I wanted to be right, so very right.

"Gable, what of Santa? We believed in Santa and his Elves. They celebrated the birth of the Creators' Son with joy and merriment, exchanging love and gifts." I asked with hope filled glee. His smile was heartbreaking, and then sorrow flooded his eyes. I could feel the disappointment that I knew was on the way.

"You speak of the Winter Solstice. Oh yes, Santa was real, but his name was actually TrA Sana. He was faery." He replied. He appeared lost in thought for a moment, but he returned quickly enough, this time with a smile.

"TrA Sana would come every Solstice to the Keep. He lived right here in these very woods. He and the Elves would work all year on gifts for the young and old alike. Once, he even traveled to the Realm of Man and offered his specialties. He brought happiness wherever he went."

"What happened to him?"

"Age, actually. He was ancient when I was young. But he remained around for quite a while longer. As the Darkeness spread and he was no longer able to reach Man he became saddened. Then as things continued to worsen here, faerylings being born less and less often . . . I remember how much it troubled him. He had said that, *"it was the loss of innocence in the world."*

"One day, not long after, he had told me that his time on Earth was ending. He passed into the Leight shortly after." Gable sat back in his saddle. He realized that he had not thought of TrA Sana in a long time. He looked over and noticed the tears in Angel's eyes.

I looked to him. "He would have been glad to have known, that not all of us gave up in our belief of him. I myself still believe. He will always be love to me."

"I do not think you could have honored him more." He said with a smile on his lips. We rode together in a comfortable silence. Things were developing, deepening between us. Our thoughts and words, our shared love had created this camaraderie between us that we'd been lacking before.

"Will we be able to see where he lived? It was always a dream of mine when I was a child."

"I think I can manage that. The place still stands as a memory to his honor, the elves keeping to the tradition. I believe that they wait, hoping to once again find the joy of such a Giver. His home is the hollowed out portion of a great tree. The roots beneath have a great birth for the many rooms that he filled with toys. I am not sure if we will have time this evening to get there, though we will definitely try to reach his home."

"Thank you!" I knew that he didn't realize how much it meant to me, but it really was the equivalence of me being able to really believe in magick in faith and in love.

Birth Right
(19)

After all of the riding, we stopped in a small area where the ground sat exposed to the sky overhead. The sun shined down in pastel rays and illuminated the earth. The grass was ankle length in depth and provided a nice cushion for our noontime meal. I was surprised at the selection that he had brought, most of it my favorites. I flushed, knowing the trouble he had gone too in order to ensure that I really did enjoy myself today. This may be a lesson, but he was showing me more of himself in this one day, than I'd been able to gather in weeks.

The meal was relaxed and offered me time to rest my limbs. I was not about to admit it to him, but I had not ridden much since I was younger, and the muscles of my lower back and thighs were a little tested from the rolling gait of the mare. After finishing, I stood, stretching strong. Feeling the goodness as it raced through the tested muscles of my body. Feeling the muscles come back alive, refreshed. Walking, I carried an extra apple in my open hand. *Whisp eR Har was bound to appreciate the sweet treat.* Walking up to her with a smile on my lips.

"Hello there beauty, would you prefer something more than that meadow grass you've been grazing on?"

"Thank you. I would love it!" Whisp eR Har replied, as she covered the distance between us in the blink of an eye and nipped at the apple in my hand.

I jumped back a mile, the look on my face, I knew, had to be one of utter surprise. I didn't speak for a moment; I just couldn't seem to recover quickly enough. Then, it dawned on me. "It was you that spoke earlier? I didn't know that horses could speak?"

She kind of laughed and whinnied at the same time. "Horses cannot speak dear, that is ridiculous. I on the other hand, am only partially a horse. The unicorn in me, no matter how reduced, will always be the more dominant personality."

"Of course." I replied, still a little stunned. ". . . What is it like? I mean, are there many others for you to talk too?" *I knew I was muttering nonsense, but I was at a loss. Completely astounded.*

"Oh, I have my fair share of intelligent conversations. Then you have this big fella over here," Whisp eR Har shifted so that she was facing Batal'Agar, "with him, I do not need any words!" She laughed again, this time sauntering off, if a horse could, to join the stallion. Over her shoulder, she spoke to me, "having feelings and expressing them are not unique to humans. You know what you want. Just think on that."

"Your heart must meet." Echoing, the words drifted from within me. The shock of her words, and I must admit that a horse offering me advice was just that, a shock, but it also made me look at my thoughts differently . . .

I turned as Gable made his way over to me, coming up from behind. "Are they . . .?" I started to ask, not sure of how to properly phrase it.

"They have been successfully mated twice now. Come next year, she will hopefully foal again. Their foals are of the greatest breeding quality."

"You might have given me a heads up." I said ruefully.

"A head's what?" He asked in confusion.

This time, I laughed, a truly comical scenario popping into my thoughts. "It means that you might have warned me. It isn't often that a horse cares to offer me advice on my . . . love life."

Now he laughed. "Forgive my forgetfulness. One just never knows with her, she will amaze you . . ." He stopped for a moment. ". . . what love life?"

This time I blushed. "It was nothing . . ." Perhaps I did need to look at this from another angle. *She had definitely shocked me into a different train of thought . . . if nothing else . . .*

Together, we packed up the remainder of our meal. We continued on, seeing things that thrilled me in the realization that they were real. But how to proceed with Gable, that was what I truly wondered? I was still embarrassed over that display. *What love life? What could he have been thinking to ask me that?*

I wanted to get closer to him, but I still needed to understand him better. There had to be a way, but I seemed to be ignorant in the area of flirtation. *What to do? I looked over at him, perhaps if I could just get him to speak more of himself, to open up. That could give me something more to work with. At least it was a start.*

"Why is it, for all the unusual names in your realm, you have such a simple name, a near human name?" I wondered.

He laughed. "It is in no way human. My máthair was devoted to the Creator and she named me for his avenging Angel." He looked at me, deep within my eyes. "Apparently, our máthairs thought much in the same way, *Angel.*" I could see the amusement in his eyes as we began to head out once again. I felt the full effect of the blush that swept through me this time. *Yep, I'd walked right into that one!*

*

As we continued on, the forest became denser, the trees around us, full of lush and thriving fruits. *I could not believe that they had just been left to set on the trees, and then I wondered if they had yet to be harvested for the winter months, or if they even were? Perhaps they were forbidden?* The great trunks of the trees had a circumference of probably twelve foot, their height beyond my ability to guess, their leaves huge, with the smallest ones larger than my own hands.

Gable noticed her fascination. "These woods are from the beginning times. They are the oldest on Earth. Their very heart *is* the oldest place on Earth. Here is where our Kind and Man started forth to populate the world. The fruit that you see in these trees," he nodded upward, "is always the sweetest. It ripens late and lasts long after harvested."

I looked around me, taking in the sight of the unusual, yet amazing view. "Back home, they believe that humankind began in Africa. There are all these fossils of smaller species that resemble humans. They all have these technical names that I couldn't say to save my life, but all of the evidence that they have unearthed, points to Africa."

He laughed for a moment. "Just like humans, trying to put together a puzzle with half of the pieces missing!" He shook his head, before facing me with laughter in his eyes. "But of course, they do not realize that half of the pieces are missing. Nearly half the world is hidden from them. It does not surprise me that they are getting conclusions like that, if they are not able to get the whole view. What does surprise me is this nonsense about humans coming from something else. Humans have always been humans."

He continued. "In the beginning times, there were so many different varieties with their own uniqueness'. Of course, they also had their differences, like build and temperment. Some combined and reproduced, some differences were that slight, but most of them have died out, some only a couple thousands of years ago. Humans themselves have not been kind to those that were different, even if it was only small differences." He shook his head again. "Life is life, regardless of its many aspects."

"Could you tell me of some of these many varieties?" I asked. "I am more curious than you know . . ."

*

We followed a path that appeared well worn upon the ground. Soon, the sun itself was no longer visible through the canopy overhead, though the light penetrated deeply enough to keep the path visible. I knew that the day had to be wearing thin, while we had only moved farther and farther from the Keep. It had to be getting close to evening time.

"Gable, how much longer until we return home? The evening meal will be served soon and Caitrin will worry if both of us are not there."

He pulled upon his reins, waiting for me to pull alongside. "There is something up ahead that I wish to show you. This is my place, a secret place, something that very few have ever seen. I wanted to bring you here. I already arranged to have MadaREn care for Caitrin for the evening. She plans on taking her to her cottage for the night."

I was warmed by his admission. "I must admit that you have me intrigued. I'm glad that you thought to take care of Caitrin beforehand though.

Thank you, for thinking of her. After all that has happened, I cannot bare to give her more to worry about ."

"You are welcome. I did not want to spoil your surprise by telling you earlier." The smile on his face was breathtaking. He waved for me to ride ahead of him.

Watching, I noticed for the first time that the world around me was changing. The blazing autumn of the leaves were reversing to emerald green. From the horse's hooves, the smell of the earth was pungent and the breeze that blew was warm, even as dusk had been falling only a few moments earlier. As we traveled forward it appeared more and more, as if time itself had sprung backwards and summer was returning. After a few moments more, we reached a stretch along the pathway that had it disappearing all together. We pushed through, the leaves separating for us with little resistance. A clearing became visible just ahead.

It was true; the world here was not affected by change, summer was indeed in full riotous bloom. The scents hit me first. Lilacs and honeysuckle, it was not a combination I would have imagined, but here, it was powerful. The birds overhead were large as they swooped down in merriment from tree to tree. A wondrous melody as we moved on. Then we were leaving the trees behind, pulling back upon the reins and staring in utter wonder. The trees had buffered the sound, but now I could hear the rush and swirl of water. Moving forward again, I could make out the sound of water crashing on stone. The sight was so intoxicating, the clearing swept off into a cliff face. Immense in size, it jutted out. Before me, high up as I arched back my head to get the full effect, were twin waterfalls.

I left my saddle, my steps bouncing in my excitement to get closer. The first was gigantic. It fell at least a hundred feet before it hit a small plateau, where a large pool sat. It ran for a few yards, before another decline created the second waterfall. The second descended about forty feet. In front of me was a simple wooden bridge. It covered the gap, from side to side. Stepping forward, climbing onto the walkway. I noticed at the start, that there were intricate carvings of the two main, side support beams. They were warriors, in full gear, brandishing flaming swords. I thought it unusual, something that nagged at my memory, but the thought would not surface. Midway across, drawing courage and peering down, I was able to see the pool at the bottom of the second, and from there, could see that the water continued to flow. If I was not mistaken, there was another waterfall still!

"Another?" I asked, turning to acknowledge Gable.

"Yes, and more. Go ahead, the way down is across the bridge and a little further. I will meet you there with the horses."

I raced ahead of him. Excitement giving me wings to fly. The path down was not too steep; it wound around to the side, bringing the third waterfall out of view for a few moments. As I came to the bottom, I saw that the falls veered in two directions. The first ran as a fast moving stream. This I glanced at and followed for a short ways. The second, ended as the final pool of the triple falls. I would arrive there soon, but first I let the sight before me, consume me . . .

The late sun shined down from the west, settling upon my shoulders, warming me in its Grace. The grass was fragrant, rich and tender under my feet. Wildflowers grew up all around the area. Off to my right . . . it was unlike anything I had envisioned, yet exactly what I'd always wanted. It was a faerytale cottage, right out of the storybook. Except that it was more a tower, than a cottage. It went up and up, layers upon layers of spiral stone, the top a cone-like shape, the roofing, some type of material that glinted back in shades of iridescence; purples, blues and greens. Wrapping its way up from the bottom was woven vines of roses, in full bloom, their glory was remarkable. Thick, white and absolutely delicate, the open roses were as large as a man's open hand. It was the contrast, of the solid, ancient stonework and the delicate flowers that gave the place a steady charm, one that took my breath away.

This was where dreams were created. I knew that. Were they were suspended in time, forevermore, always just awaiting the next dreamer to re-envision them, to make them their own. This was forever . . . *eternity.* But none of this could contain my attention as much as the final waterfall. It pulled me back to it. Once I actually looked at it, I could not take my eyes away. It pulled to me on a basic level, and I ran to stand at the base of the pool, nearly under the flowing waters.

*

Gable watched her from atop his horse. Her beauty was beyond compare. The look of utter amazement and then utter wonder on her face had transformed her. He had been right to bring her here, to his place. He corrected, to their place. He watched as she walked from one side of the falls to the other. She bent down a time or two to pick something up and continue on.

He saw that she stopped at the heady tiger lilies, and breathed in deeply. Sliding down from his saddle, he led the two horses over to the waiting water trough. Simple words, *"fEla ambEan,"* had it filled to the brim with cooling waters. After they were cared for, he secured the horses in the stable for the evening. Angel was still taking her time as she walked . . .

*

It was not possible! The constant refrain that kept playing through my mind as I studied the waterfall in front of me. *This was my place, damn it!* The one special place in my memory where a mysterious dream lover had come for me, he had offered me happiness and bliss, and afterward Caitrin. It had been the only explanation for her conception, the only one that had ever felt right. But here it was, right in front of me, real, somehow moved to a different place entirely. *Gable had said that this was his place?*

Was it possible that it could exist in two separate realms? I honestly wasn't sure about anything anymore, but from everything that I'd already seen, I honestly believed that anything could be possible now. My heart began to race, surreal feelings beginning to race throughout my veins. First in a torrent of cold, then the tingles continued the race through my system, a current of wonder racing through me, confusing and exploding all of my senses at the same time. I was aware for once, that the world, the vision in front of me was real and I was awake. Reality had shifted and this gift, offered in essence, all of the dreams that I had held onto for years.

It was the same as I remembered, the high water cascading down to the gleaming pool at the bottom. I could still see the crystals embedded in the floor of the water. The dimming sun casting light upon the stones, sending slivers of light flying within the glen. Little diamonds falling wherever the beams landed. There were large rocks that provided the perfect place to sit and laze the day away. It was a little piece of Heaven on Earth.

I turned around in search of Gable, needing to have questions answered only to discover that he was right behind me. My questions scattered in the wind. All thoughts pushed aside. I looked behind him, the horses were beyond that, fully cared for and resting in the stables. I turned back to face him, my breath caught in my throat. I couldn't speak, it was impossible. *He was so close! Too close!*

He watched her standing there, a testament to the faith of his Kind and all the people who still believed. But to him, she was so much more. He could feel his heart beating wildly within his chest. He needed her, to be with her. But he suddenly discovered that he was scared. After so long, so many lonely years of waiting and wanting, never knowing where she was; he would not survive it if she pushed him away now. The time had come and he needed to know. He pushed away at the consuming fear that he had never experienced before. Their time was now!

He took the final step to reach her. She was stunning. The look of surprise on her face drew a smile to his lips. He noticed that her breathing increased, the closer he had moved. So, he was right, she was definitely affected the same as him. He reached out to her.

"What are you doing?" I asked in a mere whisper.

"What I have waited a lifetime for." He leaned down and branded me with his lips. The passion surged through me, his lips working a magick that I'd never truly known until this moment. He deepened the kiss, caressing my lips with his tongue, using his hands to caress me further. I fell deeper. My mouth parted as I begged him to continue. He dove deeper, searing me with a heat, his velvet tongue caressing mine in a ritual that had everything to do with physical pleasure and a soul's surrender. I fell completely, I was lost. His touch was searing and my skin was parched, begging for more. All I knew was that this was what I wanted, what I had waited my whole life to find. This was where I belonged.

He brought the kiss to an end. He felt that his soul had been razed by the heat of the sun itself. He had never imagined that desire could be so powerful and painful in the same moment. He felt her tremble in his arms. She was not able to stand on her own, he was not even sure that he could. He picked her up in his arms, and holding her close, he flew them over to the tower. It was a small retreat, one he had used in the past to find solitude and seek respite for his soul. Now, it would be their place. Here would be the place where he made her his, and their love would grow.

The door opened as they approached, *"Briten Thi,"* the scones on the wall lighted and *"Fire érA,"* the fireplace sprung to life, all at his silent command. He slowed and placed her upon her feet at the end of a large, raised sleeping platform. He looked down at her, her face burned with her longing. He opened his heart and he knew that now was forever.

"I want you." Was the simple truth of his soul.

"I want you too." I breathed as he lowered his mouth back down to mine. I could feel his hands roam over me as he deepened the kiss. They trailed pleasure from my shoulders, down my arms and back upwards to my waist. I felt intoxicated, under a spell. Passion had thickened my senses, making everything feel stronger, more intense. I rubbed my hands over his chest, feeling the crisp dark hairs curl around their tips. His smell so potent, it was over powering me. *"I needed to feel his skin."* Burning with my need for him.

It was like he read my mind. He reached down and finished removing his shirt. He was hard, his muscles and power evident in the span of his chest. But to the touch, his skin was warm, it was soft and rippled. Running my hands from his chest to waist, sensations erupted, living pleasure along my pathway. The power of pleasure was addictive and we both wanted more. He removed my shirt next, lower still, removing my belt in a quick flick of his wrist. He began running his hands over my freed waist and breasts. His teeth nipping at my collar bone. Causing shivers of pleasure to continue racing through my parched skin.

She was pliant, soft. The work they had done over the past several weeks only making him want her more. Her bloody curves were all still there and he wanted to bury himself in them. She was a beautiful woman and she had him insane with wanting her.

Before I was even aware of it, our clothing lay upon the floor and the heat of pleasure had engulfed us. Trailing kisses upon my shoulder and neck, he kissed me again. He deepened it as his hands roamed lower. Caressing and arousing, his large and strong fingers making me feel wanton. He trailed them lower still, caressing my belly, my hips. As I leaned into him, his plunging tongue dove deeper. Capturing my scream of pleasure, his hand closed around the mound of my femininity. His grip tightened and released, over and over, stimulating my body and soul. Entwined so deeply, I had no idea where one ended and the other began.

The pleasure rocked me; I had trouble staying lucid as he brought me closer to completion. My hands searched lower, could feel him, his arousal lay hard and snug against my soft middle. My hands grasped him and stroked. The rippled flesh, the hardness surrounded by the velvet. He was huge and powerful, but gentle. He pushed forward in my hands again, seeking my touch. It was his pleasure that was captured now in our joined lips.

Knowing that we would not be able to take much more, Gable sat back upon the bedding, pulling me down upon his lap. His thumb rubbed my moistness, making sure that I was ready for him. He pulled me down upon his shaft, his body shaking as the ribbons of pleasure rose forth.

I felt him enter me, opening my eyes at the exquisite pain caused by his arousal. Pleasure was coming, but also tightness. I screamed in the agony of the combined two. I had never truly been with a man in this way and then I smiled, for he was so much more than a man could be. He was a powerful faery. Skilled at the fundamentals of war, but also it seemed, at the making of love. I took him deep, as I slid into place and stared without question into his burning eyes. The explosion of passion began as he thrust back and forth inside me.

I had always thought that making love would be like falling into something, but I now knew that it was like soaring, soaring free up above the rest of life. It was a place somewhere between Heaven and Earth that we'd collided into. He continued to thrust as I met him, movement for movement. We road higher together as the passion built, watching as his wings spread out. They came back around us and enclosed us in a near cocoon of perfect union. The burning fire, the intense pleasure as it seared outward from my womb, from my heart. Feeling the heat as it raced through my veins, as it continued to make the fire burn brighter still.

My pleasure tore at me, ripping my world apart, ripping it into shreds as I screamed for more. His embrace aroused me higher and sent me tumbling towards the edge of passion. Towards a cliff that had no bottom, no end. Here I met him, as we followed one after the other, over the edge. I threw my head back and screamed. Pleasure and power ripping through my body as it sprang forth outward in a ripple of exquisite release. It ripped through me from him, the raw power and the exquisite pain. I felt the liquid fire, rupture and crest, it sent shock waves soaring. His wings lowering.

Suddenly, fire burned my chest like a brand. A tattoo, deep and elegant, a lovers knot scroll, appeared upon my left breast. Looking at him, I heard his intake of breath as an identical one appeared above his heart. We were complete, this final brand a proclamation to our mating.

Before I knew what was happening to me, my back arched and I bucked. Power shot forth and upon my shoulders was the sign of my Right, my Birth. My wings spread wide as I rode the final crest of passion. I felt my neck snap back, a rush of liquid cold as it came to me like a memory; the knowledge, and the sudden realization. The floodgates opened. Within me, it was there, magick, so plain and simple, so real and beautiful. My status as the Chosen One, fulfilled.

As we came down, we lay wrapped within each others arms. Both beyond words at the beauty of what we'd shared, at what had happened. I was the first to open my eyes, though I closed them again quickly. I grasped tight the knowledge, the power that he'd given me. I could feel it now, the power that was mine as it traveled through my arteries and veins. The power unimaginable and wild, I felt it and I embraced it. It had been him all along. It had been the union of our souls that had been required to release the magick. I was never meant to do it alone, at least, in this measure. I felt the pleasure that consumed me, and yet, I also felt sadness. It was finalized for me. I was the One, the one to bring the end of the suffering, the pain. *The knowledge frightened me in its magnitude, in its pull, my core shattering at the power of truth.*

He felt her sudden sadness and pulled her closer to him. The bond was there. They now shared one heart and one mind; they were soulmates, their mating complete.

I could feel him, even though we were separate now. I searched within myself and I found the tether that joined us, a silver and white band of light that united our minds and thoughts. I looked for the answers and I realized that they had been there all along. We were one, body and soul. Even when we had not been together, our souls had recognized each other. I finally opened my eyes and looked at the room around me.

Looking at our haven, the small tower Keep was comfortable. It contained the large bed that we lay on. There was a small table and chairs, with a set of cupboards, placed to the left of the fireplace. To the right of the fireplace, a small desk and set of bookcases rested. Gable's personal belongings. There was another door that led out of the tower, besides the one that we had entered. Maybe, there was more to the place than I had originally thought. It was quaint, the perfect escape, a place to fall in love and find passion.

"What I don't understand is how this, what we have between us, could ever be considered a sin?"

"It never was." Gable replied. "Making love, sensuality, was never a sin. The beauty of the soul is also reflected outward, between mates. Others can see that beauty. It is there to be seen, admired even, so long as no faithlessness is evoked. No tearing of moral leight. The Creator wished to keep sorrow and pain from humanity. But Adam and Eve did not accept truth; it was the unchildlike curiosity of them that was the sin. Their nonacceptance of simple truth, which opened the door to heartache, suffering, pain and death. The door of knowledge was opened and with it came all."

"...with it came all." I thought to myself as the heat of my lover added a cocoon of comfort and an all-consuming lethargy creep over me. My mind began drifting off in slumber.

Gable watched as she slept. She had quickly become his everything, she and her daughter. He smiled, soon she would awaken and they would have to talk. He stared at her wings. They were delicate in appearance, though he knew that they would be nearly indestructible. It was very hard to damage one's wings. The fact that she now had them was a mind altering thought.

He had felt it, the moment she had embraced her power and had come into her own. The strength of it had rocked them both. But the sight of her, with her wings spread wide, was definitely a memory that would be forever seared into his memory. He had seen so much evidence of the Creator's Will lately that the feeling of righteousness passed through him. This he thought, is what it must be like to know you are going to win.

The Garden
(20)

I came awake slowly, my mind refusing to believe that reality was, as it was. That eternity was indeed ours. *"I didn't want to open my eyes. I was indeed afraid, afraid that the truth was something that I could not bear."* If that was the case, and I was dreaming, I knew that I would never survive the heartbreak of awaking.

"You can open your eyes now." He said with a laugh on his lips. "There is nothing to fear."

I peeped my eyes open only a smidgen. I had to make sure completely, that it had all been true. The sight of him naked was definitely enough to convince me, also, to get my heart racing once again. "Gable, I feel so wonderful . . . it was so amazing . . . Oh my God, I have wings!" I screamed in delight, jumping up in wonder, dancing around the room naked, trying desperately to get my wings to move.

"Take is slowly Angel. You can move them the same as you would move an arm or leg. Just think about it." He said. Her joy was highly contagious, bringing a smile to his lips as well.

I stopped jumping up and down and began to concentrate. *"Could it really be that simple?"* I thought to myself and my wings began to move. They shimmered as I fanned them out. They were glorious, wild and forbidden. They looked . . . well, like faery dust, their twinkling glow pristine with a lavender hue, the light from the fireplace causing a glimmer to reflect in their depths. They were impressive, but I was still completely feminine, their size still much smaller than Gable's. *"But wings? How was it possible?"*

"I do not know. That is one question that I will not be able to answer for you. It can only be the Creator's Will." He said.

"How are you doing that? You know what I'm thinking before I even say it outloud?"

"It is part of our Bond. Once we mated, we created a link between ourselves that allows us to communicate with each other whenever we have the need."

"I have seen it." I said. "Do you mean that it will be like this always?" I asked in surprise. I felt a moment of discomfort, but it passed quickly, replaced instead by a deep sense of thankfulness.

"It is something that we will always share, yes. It is an intense thing; it will take time to adjust to. You do have control over it, the same as I do. We can communicate when we need to and keep things private, if the need arises."

I allowed myself that moment, the time to comprehend what he offered me, some of my own identity, some of my self, amidst us. "Something like this is permanent. It means that our lives are now connected in a way that cannot ever be severed." I said. The idea of such a strong link was something new to me. I moved back over to the bed. The closer to Gable I got, the more comfortable I felt. I smiled to myself; I was not sure how this strong, passionate warrior would take to being thought of as a comfortable shoulder to rest my head on. Then it struck me! *No wonder every time I had fought my attraction to him, it had felt like I was falling from my goal, I had been.* I laughed at the complexity of it all. *"Life definitely knew how to throw some curve balls!"*

"What is so funny...?" He asked.

He took her in his arms. She felt so right there. It was time for her to understand, all of it, everything. "Faery are not like humans when it comes to marriage. We do not marry . . ." He started.

"What do you mean you don't get married? You cannot possibly believe that you could offer me bliss like that, and then say in the same breath that you can go off on a whim with someone else! Not after what we just shared!" The force of my feelings rocketed me to my feet and waves of shock and seething cursed through me. It felt like I wanted to rip his head off. It passed quickly and with a smile, he was right there, pulling me back down.

"Your emotions are stronger now. Remember, faery feel things differently? You need to let me finish Angel." He said with rare humor in his voice. "We do not marry, because when a faery finds their mate, they mate for life, as in soulmates." He paused for a moment. "When faery make love, it is at that time that they are considered Bonded. We are mates, you and I, mated for life. Once together, we never part."

"As in God's original plan?" I said to him, suddenly a lot more about life, made sense to me. Made me understand what God had been trying to do for us, all along.

Her understanding simple, he jolted at her uncanny ability and nodded once again. "Yes, it is exactly what God meant. Human wedding vows made their way towards it, but the actual understanding, the faery understanding was of one soul, reunited from two." He said. "The bodies, the flesh, may separate at death. But the souls are reunited in eternity. " *The only problem was that humans did not completely understand the concept.* He thought to himself.

"So it's true, we are one now! I feel so wonderful, so alive!" I screamed in joy.

*

I leaned back against him, still trying to really absorb the wonderful things that he'd been telling me.

"Do you remember when you awoke from the sleeping state that you were in, that you spoke to me of knowing me?" Gable asked.

I shook my head in acknowledgment and he continued on.

"When you lay there," he stopped for a moment, his breath caught in his throat, "in such horrible pain and I came to sit with you nearly every day, there was this strong pull to you, even then. Me, in my own right, I thought that I was transferring the feelings that I had developed for Caitrin onto you. I quickly came to love her. I did not see how anyone could not." He sat back for a moment, remembering. "But the more I look back on it, the more I realized that we did indeed already know each other. Since you have healed, we have been fighting an attraction that has been tearing us both apart!" It was his turn to jump up off the bed, he needed to pace, to move. "It was because we were already mates, you see. Our minds felt what our bodies had yet to feel, to understand."

"How was that possible though, Gable? I was never with another. I only dreamt of you once, yet we were not together, flesh on flesh. How could we have been together then?" I asked. Even hearing it, knowing that it was true, did not take away from the mystery of it.

"Nearly five years ago, I came to this place. I was desperately in need of finding peace. Over the last few centuries, the battle has not gone well. I came here in search of what I had always been able to find. Instead, I wandered. Peace would not come. Over and over again, in my soul, all that I could focus on was that I had never found my soulmate that I was incomplete, and fear began to settle in. I eventually ended up at the waterfall. I remembered taking off my clothes, going for a swim in the pool to cool off, and then getting out. The need to sleep overpowered me, it was so strong . . . my eyes closed on their own." He took a breath, closing his eyes now. A moment later, he looked me in the eye again.

"What I remembered next was passion. It was as if a waking dream, the passion of a mate, deep and everlasting. Though I could not remember all . . . it was enough for me to know that my mate was near. We had connected a rare but possible thing. Usually, only bonded mates can do so. So I searched. I tore my Kingdom apart, searching for my mate, for you." His look was scorching me to the core. "I feared her dead, after not being able to find her. I now know how very wrong I was."

I sat in silence and wonder as he explained the events that mirrored my own so completely. So many unanswered questions raced through my mind. But there was also anger.

"You knew; you knew that we were supposed to be together all along?"

"I was aware that it was so, yes. When you awoke, I knew you. But the feelings, the emotions you had awoken in me, even before you woke, concreted the fact that we were destined to be together. There was no other way."

"Then why didn't you say anything. I have wondered and hurt for weeks now; trying to figure out if it was even possible for us to be together."

"It was my fault. I was so worried about being a distraction for you. With all of the complications, all of the mistakes we had already made . . . I blinded myself to the truth. All those years ago, we found each other Angel. When we needed each other the most, we prevailed. Our bond was forged that day, though not in a way that I could have imagined. I had not looked for you in the correct place, but the reality is, that you were with me all along. We are mates, as we have been for the last five years." He switched topics again quickly. At first I was unsure of his aim. But in the end, I saw that he was offering me more. More than I had ever hoped to of gained.

"In the beginning, there were humans, there were animals, and then there was the many, many in between. Your view or I should say, humans views, are now so narrow. With them, it is, "you are not this, so you have to be this." The real answer was always, "if not this, then what?" Because the actual truth, the actual possibilities were large. There were many individuals, and born of these individuals were multiple species that came from the creation of the blending. They were so similar, these original species, that their differences could not be seen. It did not mean that they did not look human, only that they were not human. Perception is often based on what we do see, not on what we do not see. They were within them and not a stigma or "abnormality" to be reviled."

"On the other hand, there were those that wore their differences and were proud to be different. They were at different levels of intelligence, life and variation. Some of the blending was truly beautiful and lead to qualities you see today. Like eye colors, it was very limited before that. Mutual respect, acceptance and love had allowed for multiple species blending and creating. So, humans have always been human and yes, they have blended with others in the past, so the only differences in the humans you see now, the humans that your world thinks of as human qualities, are actually changes to humanity that were incorporated by the inner-species blending that occurred so long ago. Your world needs to think outside of the box, because their box is very small. By life and adaptation, the Creator made us all and we, as a society of many lives, have created the differences and in respect, the constants."

I wasn't sure where this was leading, but he always had a reason for everything he said and did. I knew something important was on the way. "I never really thought of it that way. But you're right. It only takes a small sequence in DNA variation, in our makeup, to make us other than human. But that does not necessarily mean that the difference is on the outside, like you said. Unfortunately for humans, I think that acting before thinking is a common gesture. I guess that my society has always just done that, acted out from the basic assumption, those always blatant and visible. Always noticeable for ridicule, but even now, there could be people who walk and talk to us on the streets, who look just like us, yet their DNA could say something more. I never truly thought of it that way." Shaking my head, I looked down at my hands, wondering.

Gable grimaced. "There would be a multitude more now, then even you could consider, if not for the intolerance and indifference that moved through the humans many eons ago. There began a virtual genocide of life, because of the differences that they began to fear instead of embrace. Now, your species really is the last true dominate one on the planet. Unless, as you have stated, there are others out there that have yet to be detected."

Saddened, I shook my head in agreement. *As of right now, color, age and just about anything else was reason enough in humanity to have a problem with one another. Just more examples of stupidity!* I thought on it more. It was an interesting subject, more than human, more than animal, in-betweens and more. I looked back up as I asked, "Is that how it was . . . ?" Then it dawned on me to actually explain what I meant. . . "with Adam and Eve?"

He smiled. "I understood your thought, or your train of thought. Yes, Adam and Eve where the first and only true humans to come to Earth from Eden. But there was already an abundant variety of near similar species populating the Earth. Their offspring, Adam and Eve's, blended with the offspring of others already there. Their differences were very slight. They were a very gentle species. It was a good match. It allowed for your Kind to carry forward and survive. Of course, as the species grew, they did once again pull together and blend out some of the differences. It seems to be a problem for them, accepting differences." He stopped talking and looked away.

"Does this mean," I said as I looked up at him, "that our children or child, would actually be a true blend of us?"

He thought about it for a moment, I could feel that exhilaration that washed through him at the thought of us having a young one, but then I felt a sudden silence in his mind. And the stupidity of my own words washed over me.

"Yes. I believe that a union of human and faery would create a blend." He was . . . stiff, like he was thinking something that was bothering him, almost like he was speaking the words of another. Suddenly, his thoughts shifted, as if finding a solution or . . . accepting of . . . truth.

Could we have a child, since I already had . . .? My thoughts drifting off. A silent dawning forming within me.

The sadness of what he had missed passed through him in torrents of pain, and sorrow. Of the years that he had lost and would never regain. But it was done . . . "Have you ever noticed the unique qualities that Caitrin possesses?"

I nodded mutely. Suddenly I felt fear, an ultimately consuming, soul deep, amazing and breathtaking fear.

"Caitrin is special, more than any of us realized. I do not just mean the fact that she is your daughter either. She is part faery. Though you have the abilities of us, you are essentially human, that is the way that the Creator made you. But with Caitrin, it is different. She is part faery. You can see it in her features, in her essence. She carries the mark of a faeryling."

"I always thought she was special myself. I called her my little pixie." The words were dry as they came out, breathy.

He nodded in agreement. "Our Bond was nearly complete for the last five years. Today, we cemented our Union in the eyes of the Creator. The only explanation is that the Creator stepped in. Your destiny was a path that was set before you, and things happened that pulled you off your way. The Creator stepped in and made sure that you were once again pulled to reach your destination, us." He shook his head, happily. "Hé is the Creator. Hé can do all things."

"That Hé can." I agreed with a smile. *That Hé can . . .*

It hit me. I felt it rising within me, the answer that had eluded me for years, the simplicity of it. I should have seen it sooner. I needed to say it out loud. Finally saying the truth, the truth that freed us all. My voice was nearly a whisper, as the words freed themselves. "Caitrin is our child." I said in acknowledgment. Then I screamed it out to the world. "Our faeryling!"

"Yes, she is ours . . . my daughter." Gable nodded. "The Creator directed us to each other. Hé gave me you to carry on, and to you, Hé gave Caitrin. She was the driving force to keep you moving forward."

I smiled. It was true. This beautiful, mighty warrior was my mate and Caitrin, my precious and bright child, was a product of the love that we'd shared. *"God did indeed work in mysterious ways."* I smiled again, apparently, even for the Faery.

*

"Come back to bed Gable. I think we need to continue celebrating our miracle a little while longer." I smiled wickedly. *A new found sense of control and contentment. And an eruption of passion surged through me . . .*

. . . shooting a jolt clear through his system. He could feel the pull on his heart, and the rise in his loins. She was an amazing woman, and she was his.

* * * * * * *

The morning sun was rising as I walked outside, naked in my glory, Gable still fast asleep amongst the bedding. I wiggled my wings, softly, as I allowed myself height, my wings spreading out in a golden glow. Flying off a short ways, planning on coming to rest at the foot of a great tree. It was different here, I felt the pull. There was something about this place, this spot that was more unusual than the rest of the realm put together.

The tree was an ancient weeping willow, its trunk mighty and twisted, the bark a golden brown. The breath of the arms of the tree was great. Glorious emerald green flowing leaves, covered in golden fuzz, swayed as they reached from great heights, to the ground below. And . . . *wait!* This couldn't be right! Some type of fruit, they were succulent, beautiful and perfect, growing in masses, at least a fruit of sorts. As the sunlight struck them, they glowed. *A golden fruit of plenty.* I thought to myself. Almost reminding me of apples or even pomegranates, and yet, not. But I only admired. The beauty of them, their pristine appearance, spokes volumes to Gods ability to create.

The morning breeze was warm on my bare skin. As I finished my descent, the thick grass wrapped around my bare toes as they skimmed the earth. It offered to me the soft earth as a pillow, my knees falling to the ground to be cushioned deeply by the moss and grass. All around me was life, in overflowing amounts. Everything felt right here, the world at peace, and the magick taking hold. The massive outstretched arms my canopy. I bowed my head, my wings at my side and back. I sought peace and I asked for forgiveness. I asked for myself, and then for the world at large. For the damage inflicted upon the earth and the innocent, seeking forgiveness for the sins that had prospered for several thousands of years, those that had come after the Blessing and had grown in severity.

To Hím I prayed and asked for guidance, for strength. The glow of the sun caressed my shoulder, a mere swipe of a caress. A hand of strength, offering me more in Hís gentle touch, more than I believed we deserved. The ability to keep moving onward, forgiveness and the knowledge that I was not alone.

I raised my head, the power flowing through my veins as massive streams. I opened my eyes and looked at the heavens above me, the elusive and violent streams of color as they struck out across the morning sky, deep burgundies, oranges and violets. It was almost too brutal, a burning scene, to be the promise of a new day, a day in which I could finally make a difference.

I stood, throwing my wings wide in their beauty, watching as they glowed from the radiance of the sun that glistened upon them. I gathered the energy within me, pulling from within myself, testing the waters of my skills. I thrust myself upward, speeding up and away. As the clouds came into contact, I slowed. It had always been a dream of mine as a child, to fly amongst the clouds. Skimming my hand through them, so thick, so overflowing, yet light and insubstantial to the touch. It was like holding water and yet, holding wind at the same time. I wove my way in and out. I could feel the dew as it clung to my skin and bathed me in a cleansing, a Baptism of sorts, a reaffirmation of my body and soul, a cleansing from the Creator. It was a new beginning for me, for us.

I was thoroughly wet as I finished. The sun's rays, a warming effect. I smiled to myself; I might as well go all the way. I laid back, my back caressed by the clouds. My face and body warmed by the sun, eyes closed, embracing the change in my world and in myself. I was finally awake, finally whole.

*

He had never seen anything like it before. She was glorious as she returned, appearing to have been kissed by the sun itself. Her skin glowed and held a new tint that had not been there before. Golden threads, nearly red, wove through her rich hair and vibrant curls set amongst the straight flow of her tresses. She was naked as she returned to him. The only thing she wore, the deep endless brand of their Union. He felt himself respond. Felt the fire as it ignited under his skin and within him. He could scorch the room, the desire running so strong.

He flew up off the bed, catching me in surprise as we sped through the doorway and back into the light of morning. "I would have the Grace of the Creator upon us, as I love you again." He flew us over to the waterfall, to our spot. The beginning of our evermore . . .

. . . he took his time. Soft caresses over my shoulders, neck and cheek, his lips following afterward, a soft nip, a gentle swell of his tongue, leaving behind a glorious trail of pleasure and fire. His head dipped lower, pulling one nipple in between his lips. I felt myself beginning to fall, passion flaring bright. It knotted tight within my belly, before surging outward, using any access possible to rupture through my being. Heavy and languid, my body began to betray me. I tried to stand my ground, but it was useless. The next I was aware, I was on my back, his glorious silhouette outlined above me. He lowered himself down, his weight settling on mine. He was heavy, thick, but not uncomfortable. I breathed deep as he lowered his lips once again to my neck. His hands roaming with free access to everywhere. I felt my scenes soar, the smell of him exotic and intoxicating. Like a dark musk, earth and more. A hint of something forbidden, something magick.

I knew I was sinking, losing the battle of consciousness to my desire and I dove deeply into the pit. Then I began to soar as he found me, ready and willing. Offering all that I had to give as he thrust inward and passion took complete hold of the both of us. Neither of us was aware that we no longer settled upon the earth, passion having driven us higher. We were soaring above, free in our fire and love, the heat burning both of us through, searing us into our passion's fulfillment . . .

The Gift
(21)

The next afternoon saw us returning home. *Home.* I sighed. Making our way on horseback through woods and fields, till the inner Keep walls of Ainys'Dai came into view. A new future awaited here for us, it was like looking at the Keep for the first time. So much depended on me for that future to be a good one and soon enough the decisions would be upon me, but for the moment, I pushed it all aside and just came home.

There was much celebration as word quickly spread of the Union of Gable from the Keep of Ainys'Dai to the Chosen One, Angelwynn of Man. Many came to the Keep to see the Chosen One, as much as to congratulate our Union. But none, none were happier than Caitrin. When we arrived back at the Keep Caitrin came racing towards us. From her small face had radiated joy, and upon her tiny shoulders sat a pair of pinkish wings. Her gift, that had appeared. Her joy then was only surpassed by the knowledge that Gable was her fáthair, truly and forevermore.

The small intended celebration, quickly turned into a week long festival, as more and more faery arrived. It had been so long since a celebration of this sort had occurred that the joy became contagious. Everyone took the opportunity to forget the Darkness, if even for a little while. *Who could blame them, we were looking for any excuse these days, to make the world appear brighter.* For once, we were surer of our own survival.

*

Gable himself showed a side that few had ever seen as he rejoiced in the happiness he had found in his love for Angel and Caitrin. He was not sure if his heart would ever recover from the dramatic expansion of the past few months. He was pretty certain that he never wanted it too.

* * * * * * *

We were not the only ones returning home, however. Past the inner walls, another family was rejoicing . . .

"ZackaRAy, I cannot believe that you are finally home, it seems like you have been gone forever." She threw back the door in her haste, throwing her arms around him. *"He was home, safe."* "I worry every time that you will not come back to me. Things have gotten so much worse."

He could hear the fear in her voice, the way it trembled as she spoke. But her thoughts called to him more. *"Always safe for ya."* He returned. Reaching up, he began to stroke her arms, her sides. Speaking, he moved IllEna steadily inside the cottage. "I know tha ya fear for ma, for us. But know tha tis your love that will always bring ma home. Nothin' shall ever happen ta ma, for I know, tha I will always come home ta ya!"

She tilted her face upward, "I love you ZackaRAy!" Passion flared as his mouth took possession of hers. The kiss deepened as they put all of their emotions, all of the love and fear from weeks of not seeing each other, into that very earth shattering moment of his lips on hers. Aroused higher as he removed her clothing so quickly, IllEna could feel her dress slide to the floor, feel his hard muscular body pressed closely to hers. Knowing that in moments, they would become one.

He pulled her up, wrapping her long legs around his waist. Thrusting deeply, he sought their union, only what she could offer him, and she met him, heat on heat. The earth shifted as molten lava poured through his veins. With each thrust, with each blend of their thoughts, the fire spread and intensified. He knew she was near, could feel her tightening, her subtle resistance. He lowered his mouth back onto hers, calling to her, branding her as his. His strength giving; his body thrust deeper, faster, pushing her to meet his own needs, his own powerful release.

She felt the explosion, felt their worlds shift and collide as they truly became one. They floated together, whole, complete, yet somewhere insubstantial at the same time, an existence that transcended reality. As she came back, she felt him rubbing her abdomen, and she stilled . . .

. . . His hands slide upward, from her thighs and buttocks, to her stomach, loving the feel of her silken and smooth skin. Missing her softness, her smell. He felt her stiffen, and then he felt himself do so. Where she should be soft and pliant, there was substance, there was a swell . . .

* * * * * * *

"Gable, could I speak with ya?" Gable turned to see ZackaRAy's approach. Something about him appeared different. It was like he was barely containing himself, like he was ready to burst. And his expression, there was definitely something going on.

"I had not realized that you had returned already. Is everything alright? You do not seem yourself."

"I have na been back long; I stopped ta see IllEna before arriving here. I have . . . news? I am na really sure how it happened . . . thank the Creator!" He yelled in joy, jumping up and down.

Gable stared in amazement. He could not believe his eyes. He had not seen this side of ZackaRAy since they were faerylings. He even had a crazy grin on his face. *What was going on?*

"Tell me, what has happened?" Gable said in wonder and perhaps, a little alarm.

"Tis IllEna, she tis . . . tis . . ." The words failing to come.

Gable's face changed, fear clouding his features. "What is it? Is she alright? Has something happened to her?" But no, ZackaRAy was . . . excited! *What could it be?*

"Na, she tis wonderful, she tis with faeryling!" ZackaRAy's smile was huge; tears began falling from his eyes. "We are expecting a young one. I can na even . . ." The tears began to fall in earnest, his speech clouded by his wonder and happiness.

Gable looked at him like he had never seen him before. *A faeryling? Here, now?* It was beyond miraculous, it was unbelievable. "Are you sure?"

"I am pretty sure, tha she tis pretty sure." He replied, disbelief still registering on his face. "I have seen ta evidence tha she carries."

Gable walked over to him, feeling as if his own chest would burst from the wonderful news. "My brother, do you realize what this means? It means that things are indeed changing, that the end of this is coming. The honor that the Creator has bestowed upon you is something that I have prayed for you, for all of us, myself. I cannot tell you of the extent of my happiness that it was you that this gift was given too. The Creator smiles down upon us." He finished by wrapping his arms around him, giving him the love of their brotherhood, both of them smiling. "We will have to honor IllEna."

"She wa like tha. We wa both be honored by ya support. We have talked, she wa like for ya ta be "Guard*É*an," in honor of our bond as brothers. She tis so happy. Ya should have seen her face when she told ma."

Gable was speechless. This life . . . such a short time ago he had had no family, now it was growing and coming at him in all directions. He closed his eyes, prayers on his lips. He had been blessed, truly blessed. "Thank you for this gift. Your faeryling shall never go without. "

They walked together for a little while longer.

"Have you told TazaRine yet?" Gable asked.

"He tis ta very next. I am on ma way now. Afterward, I return ta bring IllEna here. I wa have her within ta safety of ta inner walls from now on."

"Excellent! We will make the announcement tonight. This is a night of celebrations!" Gable said.

They separated and went their own ways. This was a blessing that his entire Kind needed to be aware of. There had not been any young born in such a long time. Everything was changing, thank the Creator, everything was changing!

* * * * * * *

It was as he was walking through the fading light, that he saw her seated amongst the Sprite Stumps. Angel was exquisite in the fading light, her hair falling to her waist, in a shift of some flowing material. He watched for a while, before he actually approached her.

I looked up as I heard him approach. "Did you know that I have been here all this time and I was never aware that these were full of life. I just assumed that they were all that remained of felled trees." I said, pointing to the stumps. The faint glow that announced them, getting stronger as the sun set. I could see now, that they were actually homes. They were carved out, the tiny front lights illuminating their doors and windows. Movement was coming from inside, and soon one of the small doors, no more than five inches high, swung open. Standing in the archway, a small Being, it was very similar to human in its shape. But the hair was a fiery red that was wild and free. The female, for she was very obviously so, waved to me, before she lifted off on wings only slightly larger than herself.

"You have never been out here in the dark. They are night creatures, the Sprites. As you can see, they are all awaking for their time of day."

Indeed, tiny lights were turning on all around the stand of stumps. Soon, a small town of life was evident. Some came out, some stayed in, but all appeared ready for merriment. "I'm glad that I finally saw this, they are brilliant." I stood up, preparing to enter the Keep for the evening meal.

"There is news Angel." His look one that drew my interest immediately.

"ZackaRAy has returned."

"That's wonderful news. I assume this means that all went well for him."

"Yes. But he has brought news to us of his mate, IllEna. I know that you have not met her yet, because she prefers to often remain within her own home, which is outside the walls. Their home rests on the cliffs shore. The news is hers, but involves us all."

"Now you truly have me curious. What is so powerful that it could affect all of us?" A prickle of awareness swept me. "Tell me. I would not want to have to add more worry to anyone within these walls."

"Oh, it is truly good news indeed. She is with faeryling! The first that we have known of in long years! You coming to us, it has set into motion the seeds of change. This means that our world is progressing again. We have the ability to begin rebuilding families, futures. You have brought much joy with you, and the extent of it keeps growing."

I could feel the excitement flow within me. "I don't know what to say? When will I get to see him, see them?"

"They will come to the celebration tonight. He went to bring IllEna here; the evening meal will be served a little later tonight, in order for them to arrive. It is a blessing for us all."

He reached over to me, pulling me close to his side, sliding his arms around me and pulling my head up to meet his. The kiss was shattering. I could feel the passion as it flared through me, my blood consumed in flames. He deepened the kiss, my head spinning and it sucked me down further. His head came up slowly. I could see the purely masculine smile on his lips. He was devastating me, it was that simple.

"If you keep that up, we will never make it to the meal." I could hear the huskiness in my voice.

He laughed, my stomach fluttering once more. "We will make it. Though, we might not make it to the morning meal on time."

* * * * * * *

Faery were gathered throughout the hall as they awaited the arrival of the last few. Gable and Angel stood in the main hall, waiting as ZackaRAy entered with IllEna on his arm. Each acknowledging the other, they offered congratulations, each on their own terms, for their own reasons. Surrounded by various other faery, what had become a close group of friends, quickly took shape.

Caitrin walked over to the group of faery, after making her way down the staircase. She wore a dress of pink satin that emphasized the color of her wings, which she fluttered here and there, still trying to get used to the glory of them. As she watched, she saw a faery that she recognized. Increasing her speed, she stopped next to ZackaRAy, who was close to her máthair, and who had a female on his arm that she did not know.

"ZackaRAy, I'm so glad to see you! You've been gone for a long time." Caitrin said.

Turning to acknowledge her attention, he leaned forward, offering her an adept bow. "Oh, well hello, wee one," ZackaRAy began, "tis good ta see our own little Guardian Slayer. I wa like ta introduce ya ta ma mate, IllEna."

Caitrin blushed, offering a nearly mute reply in response to ZackaRAy. To IllEna, she offered a large and brilliant smile. "You are very beautiful, I am glad to meet you."

IllEna blushed as well; a blossoming smile crossed her features. "Thank you, young one. It is nice to finally meet you."

As the strange introduction had begun, I turned to bring myself into the suddenly, interesting conversation. Turning to ZackaRAy, I directed my question to him. "*Guardian Slayer*...what do you mean?" I asked, slightly startled at the name.

ZackaRAy turned his attention to me, seriousness written across his features. "Oh, tha tis a wee bit of a sore spot around here." He said as his eyebrows rose in humor, then winked as his eyes settled in TazaRine's direction, the other faery stiffened, looking mutinous for a moment. Like a challenge being laid down, though not. Then ZackaRAy bowed to me, before he turned around and walked the other way, with an equally confused IllEna still hanging on to his arm, his laughter coming back to us on the air.

"Can someone explain to me what that was all about?" I asked. No one replied, as the warriors conveniently dispersed. With no response, I threw my hands up, but I let it go for now. I would find out sooner or later what was so funny. Following Gable, we went to sit on one of the thickly padded benches.

Gable brought the hall to order, everyone silencing as he stood and all eyes fell to him. "Today, I received news that marks the change we have waited for, for a very long time . . ."

A Burning Question . . .
(22)

As the meal was served, I noticed that Caitrin's attention was held fast by RandelfSon. Again and again, he said something that continuously drew her in. I watched the way that they were together, almost as a single unit. I had never actually had the opportunity to speak with him. It was so seldom that he came to the main hall when all were together here, turning to Gable I sought for some answers.

"They really do seem to get along well together." My head inclining in their direction. RandelfSon was much closer than when I normally saw him, he looked like he might have been handsome once. But you could tell that life had left a mark on him. His face and shoulders bore his burdens heavily. He was honestly, the only faery that I'd ever seen, that looked old.

Gable looked in the direction that I'd implied. "Yes," he said with a smile, "they are an interesting pair. I am sorry that I never thought to introduce you properly to him, with his ways, it makes it kind of hard to. Over the years, we have always just let him come to us if he was interested."

"That's no problem, I'm sure that when he is ready, he will speak to me. I'll get the opportunity soon enough. However," I began, "I am curious about him, about his past. Is it possible for you to tell me? I know of the few things that I have heard, but it is not much. I know that he has suffered tragedy. Isn't it unusual for faery to be such loners? Your Kind always seems to be in groups and family structures, is there nothing at all like that for him?" I asked in curiosity.

"True enough. RandelfSon is the last of his lineage. His family, an old one, was full of powerful faery in their day. But the Darkeness has taken all from him. It attacked his protected Keep when he was away. He returned swiftly upon learning of the attack, but the end of the battle was already near. It did not stop him; he rushed in, attempting to save any that he could. That was when he learned that it was too late for his own family, they had fallen. It was one of our worst battles; nearly everyone in the Keep fell. Only a few managed to escape and find shelter in other Strongholds." Gable looked over at RandelfSon as he paused in his speech. The old faery sat close to Caitrin; now and then he smiled at something she said. Once he offered her a sweet treat.

Gable looked back to me. "He did not arrive directly after; he was missing for quite a while. He was never the same after he did come back though. He stayed away from most, keeping to himself, helping around the Keep. It was not until Caitrin arrived here that he has made any effort to be a part of real life again. I think she is good for him. She is good for all of us." He finished, returning to his previous conversation as food began arriving.

Fascinated with their attachment, I continued to watch for a while longer. *He seemed to follow her, almost like a shadow.* The thought of something dark startled me! A solid jolt of adrenaline to the heart! I had never felt a comparison of this nature since settling into the faery society. I was not sure why I thought it now; nothing seemed to be amiss at all. Keeping my thoughts to myself. *I decided that I needed to think on it, when there was more time to do so.* Turning back, the food before me was a welcome temptation. Washing away the unease in friendly companionship. Shortly afterward, MadaREn came to join me, along with IllEna. Gable was caught up in an animated discussion with the others, and we were given time to speak amongst ourselves.

*

"I see how you watch them." MadaREn said. "It is a miracle, the way that she has brought him out of his seclusion. Has brought life back to him."

"Gable told me his tÁle, of how the Darkeness took his Keep."

"Yes, he has suffered much more than most. But that is actually only half of his story."

"Half? What do you mean?" My interest along with IllEna's, was piqued.

"I did not know that there was more that happened to him?" IllEna said in her shy, quiet voice.

"His tÁle actually starts much farther back than that. He had an unusual beginning. You see, RandelfSon and his mate were born at the same time."

"His mate? I had not realized that he had one." IllEna said.

I nodded my head in agreement.

"He no longer has one. She has been gone for nearly 1500 years."

I thought about that. *It seemed impossible to think in terms of that many years, and to live that long without a mate? The idea actually terrified me, to be that long without Gable?* I couldn't imagine it. "From what I've learned, isn't it rare for one to survive without the other?"

"Rare? Definitely. The mate can survive, but the living is taken out of the life. But let me tell you the tÁle first, so that you get an idea." MadaREn began. "It is very rare that a set of soulmates are born at the same time. What usually occurs is that one is a few centuries older than the other. For this reason, they recognize each other and the younger one develops with the older one alongside as confidant or mentor. Those feelings of deep love have a long time to develop. When they are born together, they grow together, learn together. The bond that is forged from this experience is much deeper, much greater than any of us could expect. Such was the case with them."

"RandelfSon and SaraFen were only born a few weeks apart. Their families were close and they recognized their bond as faerylings. They were always together, their lives interwoven as a continuous knot. Then, when they were leaving faeryhood behind, there was a tragic accident." MadaREn cleared her throat. Her words hitched.

It was easy for me to see that the telling touched her deeply. *There was something that she was not saying, I could sense it as easily as breathing.*

"They had been planning on spending an afternoon out together, racing horses. They were supposed to meet in a field midway between the Keep and his cottage. RandelfSon was detained and it made him late in arriving. SaraFen decided to take off on her own for a while. She was always stubborn like that." She said with a smile. "Always reckless."

A reckless faery? I thought to myself. Not something you hear of everyday.

MadaREn's voice broke, as she continued. "He went out to find her, he knew all of her favorite places. What he found . . ." Her words were choked off, breathy. ". . . was, was her lying at the bottom of a hill. She had been thrown from the horse. She was . . . she was . . ." It took her a moment to regain her composure, tears pooling in her eyes. ". . . the damage inflicted on her from the horse was massive. We never found out why, but apparently, the horse had thrown her and then . . . continuously beaten her into the ground, each blow, worse than the one before. The damage was beyond severe. She held on until he got to her, he could only recognize her by the necklace . . . the necklace, she wore. He was not able to get help back to her before she . . . she faded. She only asked for forgiveness, before passing on."

I sat for a moment. The words I wanted to say, just not right to my own ears. I could see IllEna, the tears flowing down her beautiful features as well. "How did he survive?" I finally asked, my voice shaking with unshed tears.

"No one really knows. Everyone expected him to pass, he just gave up. But no matter, he survived. We were all surprised, more than I can say. Some thought that he must have a greater destiny in store, but then he was once again ravaged when the Darkness took his family. He has never been the same since, though he is still here. Only the Creator knows what he still has yet to do, before finding his peace."

"I might be wrong, but I sense that there is more than you just told us. Why does this affect you so deeply?"

MadaREn smiled through her tears. "She was a sister to me, my twin sister. I loved her deeply."

"You were an exception." I replied under my breath, clarity dawning.

* * * * * *

The meal ended much later than normal, many conversations carrying on in merriment and laughter, no one else privy to our earlier one. As was tradition at feasts, the StorÀtellers began to unravel their tÀles, the tÀles of the previous Faery Kind that had come before and gone. Towards the end, one female came forward to tell the TÀle of the Darkeness.

Her ability to weave the tÀle was spellbinding. I noticed that most were captivated by her. Looking over to see that Caitrin was, just as much as the rest. When I looked at RandelfSon, I noticed though that he appeared agitated by the telling. Feeling pity for him, for his loss. The idea of losing his family and his soulmate was heart wrenching. As the tÀle of the StorÀteller came to a close, I listened to the Prophecy, spelled out the same as it had been in the book that Gable had read to me. Once again, my attention became caught by the odd behavior of RandelfSon. He appeared to be angry as he had listened to the end of the Prophecy. Others merely nodded a silent assent to the tÀles end, but he was furious. I could see it in his eyes, in the set of his shoulders. He got up and left the gathering, heading off into the night, alone.

*

RandelfSon saw red as the Prophecy was replayed for him by the StorÀtellers. *"Stupid faery."* He thought to himself. He shook his head, a buzzing sound ringing in the back of his mind. His thoughts started confusing him. Sometimes, he would see something one way and at other times, it would be very different. He felt crazy; he knew that he was close . . . but no . . . he was fine. It was only stress; stress was making him this way. He was just confused right now. Confusion was making him forget things . . . times . . . . places . . . . . . He grasped on tightly to his anger. He was alright. He just needed fresh air to clear his head, everything would be alright then.

*

What could of possible have set him off? I wondered. Keeping the incident to myself as we prepared to retire for the evening. His ways had not seemed to bother anyone else. *Was I making more of it than I should have?* I decided to see for myself if I could find out the answers I sought. For some reason, it seemed that there was a lot more going on, than others realized.

Elements
(23)

The days flowed effortlessly for me now, one day blending with the next. Every day came as quickly as breathing, no confusion, no more worrying, my mind, body and powers, all working together in near perfection. Several weeks passed and now, I was pushing myself to an extent I'd never imagined before. During the day, the TA Archers moved into magickal application with me. Teaching me as much of the magickal language as I could digest, in my own way, learning ways in which to incorporate information on magickal defense for myself.

My mind and thoughts, easily expanding on the new knowledge and understanding that I gained with the Right that I'd embraced. Often times, Caitrin would now join me in practice. IllEna was most often a companion in these times. We had struck up a quick friendship. This allowed the two or three of us, to spend more time together, something that at least Caitrin and I had been sorely lacking in, in the previous few months. Even with the heaviness of the load we shared, we now smiled and laughed more often. It was only yesterday that I'd put into use the theory that Caitrin had awoken in me, sought to push forward in my skills. I'd been in the field, waiting for Caitrin to arrive when . . .

. . . Sitting there waiting, realizing that I had no idea how long it would take for IllEna to find Caitrin and send her this way. We had considered a short walk beyond the walls. Deciding that with my small amount of unsupervised time, I would experiment with something that I had been wondering about. *Calling on the Elements.* Using my ability of manipulation to see what could be attained. It was nothing great at first. Realizing that I would need to put more into it. Closing my eyes, focusing on the wind as it blew around me. It wasn't strong at this point, only mild. I breathed in, and then out, imagining the wind picking up with each exhale. With each continued breathe, I increased the strength and speed. Soon, feeling the wind as it whipped around me.

With my eyes closed, the wind pick up as a tempest, the hair around my shoulders blowing wickedly and getting stronger. Opening my eyes, watching as the sky around me darkened, the clouds flowing in a swift circular pattern, their color that of slate. Pushing harder, trying to control just one small section. Pulling gently, separating the smaller section of clouds from above, pulling them down, offering more wind for their swirling action. Watching as they took their final shape upon the ground, not more than several feet high, but amazing all the same. The thrill of exhilaration moved me as it raced through my blood. *I'd done it!* In front of me was a mini-cyclone. Looking around, seeing that the rest of the environment was unaffected, the small area was totally in my control and contained. *I could do this!*

I needed to see what else could be done. Knew I could do better, so pushing my thoughts out farther, focusing on the dirt in front of me. Watching as the wind shifted and pushed at it. Straining, imagining the wind twirling, adding power and forming another small funnel. The second cyclone, no more than two feet high rose up from the earth. Concentrating harder, I pulled more air, added more wind, sending it to another location and another. Soon, four small funnels sat upon the earth, each spinning in contrast to the other at its side. Watching as the debris was gathered within them, the swirling air, brown, changing with the confetti of the debris. I smiled, putting my hand out in front of me, feeling the twist and pull of the air on my palm.

A sudden noise behind me, faltered my thoughts, and the four fell back to earth. No evidence of their power remaining, except for the swirling trail at my feet . . . and Caitrin's. Caitrin screaming in delight at the scene she had stumbled upon, IllEna staring alongside her in wonder.

* * * * * * *

In the evenings, Gable or one of his trusted Guardians would join me in the fields. Pushing me physically in ways that required me to put into use the magickal training that I was working on with the TA Archers. We were working flying maneuvers for flight and defense, my speed increasing to meet that of the faery themselves. Alongside, my skill with the blade grew. I could protect myself fluidly from attack. What I couldn't manage with the sword, the magick provided for me. My ability to adapt and learn made me an adept pupil. Now, I was beginning to even surpass my instructors.

I was better equipped to fight than many of the warriors. With this honor upon my shoulders, I knew that soon I would be receiving my sword. Sitting back, allowing my thoughts to drift. Imagining what it would be like to receive the honor. The ceremony would be for me and Caitrin, both of us ready to move on, our skill advanced to the level of Learned . . .

* * * * * * *

Not far away, RandelfSon was heading to meet Caitrin. He had done well, finding her the precious stones. She would love them; they were a rare gift, special. As he walked through the gates, he noticed Angel walking slowly from the field. He quickly shut her out of his thoughts, she was not important to him.

Caitrin would be with the horses in the barn, waiting for him as he had asked. He walked the remaining way, the building open and inviting. As he entered, he could smell the aroma of hay, sweat and dung. It was not strong, or even unpleasant. To him, it was a reminder of safety, of his days spent in elusive peace. As he looked, he could see Caitrin sitting, a couple of the new kittens adorned her lap and clothing. He smiled as he approached; she had a way with the animals.

"Caitrin, I am glad to see you here. Have you been waiting long for me?" He asked.

She laughed as one of the kittens began nipping at her fingers. "Not very long, as soon as I got here, the kittens came to play."

"I am glad that you have had a good time then. I have something special for you. Come to me now and I will show you."

She petted them a few moments more, loving the feel of the silky fur beneath her fingers. She sighed, and then rose; walking over to see what he'd brought for her. She approached, watching as he pulled his hand from behind his back and placed it in front of her at eye level. Opening his hand, she saw several circular stones, each of a different size that rested upon his palm. *"They were beautiful."* She thought as their surface changed while she gazed upon them.

"They are moonstones from the river, blessed with the powers of the Moon." For a moment, his expression changed. When he spoke to her, his voice was noticeably different. "I know that they have always been your favorite." He reached out, twisting a strand of her silken curls around his finger, before letting it go. His expression returned to normal and he continued. "What do you think? Are they not beautiful? Just like you!" He said with a smile. *How they would increase her power.* He thought to himself. *"To help her to get ready for when the time comes."*

She smiled back at him. Accepting the gift for what it was.

"You must keep them with you at all times." He said.

She shifted from one foot to the other. "When the time comes for what?" She asked.

He answered before he even realized that he had not offered his words out loud. "To end all of the trouble. To bring freedom."

* * * * * * *

I was exhausted sitting on the bench in the courtyard, my head starting to droop. Startling awake at the sound of Caitrin's approach. I'd been neglectful these past few days, only seeing her for a few stolen moments at a time, it made an immense sensation of guilt wiggle deeply in the pit of my stomach. I knew that I wasn't a bad máthair, but right now, I didn't feel like a good one either. Being so tired, all this time spent working and my daydreaming had put me at such ease that I hadn't even realized that sleep had claimed me.

Caitrin was fidgeting as she walked up, excited. "Máthair, I want to show you what RandelfSon gave me!" Pulling her hand from behind her back, she showed me several opalescence stones that glowed in the palm of her hand.

I watched as Caitrin began to move the stones with her magick, in them I could see a gentle shifting of color, reminding me of sand, shifting in a glass. *Similar to opals.* I thought.

"RandelfSon told me that these stones are very special. These are moonstones. They sit on the earth and gather the energy of the Moon, who says Its own prayer over them at night. To find them in this nearly perfect condition, is rare and that makes them more special." She said. "Just like me."

She was blushing from the words; I could see the flush to her cheeks. "It's OK to tell me Caitrin, you can tell me anything." I looked at her more closely for a moment. "Did it make you uncomfortable, what RandelfSon said?" I asked her, suspicion coloring my thoughts. I didn't want to think such a thing, but I was a máthair and it was in my nature to protect.

"No Máthair, it's not that. It's just that . . ." It seemed like she was having trouble finding the right words.

So I gave her time. Feeling my own anxiety building as the moments passed by.

"Well, he said something funny. It's not the first time that he's done it, but I cannot figure out why he does it." She replied. "He said that the stones were special like me, but it was the other thing that has me upset."

"OK, what was it?" I asked, trying to keep a straight face, trying not to get apprehensive. I felt like I was making a mountain out of a mole hill, but I could not understand why.

"After he gave them to me, he said that he remembered that they were my favorite, that they were the ones that I always looked for down at the river. But Máthair, I have never been down to the river with him, what did he mean?"

I thought about it for a moment. Then felt the cool rush of relief as it coursed through me. It was a simpler matter than I could of thought. I could not give her the specific reason for it. So I told her the simplest thing that I could think of on the spot. "RandelfSon is older Caitrin. Sometimes his memory just doesn't work for him. He is probably just confusing you with someone else from his past." For a moment, a nagging sensation reared up in my mind. I had this overwhelming feeling that I was forgetting something important. Then it was gone again, passing through my memory too quickly for me to grasp, too piece together. Shaking my head, thinking that it would come back to me if it was important.

"Was that the only thing that bothered you then?" Questioning her.

"No. There was one other thing. He said that I needed the stones for when the time came."

"The time comes for what?" I asked, confused. *What could there possibly be for Caitrin to do?*

"The time to bring us all to freedom." Caitrin said.

The shock of it hit me to the core. I could feel the punch in my gut and the blood in my veins turn to ice. *What was he talking about? Caitrin had no part to play in the coming war. Why was he worrying her when they'd all been working so hard to keep her safe and unafraid?* I felt my anger begin to burn. It boiled below the surface and replaced the ice cold. It was not right for him to have done this. I was careful speaking to Caitrin, my voice even and calm sounding, even to myself.

"Don't worry. Everything will be alright. I think that he might just need some time and rest. Why don't you give him a few days without your pestering and maybe he'll be better?" I said to her, a relaxed smile on my face. Watching as her small shoulders lifted at the request.

Caitrin smiled at me, relief flowing through her. *This was a good idea. It seemed that lately RandelfSon was doing it more and more often.* She didn't tell her máthair that, because she didn't want to get him into trouble. But this way, everything would work out alright.

"Thanks Máthair. I'm glad I told you."

Returning her smile, we held hands as we walked into the Keep together. Keeping Caitrin protected was my job as her máthair. But I could not deny that I was deeply bothered by this. The implication that Caitrin was the Chosen One was one that was now long dead and I didn't want the fear of it settling on Caitrin's young shoulders, as it had done on mine. We would make sure the clarification was made. I needed to talk to Gable as soon as possible. Get his perspective on the whole situation. I didn't want anyone scaring Caitrin with information that was not meant for her, especially with all of the things that she'd already been through.

*

I took my time searching for Gable in an inconspicuous way. I didn't want to draw Caitrin's attention to what I was doing; it would only upset her more if she knew. Disappointment set in for me, upon learning that Gable was not at the Keep. He had been called away to deal with other matters. It would be later before he was to return. So I was forced to wait to speak with him. But it would be my first priority when he did come home this night. And I was not about to waste this time that we now had. With all of the things that had been keeping me so busy lately, I'd missed out on so much with Caitrin. Well, we could fix that. And I decided right then and there, that we were going to spend the rest of the evening together. It was going to be a surprise for both of us.

Childhood
(24)

We walked together, going to the kitchen to make arrangements with the ChAEfen to have dinner sent to Caitrin's room later. Then the two of us headed off to the healing springs. *Caitrin had never been to them! I couldn't believe it!* Well, we were on our way now! This was something that we could do together. Relax, take the time and just be máthair and daughter.

The Faery had built the beautiful two room structure around the springs. In truth, the entire Keep had been built around the Old Temple and the Springs. *"With such a magnificent faerytale, I prayed that all worked out in the end, because I planned on writing the story down myself, my own contribution to the Archives of Humanity, "The Greatest TÁle Never Told."* I sighed. *If we survived.*

My thoughts actually drifted back and I could remember my history classes, about how the Vikings and Norse had harnessed the mineral springs for their daily use as mineral baths. Everywhere in the realm, I could see where humans had borrowed the knowledge of the faery. But where the faery actually lived what they believed, the humans had twisted their knowledge, using it in unhealthy ways. But, back to the Vikings, boy, my mind really was beginning to wander these days. Where the Norwegian springs could have strong odors associated with them, due to high mineral content, this spring was clean and odor free. When I had come here the first time, I'd asked MadaREn how it was possible. She had explained that its very structural concept led to its unique abilities and results.

As we walked into the antechamber, we closed the wooden door behind us, the scones on the wall jumping to life as we entered. Around us were several wooden tables with towels. The chairs were covered with thick velvet padding and decorative throws. The enormous structure was composed of two rooms, an antechamber and the main chamber. The first room provided the faery with a place to dry and rest, before and after using the springs themselves. The main chamber was magickal. The pool itself was recessed into the ground. Rings of stone encompassed the entire spring. The stone steps were two deep, the first outside of the water, the next, right below the surface, used as both stairs and a bench to rest upon while soaking. What was unusual about the chamber was the amount of moss that appeared to grow all along the back, side walls and floor of the chamber. There was no source of sunlight, as the room was entirely enclosed. Though the moss was green as usual, it emitted a soft glowing luminous light, providing the light source for the room. It was mysterious looking and quite beautiful.

"Oh Máthair, it's so . . . wonderful. How are the walls so alive?" She asked in a near whisper.

When I had come the first time, MadaREn had confirmed that the mysterious moss was the source of the waters purity. "They're AmossAa." AmossAa was a living, breathing entity that survived on the minerals. Their byproduct was free oxygen, which, when reaching the air, glowed at its release. "They live in this chamber and are provided a home in exchange for the light they provide." This was the way of the faery, all working in harmony, all together, providing life and sustenance without harm or waste.

"So the moss makes the light, Máthair?"

"Exactly!"

"I wish I had some of this in my bedroom. It would be so neat at bedtime."

I laughed at her. The thought was interesting, though I highly doubted that it would work.

"This is a very special place Caitrin. The waters here will heal our aches and pains from practicing and the water also relaxes the mind, helping us to remember what we have learned."

*

Caitrin took her time wandering around the room. I took the time to look again myself. The décor was done in a simple matter, but with taste. The enchanted theme, continued here as well. I thought it odd, how the faery continued to decorate with faery theme, while Man, in his entire search for answers into the world of technology, also fell back to a more magickal style a majority of the time, always in such a whimsical way. Though only allowing it in the mythical sense, while still pushing it away in all other areas, as much as they could. Like magick was the evil.

"Máthair, it's so pretty in here!" Caitrin said happily after a few moments. Her máthair had been so busy lately that she'd been missing her horribly. She wasn't sure why, but she knew that her máthair was upset a lot and Caitrin only wanted to comfort her as much as she wanted to be comforted herself. She understood that something had been happening here for a long time. All she knew was the stories she had heard. The bits and pieces that she had been given. The stories spoke of sadness and despair. Pain for the Faery and death. She sensed the fear within them. In her heart, she knew that RandelfSon had tried to explain some of it to her tonight, but that it had upset him. He'd been unable to finish telling her. The adults were always so sad it seemed. She missed the days of smiles. But even then, she wouldn't trade this place for anywhere else in the world.

"Are you alright Caitrin?"

Shaking her head, she smiled. "Yes. I was just thinking. So, what do we do here Máthair?" She asked.

"First, we take off our clothing and leave them in the baskets at the ends of the table. These will be taken and washed. The towels and robes on the tables are for afterward, so that we are able to return to the Keep." I said as I began removing my practice clothing. Caitrin did the same, following my lead.

"Máthair, what's that?" She asked as she pointed to the tattoo on my breast.

I startled, the tattoo had become so much a part of me, that I had forgotten that Caitrin had never seen it. "You know when people get married and they give each other a ring?" She nodded back at me. "This is what the faery do. This symbol is called a . . . a mating knot," I paused, "when the faery join together, the mates each receive a matching knot, signifying that they are together forever."

"Do I get one of those one day?"

"Oh yes. One day, very, very far in the future." I said with a laugh.

Caitrin didn't know what was so funny, but she smiled anyway.

It made me think though, would she have one, one day. I had no idea how it would work if she mated with a human or a faery. Looking at her, suddenly, I didn't want to know. *Let her be a child.* I told myself. *Right now, who cared what was later.* Smiling at her, we both wrapped up in our towels as we headed into the chamber together.

"I'm so glad that you let me come here with you."

I nodded my head. "I've missed all the time that we used to spend together. Here, in this place, there is so much that goes on, that we've not been able to keep each other company." *Like we used too.* Thinking sadly to myself.

"At least we are together now." Caitrin said, sounding more like an adult than a child. Walking over and picking her up, she put her small arms around me as I hugged her with a fierceness, from my very soul. The need was so strong that it scared me. But once Caitrin was in my arms, everything felt right again.

"We're always going to stay right here, right Máthair? This is our home now." She asked.

I could see the sudden fear return in her features. God, how I hated to see it like that. "Absolutely!" I agreed. It blew me away at that moment, how adult like she could be, and in the blink of an eye, childlike again. Caitrin was so like I had been in my earlier youth, full of life and laughter. *I'd forgotten that.* It made me feel so much closer to her at this moment. I didn't want to step away from it, didn't want to lose those feelings.

*

We spent the time together; soaking, splashing and laughing at each other. For nearly an hour, the outside world didn't exist. There was only the two of us, máthair and daughter. We stood up, the water washing down us in rivulets, our wings were a shining web of beauty. After we finished, we used the plush towels. Caitrin watched me as I pulled my hair up and decided that she wanted to do the same. Watching as she struggled, she was not able to accomplish her goal. I took mercy on her, and together we pulled her hair up, helping her to look more like the big girl she wanted to be. We put the robes on and headed back to the Keep. The sky was starting to darken as night fell upon us.

"Máthair, I had so much fun today. I've really missed you." Caitrin took my hand as we walked together. The night air was starting to cool as winter prepared its approach, both of us shivering into our robes.

"I know. Soon this will be over. Things will get better around here and hopefully you will get to make more friends that are your own age."

"It was so cool, getting to meet ROhAne. I like not being the only little one around here anymore."

I laughed. "So, that was his name. Gable had not mentioned it to me. Well, there's only more of that to look forward too. Remember, it is not so unusual for the faery. They don't have children as often as we're used to seeing back home. There won't be large numbers, but there will be more. Soon, IllEna will have a young one of her own."

"Do you think that I could invite ROhAne to come and play again? I know that we've been really busy. But it was so much fun. He is so unusual, special. " I saw the pleading in her eyes, the pout to her lips.

I caught the oddness in her speech, in the way she spoke of him. *He was similar to her.* I thought. I really looked at her, looked at the child who was simply asking to be a child. "There's always time for fun, especially when you're young. You can definitely have the time to play. I think that is something that you need to do a lot more of from now on. Play to your heart's content."

"Really! Thanks Máthair." She ran up, throwing her arms around me in a gigantic hug.

"I would do just about anything to make you smile." I said with a smile of my own. We hurried up our pace as we entered the lower portion of the castle. Following the path, we took the side entrance, following a pathway that led to the winding staircase and the passages above. We headed to Caitrin's room. Soon the food would arrive.

"I'm starving!" Caitrin said.

"Me too! Let's get dressed and we can sit by the fire to wait."

I took off quickly to my own room, returning in a long, cream colored linen gown. The robe belted at my waist was soft velveteen in midnight blue. Silver stars twinkled in the depths of the cloth. Caitrin's gown was similar, though in a shade of lavender, her robe a darker shade of primrose velveteen. We took hands as we walked over to the fire for more warmth, MadaREn arrived shortly after.

"Tonight was the ChAEfen's special. He prepared a breaded fish with herbs, and a potato side with greens. For dessert," she said with a twinkle in her eyes, "he has prepared blueberry tarts, especially for you Caitrin."

Caitrin screamed in delight. Blueberry was her absolute favorite, even before chocolate and ChAEfen knew. She jumped up and hugged MadaREn and then me. She was so happy that it was bursting forth from within her; a cascade of leight escaping her form. Both of us were shocked at the sudden display, but we quickly joined in and laughed with her in her joy.

MadaREn left soon after, as she said, "allowing us "girls" to our merrymaking. It was good to see such happiness in times like these." She finished, as the door closed behind her.

We bowed our heads in prayer, thankful for all we'd been given. Then we dug in, talking of many things. After filling ourselves, Caitrin settled down in my lap. Well-fed and ready to sleep, though fight it she did. I knew that she didn't want the evening to end, because neither did I.

"Tell me a story Máthair. I miss them so very much." She snuggled deeper into my arms, her head resting on my chest.

Smiling, I began:

"Once upon a time . . . there was a great Healer who walked the land. The quest set before him was noble and true. But though that was so, it was not easy for him. He had been sent to us to deliver a message. His message terrified the people of the times."

"What was his message Máthair, why did people fear him?"

I looked down at my daughter and a smile graced my lips. "Love." I said. "Because he taught us that love is what life is really about. And that real love is about sacrifice." I turned back to the fire and began. "And this Healers name was Jesus . . ."

* * * * * * *

That was how he found them, as Gable returned that night. They both lay asleep on the rug, snuggled deeply within a thick blanket, the fire having burned down to embers. They were oblivious to the world around them. He smiled, within his chest, the love for his family overflowed. It consumed every aspect of his being. He had not imagined that this depth of love was possible; it went far beyond anything that he could have put words too. But he embraced it, heart and soul. Smiling again, he raised his head in gratitude to the Creator. "Thank you." He said out loud. To himself, he added. *"For all that you have given me."*

He lifted Caitrin gently, settling her into her own bed. He pulled the covers up to her chin, keeping the chill at bay. Leaning down, kissing her forehead, a tingle left him as his love crossed over to her. She slept on; apparently her evening had left her exhausted. He straightened back up and headed over to Angel. Her sleep as well, appeared peaceful. Before moving her, he looked into the dying embers. *"Fire érA."* He whispered the words, awaking the sleeping hearth.

He picked Angel up with ease, not wanting to awaken her. Though she was thicker, he loved her body. She still weighed no more than a feather to him. He nearly laughed out loud at the way she would respond to that remark. Though so much of her was faery now, her basic self was still human, and it only made him love her more. He reached their chamber quickly; as he placed her on the bed he noticed that she watched him closely.

"How did things go? You were out so much later than you'd anticipated."

"Actually, we were fortunate. Not all of the damage to the storage sheds that we found was permanent. We were lucky this time. The problems that developed were able to be managed, and it will prevent any other foreseeable issues in the future. Our food stores will be safe through the winter."

I nodded to him. He left my side of the bed to reach his own. There he undressed. His beautiful body put into light and shadow as the flames from the fire cast upon him. "I've been blessed with all that I've been given." A smile upon my lips. "Let me show you how much I love who you are." I needed say no more.

He actually growled as he leap onto the bed with me. My gown quickly discarded upon the floor. "You tempt me as none ever has. Did you know that? The very sight of you heats my blood and makes me forget anything else. You are a temptress, a sorceress." He said through clenched teeth. Already, his body was pushing at mine, seeking out that which only I could offer him.

I threw back my head as passion gained control of me. "No Gable, I'm your Chosen." I said. Fire raging in my eyes as he claimed me. Each of us, showing the other, where we belonged.

Destiny
(25)

"Good Morrow, Caitrin. It is time for you to get up. We need to leave." RandelfSon said. He looked down at her sleepy features, his heart stuttering in his chest at her beautiful innocence.

"Are you sure? It's yet dark in the Keep." She asked sleepily.

"The time has come to end this pestilence. I have seen the Prophecy. I know what the others do not. You and I, we will end this today. You are the One."

Caitrin stared at him. She could see the wariness and the haggard expression that he wore. RandelfSon, he had made her feel like she belonged here far faster than anyone else, even her fáthair. She wasn't sure how, but she could see the battle that he was fighting within himself. She knew that he was damaged, that he was no longer right. But it was also at times that she could see the little boy, the innocence in him. When he told her the stories and snuck her treats, the boy would return and the two of them would spend hours together in exploration. This was the secret, the one that no one knew, the one that she had not shared with the others. But she also knew that she loved him and that he would never hurt her. In her heart, in her soul, she knew that she had to go with him. His life depended upon her now. She had to go with him; it was her destiny, the way it was supposed to be. "I'll be ready in a minute RandelfSon. I just need to change into something warmer." She jumped down from the bed, going to her belongings in her chest of drawers.

"Good. We will leave as soon as you are ready." Turning away from her, he gave her privacy. He reached down, placing a note upon Caitrin's pillow. Soon, MadaREn would come and soon, it would be over.

Darke Ones
(26)

We flew with all haste, knowing that we were flying into the Darkness and not away from it. Passing into the shimmer was like passing through falling water, though you didn't get wet. As we moved, the Realm of Man moved around us. I watched the world as we passed them by. *Now I understood what Gable had said, about them being able to watch humans over the years.* The view was distorted slightly and we were able to pass through solid objects, but it was easy to see and watch events occurring. I was distracted for a moment, but quickly came back to the time at hand. A shiver of fear raced through me. Ice racing through my veins as the terror of not knowing pushed at my mind. RandelfSon had taken *my* Caitrin into the heart of the creeping Darke. Even now, he was racing ahead of us to reach his goal before we could stop him. Not even an hour had passed since Gable had awoken me with the news.

In the night, RandelfSon had taken Caitrin. He'd left a note, the crazed ramblings of a deluded mind . . . *"I go to end this evil now. Caitrin is the Way; she is the Heart of the Chosen, her sacrifice."*

Once again, the fear rippled through me, making my heart race and my blood run cold. It was true, Caitrin was my everything, but she would not become a sacrifice. This would not be the answer to solve this war. These words, these thoughts, were just the ramblings of an unstable old faery.

"Words cannot live up to the horror that I feel right now Angel. I never imagined that RandelfSon was so far gone." Opening our bond, I felt the sorrow and fear that flowed inside of me from him. *"He must have been infected, there is no other explanation. But I do not understand how it is possible. How could he have been infected all of this time and not bear any symptoms of the disease. It just does not make any sense!"* Gable said, the anger making his thoughts vibrate.

Though he appeared calm to the others, I was fully aware of the turbulence running through him. He had thought that Caitrin had been helping RandelfSon, maybe even helping him find his place amongst the faery again. Instead, he had been plotting to hurt her, to use her as a weapon.

Gable's thoughts rippled through our minds. *He had let this vile and evil creature near his daughter, and now her blood could he on his hands because of it.*

"Gable, this was something that none of us suspected. We just need to get to Saery's Tower, how much longer until we reach it?" I kept my thoughts from him. The suspicions that had clouded my judgments recently. He did not need to feel them right now.

"It is still further to the south, then on to the west. We pass through the shimmer of the outer wall and travel within it until we reach the outer wall of Saery's Tower. We will travel for another couple of hours."

"How many faery live within its walls Gable? How many lives is the Darkeness going to consume if we do not get there in time?"

"The tower is only basically manned. Most of the inhabitants have moved into the larger Strongholds. Only four warriors are there at present."

I closed my eyes, imagining random faces and bodies. Looking back at him, "We need to get there quickly! That is still not good enough. "

I reached out; throwing everything I had into my search for her. Having no real idea of what I was doing, only that I could not bear the thought of not making it in time. Everything I was, was wrapped up in my family. *Having to survive without her? If anything happened to her, it was not something that I could contemplate. My existence would be dust and I would not survive.* I knew this. Closing my eyes and praying. Erasing all thoughts from myself, focusing on the back of my closed eyelids, seeking her out.

It started as a sparkle, a small glimmer of leight in the surrounding darkness. I could see the pulse, the emitting glow of a golden form. The innocence, the beauty of one so pure as it raced across space and time, pass all the taint of humanity and the shimmer. It was Caitrin, her essence. It responded to my search, a silent beacon of reality, of life amidst all of the fear and unknowing. I pulled it close to my heart and I opened my eyes.

"She is still alive and we will make it. " My thoughts returned to him.

We flew the rest of the way in silence, the other warriors following in our pursuit. Getting there was the only option.

* * * * * * *

We left the shimmer, its bubble-like quality falling behind us as we stepped onto the earth and dirt again. This part of the Faery Realm was definitely smaller than Ainys'Dai. One could actually see from shimmer to shimmer. "What's the purpose of such a small stretch of land?" I asked. It seemed pretty insignificant when compared to the size of Ainys'Dai.

"It serves as a basic pass through for larger Strongholds, as well as a place to rest and seek shelter. Only a handful of families came from here." Gable said.

But as we stepped out of the dense foliage, I was shocked by the world I'd stepped into. We studied the area around us. We'd come out near a full stand of trees, the area heavily wooden and enclosed. A rough and tumbled landscape with a tree line ending abruptly at rock and coarse dirt. Forty feet out, the tower itself looked to have been forged from the rocky face of the cliff. The intermittent crystal clusters the only break in stone. The tower was smooth, wrapping back in on its self to create a wall of protection before another towering rock face and tree topped canopy rose further to the north of it with a small mountain of sorts rising up.

I visually followed the trail of rock along the back side; the cliff recessed more, here was more ground. The cliffs small trail, nearly to edge, wrapping back in on its self, following the natural curve of the mountainous area and leading to a large boulder outcropping. Huge chunks of the upper cliff, giving way to rest in a type of graveyard of rock and dust. There were dozens of boulders. Taller than myself, taller than faery. Haphazardous as it wove a maze of passageways between them. A labyrinth before the cascading fall of the drop. What went beyond it, I could not be sure from my vantage point.

As we watched, no one good or evil appeared visible, so we moved forward slowly and prepared to advance on the tower. Though not huge, the tower was impressive. It stood several stories high. Its only openings were the gateway and windows, floor by floor to provide light into its interior. Built solidly of stone and reinforced with magick. There was the fluid inner wall to provide resistance to invaders. As long as help was on the way, it would offer enough resistance to keep the evil out, or at bay. *Unless,* I thought, *someone was letting it in the front door.* I looked down, the glint from the sunlight, coming off of my borrowed sword. This was new, this feel of steel instead of wood. But it would not deter me.

As we approached, we noticed that the gated entranceway was wide open, the solid wooden door appearing to have no damage to its integrity. This didn't bode well and we all placed our drawn swords in battle ready position. Gable remarked, as we entered, that the sky to the south was beginning to tinge with darke. The evil had not yet arrived, but soon the Darkeness would be upon us. It made us move faster. But not before rounding the edge of stone. Before the sight of the mountainous drop, the precipice caught my view. *It was desperation.* A desperate landscape, but breathtaking in its dramatic beauty. Deep below a valley opened wide, the rich green of the trees and the blue of water, hidden before, met head on by the rough outcropping and stony deposits of the cliff face directly below. Fertile, fresh. You could see all the way out, all the way to the shimmers edge. From there I could see out past the shimmer, Man's Realm. What I saw was . . . what I saw was destitute and barren. Wasteland. The desert. It was like the richness of this side, died at the border. Died at the World of Man.

I shook away the despair as we entered the tomb. We found what we'd feared. Two faery lay prone on the ground, their backs to our group. *Useless death and cold . . .*

But we were much surprised however, when we realized that both were still alive. Their breathing ragged, though their hearts still beat strong. Both were swathed in magick, blows evident to the backs of their heads. Their hands tied behind their backs. Turning, TazaRine and another Guardian secured the door, while reinforcing the spell of protection on it. The two fallen warriors were roused and offered aide, two more taking their place to stand guard, should the dark*e* fa*e*ry get through the wall and continue their attack on the tower. Gable and I led the way, as we climbed the ancient spiral staircase higher.

At each floor, we stopped to check. Most of the rooms had been neglected for a while, the others were the ones that the resident warriors were using. We came into contact with no other fa*e*ry. Making it to the top floor, the door to enter outward onto the guard walk above was in view. The door was pushed closed, though not secure and lying at its base was like before, the remaining two warriors. I noticed for the first time, that one of them was female. Both were unconscious, but alright. We left someone to awaken them and carefully entered through the open guard walk door.

Gable pulled the door back slowly. It moved fluidly, no sound escaping as it came to rest against the wall. Climbing, we could make out RandelfSon, pointing to the sky in the south. He was showing something to Caitrin that we were unable to see from our vantage point. Slowly we crept out, trying to get as close as possible before we attempted to get his attention. I held my breath, knowing that the faintest sound could give us away. We were so close, when he spoke.

"I know that you are there." He turned around to face us, surprisingly there was a look of utter serenity on his face.

"What is the meaning of this RandelfSon? What have you done?" Gable demanded. His sword was drawn in front of him, hanging in the air to place home the deadly threat for what it was.

As we watched, Caitrin came to the forefront, situating herself directly in front of him, her hands clasped in his much larger ones. RandelfSon began again. "I knew that you would come. But this had to be done. None of you understand what I do. Do you not see, you have all been wrong, wrong this whole time! It is through Caitrin that all of this will end. It is her blood that will end this war. Her sacrifice that will make the Dark*e*ness go away!"

"You are wrong RandelfSon. It is Angel that is the Chosen One; it is through her magick and power that this evil will be purged from our lands."

"I do not wish to hurt anyone. But the time to end this is now. No more should be lost to this encroaching Dark*e*. We are falling, soon there will be none of us left, our world, obliterated, and why, because of the horrific humans. I am not wrong. I have seen the truth; I have seen it as it was written thousands of years ago. The Old Temple speaks the words as the Creator intended them. There the words have not been washed and used. Caitrin will end this war. It is her destiny. You could not stop it even if you wanted too. You see," he said as he spun his arm out to the south, "it is too late, the dark*e* ones have arrived."

Sure enough, they came. It appeared as if a hundred strong, dark*e* faery flew upon the wind toward us, their dark*e* and cold countenances not more than seventy-five feet outside the tower walls. Even as they came, the world around them seemed to wash out at their very presence, grey bleeding into the surrounding areas. None of the descriptions I'd received had really prepared me for the sight of them, *vampires*. That was the only comparison that my mind could pull forth for me. Vampires with wings, their flesh was. . . I was sure they'd feel cold to the touch. All had hair of black, growing long and wild.

They were bound in black leather. Their bodies covered from neck to wrist, to I assumed ankle, with black boots that came to knee height. The skin that was visible, pale. Carrying weapons of various type and design. Though dark*e* and menacing, you could still pick out some semblance of individuality from them. They were not drones, at least not in that sense. They were just soulless, without l*e*ight. And as I watched, I could see the coldness of their blackened eyes, all the brilliance of life seemingly removed, seeing something that I had not expected. In my own mind I'd thought of them as zombies, soulless creatures, doing the bidding of their master, instead I saw cold calculation. They were very much in control of themselves; only they were influenced by the Dark*e* now. There was no L*e*ight left in them to rein in the evil. They were frenzied in their bloodlust. Twisted smiles that were crazed and maniacal. They were by far, worse than even I'd been able to imagine. This was real, what we were really going up against. The dark*e* ones flew quickly, with their swords held high, ready for attack. Their blackened, shriveled wings a mockery to the faery they'd once been.

"You are too late!" RandelfSon shouted to our group. Lifting Caitrin high with a speed unexpected of him, he screamed outward. "Come to me now Dark*e*ness, I have what you seek. Here I have the Heart of the Chosen One." And up he flew on his way to meet the evil face to face.

Quickly the scene shifted as Gable and I took off after Caitrin, our fear giving our wings more speed. The Guardians right behind us, we burst into the air in a flourish of gossamer and silver. I could feel the power of the wind as it gave me strength to fly faster. Chaos broke free as we shot forward towards them. The battle ensuing as Gable surged forward to save our daughter from the hounds of hell. His attack was swift. Instead of going for RandelfSon, he went for the dark*e* faery that RandelfSon was handing her off too. Gable knew that I could deal with RandelfSon. His men and he were now outnumbered three to one; it was his job to protect his family from them, his whole family.

Crossing the boundary of the inner wall, we left its protective magick behind. I heard the resounding, thunderous crash of sword on sword as I reached RandelfSon. The grating sound, was one I would never forget.

RandelfSon appeared momentarily dazed as the events were shifted from what he had expected. He recovered directly though, rethinking his strategy. He took off in flight with Caitrin, as Gable attacked and Caitrin was released by the dark*e* one. His hold broken for a moment.

*

RandelfSon fought to keep Caitrin with him. She was the key; he would keep her close until he was able to pass her off to one of the Dark*e*. *He had too; she was the only thing that would end this for all.*

*

I watched as RandelfSon raced ahead of me. His wings a blur, Caitrin grasped tightly within his arms. He was heading west, across the open field, the only thing visible ahead was the large rocky outcropping. As I drew nearer, I could better see the large groups of humongous boulders that had once been part of the cliff itself. They were clustered together, the spaces between them narrow enough to allow only minimal movement. *I could reach him quickly.* I realized as I pulled from within myself. Reaching from within my core, gathering strength and power. I shot forward swiftly, the world around me becoming the blur.

Shattering
(27)

Within moments, I was upon RandelfSon as we landed on the gigantic boulders. "Hand her over RandelfSon. It's over. Let me save her and let me save you."

"You do not understand! This is the only way to save us all!" He screamed. I stepped forward, trying to set aside my fear, my sword arm out as I prepared to do battle if necessary. Nothing was going to get through me and I would get through whatever was required to finish this.

"Máthair stop! You must stop, you can't hurt RandelfSon!" Caitrin suddenly shouted, jumping forward and placing herself in front of him.

"Caitrin, he is trying to hurt you. He's not right. He's crazy." I screamed out, more afraid now as she placed herself directly in the line of danger.

"I know Máthair. But this is not the RandelfSon that I know, this one is." Turning slowly, she took RandelfSon's hand in her own, placing it upon her heart. Caitrin looked into his eyes and said. "It is time. Come back to me ElfSon. You must come back. You will not hurt me, for I love you and I know that you love me. It is our time now." Tears slid down her cheeks as she used her magick to command her words into his heart. *"Freedoma Á thee."* She reached through the damaged portion of his brain, to break the bindings that were in place, to free his true self.

*

I felt it, the change. How it radiated from him. Then I watched in wonder as he changed before my very eyes. It was a complete physical change, it was dramatic in its scope. His youth had returned to him, his features once again a vibrant, adult faery. The real change however, came from his soul. From the depths of the faery, came the faeryling, the young innocence of faeryhood. He looked around, trying to figure out what was happening and where he was. It seemed as if he was awaking from a dream.

"I knew that you were still in there ElfSon. I knew that you would come back to me. There was no way that you could hurt me." Caitrin said as she grabbed hold of him in a hug.

He returned her hug, the expression on his face one of wonder and amazement. "I would never hurt you Moonbeam! I love you!" He said. He looked at me then, his eyes and mind clear for the first time in over a thousand years.

He shifted. "I recognized her at once. But I still did not understand that we were being given a second chance. It was impossible, never heard of before. But I would recognize her anywhere. She was mine and I was hers. When I lost her the first time, I was literally split in two. Then, when the Darkness invaded . . . it was not more than a moment, only one moment of wanting her, and I let it in. It swarmed through me, but it was not her. There was still no her, and I fought it."

I felt him cringe, understanding on some level, his pain.

He continued. "It was already too late though; it was able to taint a part of me. I was trapped, but I was able to keep it from completely taking over. I fought it like nothing before. It was like there were multiple sides to me when she arrived, there was the innocent and the evil. One wanted to use her as a weapon, twisting the darke back in on its self at any cost. The other sought to protect her, to love her, for she was the other half of my soul." He shook his head. "I could not let my true self show. A mere lapse in my struggle, for even a moment, and the darke would take complete reign. As it was, the darke came through at times, before I could reign it back in. It was getting stronger all the time."

*

I could barely comprehend what I had seen, little less, what I was hearing and yet it was there, the signs. The proof that they were meant to be. Reviewing them through my mind in memories of the past few weeks. The proof had been there all along, but I had been blind, or unprepared for this part of Faery life. Either way, I was only wrapping my mind around it when Caitrins scream pierced me through. Swinging around in time to meet swords with the first of three darke faery that attacked, the ringing of sword on sword shattering the quiet. Quickly, yelling over my shoulder. "ElfSon, get her to safety. Hide amongst the boulders." And I faced off with the darke, knowing that I had to keep the two of them alive. Gable and his warriors were fully entrenched in their own battle above the tower. No help was on the way.

The three of them circled me, preferably not wanting to go after the two in the boulders, yet. I cleared my mind; I would need calm and concentration to get through this.

"You should surrender now. Your chances are nothing." The one in front of me hissed, his voice rasping and strained. Finally, seeing them up close like this, sent prickles of fear along my flesh. Gable had not exaggerated about their appearance. Indeed, they were the living dead, an evil taint on the existence of life. They seemed consumed by a burning hunger, one that wanted my blood, my soul.

"You don't want to do this. We have so much to offer you, to give." It was hypnotic, the rasp of its voice, agonizing, the flames licking away at my resistance, coiling through my senses and flesh. *A caress . . .*

. . . Then it was even more, the sway, the dizzying effect. I could feel it pulling at me like a velvet caress. Calling to me, seductive, calling me in. It could give me so much. Darke desires, darke pleasures. The ribbons of pleasure rippled through me. A sirens call. The desire flared as the seduction pulled me down. Touching me, stroking, bringing me pleasure, with the pain . .
.

I flinched as if slapped in the face. I felt unclean. Felt the silent rape for what it had been, an invasion of my soul. The tears flooded me, but only a bare blur before using all of my resistance to shut them in, to shut the Darke out. Shutters of withdrawal cursing through my veins, a junkie coming down from a high, that was how potent the Darke was. I understood, I now understood what everyone faced and fell into, the icy shock of my resistance striking me so suddenly, my soul screaming a denial at the evil. Washing away the stain of filth, I shook my head . . .

"You have no hold here." I said firmly.

He struck quickly, swinging his sword high, attempting to get me to back up, to succeed while I was distracted. *But I was not distracted. I was furious! Dangerous! Far more than they knew.* His swing should have caused me to arc into the sword coming at me from behind. I saw the look of surprise on his face. They had not realized that I was Learned. Quickly, I shifted to the right and then rolled further away. This allowed me to miss both swords, but also allowed the third to make his move. From here, cat and mouse developed, each one stalking me, hacking away at my defenses and strength, seeking a weakness that the others could exploit. I met each swing as they reigned down upon me. They rotated from ground to flight and back again, each advancing with their own variation. I figured out pretty fast that their strategy was to try to wear me down quickly, once they'd discovered that I was an equal advantage to them.

"Gable," I thought within my mind, *"I need you."* I sent the message straight, using our bond.

*

In the distance, he looked up quickly, finding the source of her distress. They had boxed him in, keeping his back to her and obstructing his view of the west. He had not realized the extent of her danger and fury filled him. Quickly, his arm shot out with his sword, the head of the darke faery in front of him severed from its shoulders, the body falling to the earth after it. "Guardians quickly," he yelled, "our Chosen One is in danger!" His scream was full of rage. The ferocity of it, knocking some of the darke faery back in their stances. It gave him the opportunity he needed for advancement. Swiftly, he was advancing on his way to Angel's side, the darke in tow. Knowing that he still had a heavy group of fighters to get through in order to make it to them.

*

I used my powers, pushing at the minds of the evil, causing them momentary confusion. It gave me the advantage of staying ahead of them, though not by much. Sword raised high, I shot quickly over the head of my opponent, doing a somersault in midair. Bringing my sword across in a clean arc, slicing through the skin and muscle of the neck of the darke one. It was like butter, no resistance was offered my sword. The head slicing off cleanly, falling below. It brought my opponents down to two.

Seeing their advantage disappearing, one of the remaining dark*e* faery took off after Caitrin and ElfSon, while the last one engaged me in battle.

"ElfSon, if you can hear me, protect her! They're coming!" I screamed as I faced my remaining opponent. I could see Gable getting closer, though he still battled dark*e* ones as well. I prayed to the Creator. "Dear God, please let him get to us in time." As I turned back to the battle at hand. *I'd never expected, for the first time, to face them alone.* The thought flowing through me...

*

ElfSon looked at Caitrin as they hid amongst the boulders. They had traveled deeply into the pile of rocks. Now, they hid among the cropping, praying that no one would find them. They had no weapons, but ElfSon knew that he would protect her to the very end, even if he only had his hands to do so.

"I am so sorry for this Moonbeam. I tried so hard to get free, to stop this. I was just not strong enough. I would never have done this to you." ElfSon said, tears streaming down his face.

"It wasn't you. It was the dark*e*, hiding in the broken part of you. You were strong, or it would have taken you a long time ago."

"But I put you in danger! I will not let anything happen to you Moonbeam, I promise. They will have to get through me first."

Both of them looked up, as they heard the scream from Angel in the distance. Blood running cold as their fears raced down upon them.

*

I increased my power. Watching as the other dark*e* faery disappeared over the top of the boulders, knowing that I didn't have much time left. Increasing my swing, bringing my target closer and closer to the mark. I dodged swiftly, swinging and swiveling, using my momentum to strike out at my opponent. Within moments, I had him on the defensive. Soon, my opening appeared. He got sloppy.

He swung wide from the right; rolling on my feet at the same time, dodging, while bringing my sword upward in an arc. I made contact with Its throat, the same as the other one. As my arm went down, his own sword sliced a gap in my upper shoulder. My skin provided me with protection, but not completely. I saw the flash of crimson seep through, only registering the pain for a moment before I was off after my daughter. Gable was almost here, but one opponent still stood in his way. I could not wait.

Moving quickly, looking behind one boulder to the next. The outcropping was continuous, with no end. *It must circle back.* I thought. They were excellent places to hide. But it was also too many while searching. Looking for several minutes more, keeping my thoughts tuned in for the approach of the last dark*e* faery . . . or Gable. Finally, rounding a boulder that was abnormally larger than the others around it, I walked into a nightmare . . .

. . . Caitrin lay at the feet of the dark*e* faery, blood spread out across her forehead and temple, her eyes closed and unmoving. The dark*e* one had the battered and bruised ElfSon in one hand, a sword pressed to his throat with the other.

"You have betrayed us. You promised us the child and then you think you can keep her, go back on your word? The Great One will not be pleased by your duplicity. He already prepares to march this way. Your time has come to an end."

"You will not have her. She is not yours to take." RandelfSon turned his attention to me. Looking deep into my eyes, he said the words that he knew would free us all. "You must go back to the Old Temple. The answers are there. Go back!" Then he pushed at the dark*e* faery, giving me the opportunity I needed to get Caitrin away.

As I raced forward, Caitrin was in my hands in a mere second, moving back, my mind racing at what to do next. Lifting us up, my wings singing as I prepared to get us both away. Looking back, I watched as ElfSon and the dark*e* one struggled. Looking into ElfSon's eyes, watching as the blade of the dark*e* one pierced his heart. Caitrin jerked in my arms, as we both felt his pain. The blade pulled free and RandelfSon slid to the ground, his eyes revealing his terror.

*

The dark*e* one turned his attention back onto me, a feral smile across his lips as he moved forward. He only got two feet, when Gable somersaulted over the top of the adjacent boulder. As he reached even with the dark*e* one, his blade cleanly sliced Its head from Its shoulders, the look of surprise on Its face, the last thing that I saw.

Moving fluidly, Gable knelt down over the fallen RandelfSon. Shock registered on his face as he observed the young faery, instead of the old. He pulled RandelfSon up slowly, blood flowing in rivers down the front of his shirt.

"I loved her." RandelfSon said. "I would never have let them have her." He closed his eyes, the last of his life flowing to the earth below. His soul set free.

Tears filled my eyes as I looked down at RandelfSon and back to Caitrin. My daughter still breathed, so there was still hope. "We need to get to the Atrium Gable, quickly!" Gable took Caitrin from my arms.

"I do not understand?" The confusion was evident on his face.

Shaking my head, we flew to join the Guardians at the tower. Two of his warriors, those that had been stationed at the tower, had received mortal wounds, death quickly taking them. "Bring their bodies back and I want the tower abandoned. We need all of the warriors we have at Ainys'Dai. Now!" His last was a ferocious snarl.

"I want RandelfSon's body brought back as well." I said. Gable turned to stare at me in disbelief, but I shook my head. "It's important Gable, that's all I can say right now."

Quickly, orders were followed and we headed back, racing against time. *I could feel my world shatter, no, it was more than that, so much more than that. It was my heart and soul shattering. I could feel the slivers ripping my heart apart from the force of my sorrow.*

* * * * * * *

Our arrival was marked with sadness, as Caitrin had yet to awaken. She was taken to the Atrium immediately, CalOwAy and the other ArtimA quickly going to work on her various injuries. RandelfSon was laid out in the Temple, alongside the bodies of the other two, fallen warriors.

Gable turned to look at the broken faces of his Kind. "We prepare for battle. I want all of what is left of our Strongholds and Outposts to abandon and come to Ainys'Dai. The Evil One comes and we must be ready." His words were heard throughout the walls and soon, throughout the Realm, as all prepared for what was to come.

* * * * * * *

The next several days were an influx of activity. Faery from all over the realm arrived at the Keep. Soon, other magickal creatures arrived, the Elves, the Sprites, WÁ Táren's, several Unicorns and even an entire herd of small Merryflyers. Some arrived in which I had no idea of what their classifications were. But all were brought within the walls. The walls of the Keep came close to overflowing, but magick had its advantages, as it was used to expand and multiply, allowing room for all. A rolled parchment, in the hands of a single Centaur, saying they would arrive when the time came. The only ones to not arrive were the Dwarfs and Dragons.

"If this is to be our last stand . . . than we will hold out in our mountains." The Dwarves stated. While no reply arrived from the Dragons at all. Gable took it all in stride, while I spent all of my time in the Atrium.

The ArtimA brought only grim news. They were unable to say if Caitrin would awaken or not. The damage was severe on its own, a fractured skull, two ruptured arteries and swelling of the brain. Caitrin the entire time, remained unconscious and unaware. They were able to heal her. The only remaining evidence, the superficial bleeding that was the dark bruises across her temple and cheek; however, there appeared to be more to it than that. They could not wake her up. It was like she was giving up, but it made no sense. She was so young, the brilliance of youth alone should have kept her fighting. But it was not so.

All I could do was weep. I knew why Caitrin was, as she was. I also knew what the chances were that she would awaken. *And I could feel my sorrow bleeding.*

* * * * * * *

Gable watched and her tears tore through him, freeing those that were within himself. He gave Angel what she needed and he allowed her her pain. It was cleansing in itself and he would wait for her. He prepared, soon the evil would arrive and she would have to be ready then for all of them.

*

I sat by Caitrin's side, her small hand tucked safely within my own. So much had happened and though I'd known that war was going to be the eventual outcome, I'd never imagined that I would find such joy and pleasure along the way. My world had changed; reality had been spun upon its head. But looking at my daughter, so still and pale, the huge bruise across her temple, brought the tears. *Had it been worth it? Was this the price of my happiness?*

I sat there and cried. I cried for the pain and the loss, and I cried for the Earth. So much destruction and loss and now, it was possible that my daughter would be among the casualties. I wept as my heart broke and I struggled to put the pieces back together to make it stronger.

*

Gable came to me that evening. I had pulled a chair up next the window, watching the sun set to the west. My expression vacant, but our bond gave me away. He could feel the swirl of emotions within my mind. As he approached, I turned my head to face him.

"I wasn't able to face three of them, three! How could I be expected to face thousands? Don't you understand? I wasn't strong enough. I let them do this to her!" My thoughts screaming out to him, my agony a solid wall of vicious pain.

He braced himself, the power of her, near to driving him to his knees. "You are not fair enough to yourself. It was your first time, in battle and in seeing them, that matters." He said out loud.

"Nothing matters if I cannot protect the ones I love." I thought.

"You can and you will. You need time. Look inside yourself for what you seek."

I turned away from him, effectively closing the bond we shared. I heard him start to leave, the door opening for him. Maybe I did need to look within myself, but I wasn't sure if I was going to like what I saw.

"You never know until you try." Oh shut up, I screamed within my mind, pushing away at the voice, at the words.

"How can this be Hís plan, Gable? Have you seen what I've done? I took those lives. How can I be any better, if I'm the one to extinguish the life from them?" I asked out loud, my pain radiating from within me.

He turned back around to face me. There was anger with his sorrow. "Angel, they were not alive. There was none of the beauty of the Creator. They are a walking shell. They are the left over, the undead. All that remains until the evil shrivels them to dust."

I lifted my head, raising my eyes higher. "Ashes to ashes, and dust to dust." I said, as tears slipped down my cheek.

*

He left her then. His own soul feeling like it was shredding before him. They both needed time, she more so than him.

*

. . . Innocence sees so many things, it see's life the way it really is, as it should be. I thought to myself.

Sitting back, closing my eyes and my ears. Allowing myself to drift inward, not sleeping, only focusing. *I would not lose any of the time I had left with my daughter.* I thought back to earlier, to the battle . . . replaying it again in my mind and watching. I saw . . . my fears, worries . . . my uncertainties; it was a condition of my own thoughts . . . my own unprepared mind. There was more to me than that. *All those limits of a human body no longer applied, I was more than human, more than faery. I had placed those limitations on myself and now . . . now I was removing them. I was invincible and I would prove it. Fear no longer guided me.*

"God did." *Finally . . .* the words whispered.

Late December 2012
Finding Courage
(28)

Five days passed as the Keep came to an uneasy rest and the preparations were finalized. All of the remaining inhabitants of the Magickal Realm were now encased within the Keeps magickally enlarged walls. Guardians were posted every four feet around the inner city wall, while several sentinels had been posted on the far outskirts of the Strongholds defenses, close to the shimmer. Each located at the four corners. It was their job to report when the evil arrived and how it was enforced.

It was as the Guardians were changing post on the sixth day, that the sentinels began arriving back from all four directions. They were coming. Dark*e* faery were arriving, entering the realm from every direction. Even as they spoke, a steady glow began from the crystal clusters, a strong omniscient radiation. The boundaries were indeed breached, they were on their way. The activity of the courtyard ceased as all stood in fear, waiting for the next thing to happen. In their minds, it was simple. All areas of the Magickal Realm had fallen if they were able to come at us from all directions. Only Ainys'Dai now stood between the Dark*e*ness and the complete control of the Realm of Man, of the World.

Gable alerted his warriors and word was sent for Angel to join him at the Gate Keep upon the wall. As ZackaRAy followed those orders, he saw that the Centaurs had finally arrived. Their entire herd rode as if the Hounds of Hell were upon them. In theory, they were. As they reached the gate, they were permitted entrance. The solid door sliding closed behind them. It was then sealed with the strongest magick possible. It would only open again, to allow survivors of the coming battle to enter, if there were any. The finality of it sent shivers up the spines of those who watched and felt the impact of the gate, settling back to earth.

* * * * * * *

I heard the knock on the door. I'd gotten some decent sleep. My sleep depraved body finally forcing me to close my eyes. *I felt stronger, more alert. I wasn't really sure if that was a good thing. I liked my numb state. It didn't hurt as badly as the feeling did.* I kissed Caitrin's forehead, whispering to her that I loved her, turning and walking over to the door, opening it. The look on ZackaRAy's face alerted me quickly that something was drastically wrong.

"What's happened?" I asked quickly, stepping into the hallway, closing the door behind me.

"The sentinels have arrived. It has begun."

"All of them. At the same time." I said it more in acknowledgment, than in question.

"Yes. It is the worst possible outcome, we will be completely surrounded." He replied. "Gable waits for you at the Gate Keep."

Simply nodding, following him as he led the way. A snow had fallen, in the previous hours, a dusting to the realm. A coolness in the air. Around me, I could see the faces of the terrified, those that remained within the courtyard. They knew. They all understood that I was the only thing that stood between the Darkeness and them. So much rested on me, I took a deep breath, and held my head up high. If nothing else, I would offer them hope through my courage.

We reached the Keeps wall, extending our wings, flying upward toward the gate walk and the Gates Keep. It was not a large room, but it served as one of the strategic points for the Guardians along the walk. As we touched down, a lite snow began, a chill creeping into the air. ZackaRAy knocked, waiting for Gable to bid us enter. Waiting, I saw that IllEna was here as well. She raced over to ZackaRAy, throwing her arms around him in a kiss of fear, of love. He wrapped his arms around her, caressing the swell of her abdomen where the new life was evident. Already knowing that this could be their last moments together on this earth, but also knowing that nothing, not even hell itself, would keep them apart. I smiled, feeling the constriction of my heart, feeling it into my very soul. This was what we were fighting for. This was what would ensure our success.

She turned to me then, her look . . . *different*. Behind her, several baskets were evident. IllEna had brought me the stones, the "true diamonds." They were overflowing in the baskets. "Caitrin asked me to make sure you got these, in case anything happened. I think she knew." She said with a confident truth and sadness, her eyes near to overflowing.

I looked to her. "I think she knew more than any of us." Nodding in agreement. Turning to the baskets, I shifted the pure diamonds, hundreds of them, throwing them upwards in the wind, all together. "*Alt A*." Using a minor spell, I suspended them there. Above the fields, to where the battle would proceed. Turning as I heard Gable's reply to enter, opening the door for myself and closing it quietly behind me. Studying Gable as he looked over a chart on the table, he looked in command, fierce, indomitable. Heat suddenly flared within me . . .

. . . he felt her passion.

He looked up at me. Throwing my arms around him, bringing my lips to his, passion flared between us. Actual static flares jumping from one to the other. Knowing that the end was near. That there was a chance that everything we had done, would still not be enough and we could lose this battle. But I also realized that if I only had moments left on this earth, I wanted them to be in Gable's arms, with his strength around me and within me. Wanting to taste and feel. I surrendered. Let go of everything that had happened and opened my arms too this, too now. My clothing fell away. I could have cared less if someone had walked through those doors right now. Nothing could tear me away from him.

His hands were rough as they raced along my flesh. So much work and practice had hardened his already calloused palms; it only excited me all the more. His palms gripping the mound of my breast as his tongue swirled mercilessly around the taunt and sensitive nipple. I felt the fluid heat as it pushed itself outward from my feminine core, surging through me, pushing outward into every conceivable outlet. I was burning, burning alive in passions grip. He sat me back along the table. Raising my legs upward and spreading them as his mouth went lower. Searching out every spot, every location that he knew was his and his alone. I felt the rapture as his velveteen thickness pulled forth from me, what was impossible, yet given.

He caressed the curls at my junction while I fought to breathe, my heart thundering, my lungs working in overdrive to keep up with his continuous assault. I felt him spread me, gently for his size as he pulled back the sateen layers and with a passion far greater than I'd known before, he razed me with his tongue. An assault upon my sensitivity, a quick flick before a brazen roll of pleasure from bottom to top, over and over again. Could actually feel my heart stop as I was consumed. Felt the moment were death appeared evident, and then the tidal wave of pleasure, too intense to ever describe, ripped through me and tore me wide. Before I could scream, before I could even wait for the next heartbeat to fall, to prove that death had not claimed me yet, his lips claimed mine. And his passion, he buried it deeply within me and extended the torture to beyond what I could endure . . .

. . . I felt the tug, felt the ripple from our joined tether. Doing something new, he opened our bond, flooding me with his thoughts, emotions and lastly, with his pleasure. It was a whirlwind, an assault on my mind, as much as the one on my soul and body had been. We were beyond connection, beyond each other. We were one, the intensity of it, the completeness. There was no greater power, no greater passion than the depth of what we willingly embraced, waves of leight ripping out in a cascading effect, the vibrations of our beings, blessed in the harmony of leight and sound, in our own frequency...

. . . We were whole, complete. The ultimate creation of love, the awakening of soulmates, rejoined as one, a new level of awareness, of being. We touched the border, the very edge of our existence and we grasped the truth, the connection to the Creator, his message of love and redemption. Two souls completely merged into one, a reunion of the original. We felt and we understood. With Grace, we pulled back, back to our joining, back to us, the passion rupturing . . .

. . . Again and again, thrust after thrust of pleasure that set my soul to fire, igniting within me a pleasure beyond the intensity of the sun, beyond life. And then he joined me, a cataclysmic collision that threw the world out of balance, before the gravity of each other pulled us back together, to each other. I could feel the sweat, as our skin combined and my mind was brought back to earth, to reality, the physical human and faery side. The fantasy, the unreality was now slipping away, the Earth back beneath our feet.

I broke away first, a slight nip to his bottom lip as I did so. "I love you. More than I needed to say it, I needed to show you." I said, breathing heavily. Struggling to give him all that we had felt, knowing now that no words would ever compare.

"I am glad you did. I have missed your touch the last few days." He said, as he wrapped his arms around me, as his heart now beat the same steady rhythm as my own.

"I've missed you too." Laying my head against his chest and closing my eyes, breathing deep, taking in his scent, taking in anything that I could of him. I knew that we had no time left. But I took what I could from his arms. "Tell me, what do you plan to do?"

"We will meet them head on. We do not hide behind these walls. We have waited long enough for these days."

"What if we're not able to defeat his forces?" I asked. *Call it the human side of me asking.*

"We are not able to defeat them." He said to me, the serious expression on his face, frightening. "Only you can defeat him. We are only going to try to make it a little easier for you."

I could only nod, what more was there to say. Letting go, he reached down and grabbed my tunic and pants, offering them back to me, before a smile came to his lips.

"I have something for you." He said. "I know that this is not how we normally do this, but with everything that has occurred . . . I thought it the best way." He walked back to his table. Reaching down, he picked up what appeared to be a bundle of cloth.

I pulled my tunic back on, tying the top into place, pulling the leggins back up. As he walked closer, I saw that it actually was something wrapped that he carried. It took me a moment, before it dawned on me what I staring at. I looked back up at him. "My sword."

"Yes. I told the SmytHe to take *"artistic license"* with it, as you would say." His smile was sad.

Reaching down to take it, my hand brushed the sturdy material it was wrapped in, looking at the fascinating and descriptive symbols that the cloth held. I'd wanted this celebration to be a family event. Caitrin and myself, receiving our swords at the same time. I know that sounded funny. But it was my, no, our reality. This was our life. I hated that this was taken from us as well. Sighing, then pulling the wrapping from around the sword, what I saw, took my breath away.

Easily, the sword was three feet in length. The blade glistening with my perfect reflection, as clear and beautiful as the most pristine water, broken only as the language of the faery was emblazoned upon its center. *"En ainm De, be leivÀ en ale sa prÀ sibblé a,"* it read, in a simple translation, *"in God's name, all is possible."* The handle was intricate. From the pommel to base, it was thick Celtic knots, woven deeply in the endless cycle of the soul. It was the very base that shocked me more. Inlaid deeply was an amethyst, pure and bright, roughly the size of an egg. I was sure that I could see the fire of life burning deeply from within it. Unable to respond for the moment. Carefully, running my hand along its length, turning back to face him once more.

"It's beautiful, utterly beautiful."

"Good. It was supposed to reflect the soul of the owner, remember. I will let the SmytHe know that you were well satisfied."

I ran the short distance between us, offering in my kiss, all that I was and felt. He returned in kind.

*

A knock at the door interrupted us. Moving quickly, I placed my boots back onto my cold feet. We walked out together, ZackaRAy still hand in hand with IllEna, needing only to point. From all directions, they did indeed come. Thousands of darke faery approached. Standing with the others, we watched. Seeing the sky all around beginning to darken. It appeared as if dusk had begun to fall. But that was not the case at all. They came from every direction, a solid circle of creeping death. They moved as a unit, draining all that they could in their immediate path. *Vampiric faery.* I shuddered.

As we watched, the darke faery landed on the barren fields around the parameter of the Keep. They stood forty deep, and still they came. As it continued, trolls cleared the fields, followed by ogres and other darke creatures. They flitted through the bodies, making their way in the ranks. Taking their places. We stood tall, watching as they surrounded us, knowing that at last we would be facing all of our fears. They continued filing in, one after another, hundred after hundred, standing so deep that the fields disappeared. Watching as their Flyer's settled into position amongst the rest. We waited, knowing that our defenses would strike soon. Knowing that to tip the scale, we would need everything at our disposal. In front of us there stood at least 20,000 strong, one of the greatest armies in the world, of all times.

Gable raised his hands to his warriors. The time had come. Half of the Guardians remained on the walls, as the other half, and the entire regiment of Warriors rode out to meet the army at our door. The Warriors of Leight stood 3000 strong, the Centaurs our only Allies to join in the cause. Their swords drawn, the faery sat upon the backs of their war steeds, all awaiting the command for the battle to begin. And I watched as almost seven times our numbers unfolded. We were at a great disadvantage. But it was my magick that must hold. It was I who would have to face the Darke leader and end this curse. I pulled deep from within myself, finding the strength that I'd missed for so long. *Now was my time and I would hold.*

As the others finally came into place, we could see a disturbance moving from the back towards the front. From within, rode a darke faery, *"a Minion-in-Command."* I thought to myself. It sat upon a serpent. The serpent resembled a horse, somewhat. Its body shape was similar, but that was the end of the similarities. Its skin was scales, a deep crimson against the sea of darke behind it. It had a long tail and a forked tongue that darted in and out. I could see distortion in the air around it, like gasoline on asphalt, the noxious fumes coming from its mouth. Apparently, some type of combustion was possible for it. Even from the distance, I could see the glow of its eyes. The sight of the beast made the warriors murmur amongst themselves. Even though they had all heard of the serpents of Hell, no one in memory could remember ever having seen one. Gable held up his hand for silence. The darke faery rode forward, slightly ahead of his own ranks and spoke in turn, his raspy voice reminding me of nails on a chalkboard.

"It would serve you better to surrender now. The Darke One approaches. Those that surrender will survive and be added to his ranks. They will rule under him for all eternity. Those that do not, they shall be tortured. One by one, every male, female and faeryling, will be put to death in the most torturous of ways." He laughed then, in a maniacal way, his words washing over all those around him. In response, the horde behind him laughed, the eerie and revolting sound, causing dread to creep up the spine of even the most seasoned warrior there. This was death. Right out and in the open.

Gable's voice, reached out strong across the sea of Leight and Darke. "We will never accept your offer. We are the Warriors of the Leight and you are the filth that creeps amongst the darkest pits of Hell. We ride with the Chosen; we will destroy your master and all of the spawn that he has placed upon this Earth. Your reign has come to an end."

"Enough! Your chance for survival has passed!" The minion swung around in his saddle. He raised his sword, a blackened piece of metal and screamed his cry of attack. Bringing his arm down, the battle began. "Take as many of them as you can. Let us show the Darke One what we can do for him!"

As those words were sung, sudden, deafening screams rent the air.

From our vantage, we watched as several darke faery began swarming. They were shaking, beating at themselves, clawing at their flesh and clothing. We watched as more and more joined their ranks. It was not all, but many of the Darke became deranged, screaming in terror and pain.

"It's the lodestones?" I questioned Gable.

"Yes." Was his only reply.

We watched for a moment more, when the darke faery on the serpent yelled out amongst his own ranks. He ordered those still standing, those unaffected, to strike out at those no longer in control of themselves. They easily removed the heads of the deranged in their haste. It was gruesome, the thick blood upon the ground, as not all of the darke faery were old, their blood long ago consumed. As we continued to watch, their numbers fell, not enough to even the odds, but enough. As they continued their butchery, Gable shouted the cry for war. The Leight rode out to meet the Army of the Darke amid the chaos that ensued. We surged into them like a mighty wave upon the ocean.

I rode beside Gable as we surged forward, slicing a wide path, taking heads as we went. The zing of sword upon sword as the battle began in earnest. As I viewed the scene around me, I watched as the Leight came now from the sky, those without horses, flying out in a second wave to provide coverage from above.

Using the strategy that Gable and I had decided upon, using my powers to boost the effect of the diamond outcrops. Now the Faery of Leight had multiple circles of protection to fall back too. If the Darke crossed our lines, they were quickly disposed of, their ability to fight removed by the high resonations of the diamonds. Around me, I placed a circle of protection for myself. My main goal was to offer aide to as many as possible; my real battle would not begin until the Darke One arrived. As the battle continued onward, I sent my magick outward to the fighting warriors. Protection, firebolts of energy and thoughts caused confusion for the darke faery as their greater numbers fell and they attempted to overtake the Leight. They'd never seen this type of magick before, fighting against it cost them time and energy, something that they did not have to waste. Then I did something that no one expected, I called down the elements to face them; rain, hail and cyclones.

As the cyclones formed, I muttered under my breath, "*Fleight sans,*" shifting the "true diamonds" into them. From the height of the vortex, they shimmered in the faint light still emitting from the inner swirling, from outside the shadow of the Darkeness. I pushed back at the clouds that I was not using. Coaxing the sun forward, coaxing it to shine down in strategic points at the height of the vortex. As the sun obliged, rainbows shot forward. Multiples of them, their hues a blatant reminder of the Creator's Once Promise. I watched as they blinded those that they came in contact with. The darke screaming in pain as the leight blistered the skin and eyes. I looked away. *It may be necessary, but I could not stomach the pain I was inflicting.*

I refocused outward, throwing the cyclones in diverse paths. They threw their debris at the various darke faery, causing as much confusion as its whipping winds were able to. Many were thrown down from astride the strange animals that they rode. *Remember, any advantage, was a good one.* I thought to myself, a stubborn smile on my face. I watched as lightning reigned down, striking out to erase the darke. The smell of scorched flesh was nauseating. Then I brought rain in torrential pours. It came down in a fury, the lightning and thunder continuing to follow. The earth split were the bolts of fire made contact. It was ferocious and furious in its assault upon them. It was also cleansing in its own respect, as it washed away the blood and odor.

Soon the battle came back to back as the number of darke faery increased, those that had remained hidden, flying out of the woods and into the fields. They seemed to come in endless waves, as we pushed and crushed them under foot, more would come, pulsing forward. Blood flowed from the wounded and more than several warriors were returned to the Keep by their steeds. I could see the death all around me. I stood at the center and watched. The opponents toe to toe, the winged beasts in flight. Frozen in my sight, I saw it all as the destruction was seared into my memory. It was as if time itself stood still, the fighting, the destruction and the death.

"This was not the answer!" I felt it through my bones, all the way into my soul.

The Warriors of the Leight were littered amongst the dead in numbers equal to those of the Centaurs. I saw friends, ones that I knew and had come to love, lying at my feet. Flesh cleaved into ribbons, crimson flowing freely over the ground. I got lost in the sea of faces. Some I couldn't identify, the damage so strong. Others we struck down with our own blades, to keep the darke from spreading. *We were bleeding the life out of ourselves, in the simple fact that we had no other chose amongst the unrelenting hatred.*

This could not be right. So much love, so much beauty torn asunder and destroyed by hatred and pain. I pulled my focus away from them. I knew there was nothing I could do for them anymore. Looking around, seeking out the faces of those still standing, needing to see, to believe that there was still right and leight in the darkeness. I counted them, one after the other, drawing strength from the essence of each one. Each a brilliant jewel in the sea of despair. Sighing, I prayed the rain would cleanse our souls as much as it washed away the death and blood.

*

We pushed and pushed. The darke faery gaining on us a little at a time, their forces were just so numerous. They were able to replace a fallen one quickly. It kept us swamped. Allowing for no rest, no reserves, the battle overhead raging just as fiercely as the one on the ground was. Though I remained protected at the center of the magick, I knew that if a miracle did not happen soon, we would simply be defeated by being outnumbered.

*

We heard them first. Even over the zinging clash of swords and the screams of the injured and dying. A great swishing noise approached. They came from the North, their numbers not quite strong, but impressive none the less, this sight of the amazing beasts, causing my breath to catch in my throat. *The Dragons had come!*

Their leather skin reflected in the fading light, creating an aura of omniscience about them, a feeling of purity and strength. The largest, his wing span an easy forty feet wide, they were the essence of power and intensity. As they reached the lines, we fell back, those powerful jaws opened wide. They screamed in triumph as they released stream after stream of fire down upon the darke faery, the screams of the Darke filling the air. We were able to surge forward again, pushing back and regaining ground as the Dragons fought side by side to keep the Darke at bay. The battle continued as the side of Leight was strengthened.

*

We fought on, making impressive dents in the numbers of all the darke creatures. But the loss of life was so profound, that the very Earth bled out Hér sorrow and Hér pain. I watched as our forces were pushed back and surged forward and then pushed back again. It was a constant struggle, a few mere inches at a time. Still I gave more and more of myself; I spread out my power, my circle of protection, to the limits my mind could control, pulling more and more faery within my spell. But the evil ate away at it. The leight was dimming.

It was as I pushed out with more, that I felt it, the final blow that sent me to my knees. The shimmer shook, it actually groaned under the weight forced upon it. Then it happened, the shimmer collapsed. With its fall, Darkness spread out in a great wave upon the Realm of Man. Thought tainted with their own evil, the poison of the Darkness devoured everywhere it touched humanity. People fell, cities fell. Families ravaged in pain and fear. Some fought, some still believed in the leight of this world, in the goodness that waned. But they fell. Fell as the weight of evil crushed them within its grasp.

Within my mind, I could feel the terror, sense the death as the innocence of my old world, was becoming consumed alongside the evil. My heart shuddered. I felt it, the fear. The loss was shattering, the extent of life extinguished in those moments. The end was near and he was coming, the Darke One. For thousands of years he had ruled from beneath, from in the shadows. He now felt his victory was near and he was coming to collect. All around the edges, the Darkness closed in. Their numbers seemed unending.

Behind the last Stronghold, the mountains themselves became lost from view. And the Dragons left us. The males, those that had come, were roaring in their fury, the earth shaking in their terror. They were searching for home, searching for their families and not finding them in the Darke. Taking off in flight, great swaths of emptiness left in their wake. *I could not blame them. I felt the same. I wanted to disappear and find purity again.*

I scanned the field. Gable was not more than fifty feet away, but it could have been a thousand, the heavy casualties and the Darkeness that stood between us was that thick. He fought hard, I could feel his concentration, his strength as it flowed through him to keep moving and keep safe. With the extra I had left, I pushed more power to him, my love offering him all that I had to give. *I stood up once again.*

*

He felt the connection in his soul a mere moment before the force of power boosted his own. Her raw energy was magnificent. She recharged him back to his full potential, even as he had begun to feel himself fall. He renewed his battle, his mind fresh, and his skills nearly unbeatable. He had seen her fall, had felt her soul scream out in torture. He knew that she had to be exhausted, for a moment he had felt it, before she had shut it out from him. Knowing there was nothing he could offer her, so he sent her the greatest magick he had. *"I love you Angel. Always stay strong."* The connection was broken.

But I felt the reserves of love strengthen me, as the battle ensued.

*

I searched; I spread out my mind to find Caitrin. Feeling her familiar essence, as my range zeroed in on her silent form. Feeling that she still lived. Her heartbeat and breath. Knowing that she was still trapped within herself. The protective circle of magick that I'd given Caitrin, was at the moment still keeping her safe. I didn't know how much longer it would be though. Soon my powers were going to drain, then I didn't know whom to let go of to keep my daughter safe. I refocused my mind, watching so many of the Leight and keeping the Darkeness at bay.

* * * * * * *

Several more hours passed, when I felt the earth shake beneath me. Our bond opened in a floodgate. *"Gable, we need to pull back to the Keep. He is coming; I cannot keep everyone safe any longer."*

*

Gable looked over to her ragged face. How she had lasted this long, he did not know. Raising up his sword, he cried the sound of retreat and followed his Kind back to the gates. They opened, allowing those of them that remained entrance. The wounded, their numbers high, only outnumbered by their dead. They gathered the remaining forces upon the walls, watching as the sky continued to darken around them. Evening itself, finally beginning to fall. The end was coming at last. He looked over as Angel appeared next to him. She was still beautiful, even as the weariness and the horror of their long day sat heavily upon her shoulders. She truly was the Hand of the Creator. He could see her suffering, and from within her, he could feel her great sorrow and pain.

*

       "The battle does not go well Gable. Our forces are dwindling. More and more of us are falling. Soon the Dark*e* One will have a tight knot around us, and all that stand within these walls will fall prey." I said quietly.

       "If that is the outcome we face, then we will face it. We have done as the Creator bade us do. We have followed Hís plan and we will prevail. We will march out for the final battle as he arrives and we will make our final stand." Gable said defiantly.

       He was intimidating as he stood there, those faithful followers of the L*e*ight, surrounding him in their greatest time of need. I didn't respond, merely nodding my assent to him. But I knew. This was not a war that we could win. I was no coward, but I could see that somehow, this was wrong. War, battle, none of this was the answer; it was only a bandage, a way to suppress the overflow until the cure could be found. We were going to lose this battle, if I could not figure out what piece of the puzzle we were misunderstanding.

Without Fear
(29)

~ↄ~ **Looking back, I now realize how much Faith, God still had in us . . . ~C~**

I stood back, watching as the ArtimA rushed the inner courtyard. The wounded, laid out as they prepared to seek aide from them. It was like a sad vision from olde history. The wounded littering the fields of old. I searched; I went through all of the things in my head that I had learned over the months. There was something that held the answer; I just had to find it. Grasping at anything, replaying the events like a movie, when suddenly, it was like a light went on. *An ultraviolet light of immense proportions.* RandelfSon's words came back to me.

"Where is the Old Temple?" I asked, turning to face Gable.

"RandelfSon took over the unused portion of the Temple for his home. Truth be told, it had not been used for many a year, having become so overgrown and hidden."

"Why was that? It seems like something as important as that, would not have been set aside."

His face flushed. "I really cannot speak for my ancestors, for it happened long ago. From what I do know, it was a building that needed taken care after the Great Cleansing, and a thousand years more after that. Like all things of the earth, the structure began to crumble and ruin. While it was repaired, a newer temporary Temple was put together. The newer one actually became more common, for it was closer to the courtyard and larger. It accommodated the influx of faery that began arriving. Eventually, the Old Temple was finished and left to set as a reminder of God's Will. After that, I am not really sure what happened. It is like the world seemed to just pass it by. That is, until RandelfSon asked permission to use it. I thought it fitting that he sought shelter from within the walls of the Temple." He continued on. "If you go to the Temple we use now, continue on to the back of the Keep. You will see the area that is wild and overgrown; there you will find his door." He replied. "Why do you ask?" He suddenly wondered.

It was all meant to be. Every last thing that had happened had been for a reason, this reason. "I need some time to myself while we wait, some time to pray." He nodded his consent as I raised myself up. I made a slight detour first, finding our chamber. I needed to cleanse, to wipe clean the outside and pray for the inside. A new set of clothing wouldn't hurt either. My battle cloth. Washing the reek of death off, I felt the sorrow, watching the rivulets of red that disappeared into the basin. Now was not the time, but the loss would be accounted for, all of it. Closing my eyes, dressing in the silence. Finished, I left the room and flew to the entrance of the Old Temple, following Gable's directions.

Here the ground was covered by growth, and an accent of newly fallen snow. The earth was beaten in age, the visible plants, wild in their abandonment. The walls and the door itself, covered in vines that climbed high to reach for sunlight. The door had not been entered in a while; obviously no one had come here since RandelfSon's death. Moving aside the vine with my hands, the door shifted with my thoughts. The room was dark and musty. *"Briten Thi."* Scones upon the wall quickly lit themselves as I entered. *"Fire érA."* A fire springing to life, warming the room and making it more comfortable. I left the smaller antechamber and entered the gathering chamber itself.

Here was the oldest part of the Temple, dank and musty to the eyes and nose, the sign of the recent neglect evident. Pulling on leight, the room came to life. My breath was sucked away. The room carried the history of the Faery. The tÀle circled the room, from one wall to the next. Standing at center, I could spin in a circle to read the text. The deeply carved words glimmered with a golden hue as the ancient magick ran deep. It was the TÀle, the actual recollection of the beginning, set down by the Hand of God, Hímself. Laid down upon the face of the Earth, I read every line and thought, turning in a circle to complete the TÀle. It was not that you could read the words, it was so much more. You could feel the words, the truth in every syllable. It wasn't until the end, that the difference was found. The missing piece of my own salvation revealed. It was simple, so very simple in its requirement. Therefore, it would be the hardest thing to be done. It asked for all, would require all. It was the very foundation of life that I would give, and I knew that I could.

I knew the secret, the understanding of the Creator. My own words, from the story I'd told Caitrin, came back to me now. *Real love is about sacrifice.* RandelfSon had been right about the message, but wrong about the content. I would stand with the Leight, and I would sacrifice all to the Darkness. I would place all of my faith in God. I would give all that I was capable of giving, everything.

The Faery though, they would think it surrender, at first. They would have to hold, hold until they understood. And they would. It was faith, complete and utter faith in a loving Creator. Something that the very Angels of Heaven could give, I could do also. It was a part of me . . .

. . . I finally understood. I had the free will to make my choice to God, the heart and soul to decide it and the acceptance to carry it through. It would free us all.

And I finally understood why it had carried on so long, why this war had raged for eons.

"Í had still believed in him." Now the words were clear, the truth coming not in my words or suggestions, but from the Source itself.

I stepped back, leaving the chamber quickly, heading back to my mate. I could sense the change in the air. The Darke One had come at last and the battle, the final battle would begin and end here. I braced myself, stealing my mind and my heart for what was coming.

*

I flew up to the top of the wall, joining Gable and the others, a slight smile to my lips, a quick joining of our thoughts and minds.

Gable's heart skipped a beat. *"She is my everything."* He thought to himself.

The wind had picked up something fierce, the bitterness, bone weary. I wore my battle attire now. Having grown accustomed to the scant clothing that I now wore, they did indeed allow me more range of movement. My attire, entirely white, except for the golden adornments of belt and necklace, holding the pieces in place. Around my shoulders was a long, velvet flowing cloak, it kept me warm as the winter winds had finally arrived and began to blow. Within the teal folds, golden swirls were seen, the Celtic knots glowing with their power from within.

I knew that I would have to lose its warmth, once the battle began, but until then, I would hold it close and hold the old magick closer still. I'd plaited my hair, to keep it at bay. Golden adornments, the same as Gable's, kept the wild masses in check. I felt like a warrior princess, and I knew that within moments, I would be proving it. It really amazed me, how comfortable I'd become in my own skin. I only wished that I'd attained this much freedom years ago. It was a powerful rush, one that was needed, all of it that I could get. It was final, the faith I had in myself. Taking Gable's hand, together we turned to watch as the evil approached. Not more than a hundred yards out, it spread around us as a darke circle of hatred.

Everything obliterated. It was a mockery of the once magickal, once thriving realm. The life had been leached out of our surroundings. The once proud realm, reduced to rubble and ash. *How do we recover from such chaos?*
* * * * * * *

A disturbance up the center marked the arrival of the Darke One. He had had so many names, so many faces in history. But his mark had always been evil. He came forward, far more beautiful than I could have imagined. He stood well over 7 foot, a true giant. He was solid muscle, thick and toned, his hair, dark and wild. His skin a set shade of deep caramel, it was his eyes that bespoke his nature, black eyes with no leight. They offered no hope, no freedom.

As he approached, I watched his mighty wing span. Cast of jet black feathers, silken and shiny even from this distance. He was nearly bare, except for a black cloth worn around the waist, it hung to knee length. *We offered him no fear, that much was apparent.* As he finally came to a rest, I saw black markings upon his chest. They were different than ours, an older language; they marked his name, his true name. And I could read it. *Knowing something's true name, their true essence, gave one power. Immense power.*

He smiled as he watched me watching him, perfect white teeth in a perfect face. *No, he was not afraid of me at all.*

"He will be."

*

He held up a great staff that he carried in his left hand and a yell that terrified the senses, marked the beginning of the end. We watched as his ranks followed him in. More warriors of the darke appeared. Looking, I realized that all of their dark wings were feathers, the sudden realization hitting me like an arctic chill. These were the Angel's, the Fallôn Ones, those that had joined his ranks from the very beginning and still stood strong, behind him. They were the beginning and the end, all together at last, the final turn on the wheel.

"All of you that cower in your fear. You cowardly Leight Bringêrs. Your time has come to an end. All that stands between total Darkeness and me is the paltry few of you that hide behind those walls, your numbers crushed. You have lost this battle before it was even begun. I have come to collect. My time is now!" He raged forth, slamming his staff into the ground. It caused a violent shock wave to shoot forward and shake the earth. It breached the walls, the protection of our circle. The inner walls of the Keep shaking and crumbling from the Darke powers force. "Surrender now, your time is done."

*

"Never shall we surrender! We shall fight to our last breath! You have no hold upon us here! Here is where the Creator walks. The Hand of the Creator, His Chosen is among us now and the time of your defeat is at hand." Gable yelled across the field.

The Darke One laughed at his proclamation. "The Chosen One. Do you not think that if the Chosen One was truly that powerful, that she would not have destroyed us already? Even your Great Creator, in all His Glory, was not able to destroy me thousands of years ago. And today, today my power is a thousand times stronger! Your Creator has abandoned you in your greatest hour. Hé is not here, nor does Hé walk amongst you. All around you is my Darkeness. I will swallow your numbers whole and reign in my glory for an eternity to come." He rolled back his wings, displaying his mighty power once again. His roar, terrifying!

*

Gable turned to me then. "We will fight. We will defend our Kind, our very souls, to the bitter end. We have done as the Creator asked. If we fail now, then it never was meant for us to succeed."

I looked at Gable, allowing all of my love and feelings to show, placing my hand to his heart. Here, I could feel his love and his faith. Looking out to my left, I looked down upon the faces of the survivors. Those below were the last remaining survivors of Earth. Here, looking out from all sides, were my Kind. I was more than one, I was all. We were one large family, created from God, fighting amongst ourselves, our unity. Turning back, looking Gable directly in the eyes, I felt more than could be said. "You will not march out to him. Your time to fight and defend has come to an end. It is my time now. I will go out and I will face the Darke One."

"You cannot go out there alone!" There was terror in his reply.

"I was always meant to face him alone, Gable. It's my destiny." Rubbing his chest one last time as I prepared to take flight. "You have my love Gable and you have my soul. I could never have asked for more." I released the clasp at my neck, my cloak falling to the floor. Closing my eyes, I lifted off the wall. My future was ahead of me, and the terror I felt, I locked away. It had no place with me anymore, my time had come.

"Darke One, the time has come for us to face each other and finish this, this evil that you started so long ago." I yelled across the way.

He took flight, the same as I, to meet me on the barren field between us all. He was mighty, his frame towering over mine, but from me, no fear was apparent, I wore my faith as a cloak now.

"You should not have left your defenses. You are completely defenseless against me. All that is yours will be mine. I will have your daughter. Would you leave her crushed under my power after I destroy you?" He laughed, the sound actually pleasant, though it cut me through like knives. "Be mine, surrender to the Darkness and end all of this with me. I have what you want. I could offer you more, more than you have ever dreamt, ever imagined. You have felt nothing compared to what I can offer. Come to me now!" The Darke One said with a sneer upon his beautiful face.

And I felt the heat, felt the violent swirl of temptation as he attempted to offer me all. To pull me in and down. A savage darke temptation of lust and passion. Carnal pleasures that raced across my flesh and throughout me. Swirling, sinking in their depths. Seeking to consume.

"Afterall, if you do not stand for me, you will die." His smirk grew wider. "Of course, should you fall; it would be to your daughter that your place would fall. She would be mine, now and always."

I felt the horror, and the disgust, the loathing at the thought of him touching her. My voice was firm. "You are right there; it is my time to die." I said the words loudly. "I surrender."

*

No one moved as the words reached over the Keeps walls. The shock and finality of them, too much for most to comprehend, they stood frozen in their disbelief. Gable growled, deep within his chest and throat. "*This was not the way.*" She would never have given in. They were lost. Then he felt it, the slight brush of her mind. And the peace that she gave him. She believed that she was right. So he accepted, fighting away the fear of carnage, fighting away the doubt.

*

The Darke One screamed out his pleasure at his success. He threw back his arms and drawing his power from the Darkeness around, he screamed out his magick. He cast his staff forward, and the Darke power, the very essence of him, attacked her with a viciousness none had ever seen. He laughed as the power hit her. Straight to her belly, her core.

*

The power surged into me, the raw festering evil a burning tar as the darkeness took hold of my human form, and still I did not fight him. I felt his pleasure, felt his wicked caress as he sought to claim all that belonged to God. The pain ripped through me, I could feel the darkeness. It tore through my clothing, burning through my skin. My body exposed, stripped bare to the masses that watched. The raw power seeped into my gut, reaching into blood, muscle and organ. This time there was no seduction, only vengeance. It took a foothold and spread. I could feel the power, the strength of the evil as it devoured me, reaching for my heart and my soul. It was then that I looked into the eyes of evil, into the pits of Hell, and the darkeness that dwelled there...

. . . Without fear. "But you see, you have nothing to offer me." I said, keeping the pain from my voice. "I would see my daughter dead in God's hands long before I would give her up to you to save her." I screamed in triumph.

"Samma∂l, your Creator never abandoned you. Hé stood by and watched as again and again, you destroyed what Hé Created, in your jealousy, in your hate, and your shame." I paused a moment, the pain becoming unbearable. My flesh on fire, the pain so intense, that I wondered if my soul would indeed be incinerated. "For all Hís sacrifice, for all Hís love, Hé continued and Hé hoped. Hé offered and waited. To give up on even one soul a horrendous loss to Hís own soul. Now, for Hím, I sacrifice myself." I said. "I sacrifice my life, my daughter, my mate and all of those that I love . . . to God. I offer my sacrifice of unending love. To the end, I offer my sacrifice of faith and I embrace the Leight."

I saw it in his eyes, the one and only sign of fear before the darkeness consumed my body, it reached my heart where it deviled deep into my very soul.

*

The Darke One jerked back, her words no longer important, he threw back his head and laughed. His darkeness had claimed her soul and she was now his. Even now, his power was spreading out, taking the Keeps walls and attacking those within. He had won, finally, after thousands of thousands of years, he had won. He turned back to look at her, her body broken as the force of his magick had her suspended above the earth.

He moved closer, he wanted to collect her personally. His trophy, his final victory over the Creator and the Leight. As he drew nearer, he saw something that had never crossed before. Her eyes opened and she looked at him. They were white, completely white and the Leight from within them shined fiercely.

He felt fear . . .

*

Suddenly, the voice of the Creator rang forth from my lips. "ALL OF YOUR JEALOUSY, ALL OF YOUR HATRED. Í LOVED YOU, YET YOU CHOSE TO SCORN THIS WORLD THAT Í CREATED WITH YOUR HATRED. SO, FEEL NOW YOUR CHOICES, FEEL THEM WITH THE HEART OF A HUMAN, THAT WHICH IS SO MUCH MORE POWERFUL, THAT WHICH YOU HAVE CURSED A THOUSAND TIMES OVER. FEEL ALL THAT YOU HAVE DONE." And the thunder rolled outward.

*

A blinding white leight, tinged in shades of blue and ultraviolet, more intense than the sun, shot out from the depths of my heart. A straight line to the breast of the Darke One, marking him where his heart should have been, the leight pierced him through.

He stared at it for a moment, comprehension not yet dawning, then the intensity of the leight jerked him upright into the air. Our forms were uniform, as he took what I had received. It suspended him; arms spread wide, a silent crucifix. The burning leight, it spread through his chest, tearing through his outward Angelic form. It ripped through to his very core, to the darkeness that laid in wait. Burning clear through the shreds of what might have been a soul in any other.

He screamed in pain; the guilt, the remorse, the suffering of human emotions running through him for a thousand, thousandths years' worth of misery and torture. The torture of his body being cleansed by the Holy Leight. The pain tore through all of him, shredding him atom from atom. Until, there was only dust suspended in the air. Until, there was nothing left. Erasing his essence from ever being, cleansing the earth around him.

*

Gable watched. With a crack louder than any thunder, the leight burst forth from Angel. Before the power exploded, a golden halo of dust escaped her ravaged form, her essence lifting upward and away. Their bond . . . lost . . .

The leight blinded all and everything in its intensity. It moved with a speed so fierce, that the darkeness could not escape. It raced across the Earth, from end to end, above and below, and everywhere in between. It penetrated the very depths of the world itself, pulling upon the core for speed and intensity. In those moments, all that was, all that had ever been, disappeared as it was bathed in the Leight of the Creator's Love, cleansing the Earth of evil, completely extinguishing the Darke forevermore.

In the Year of Our ReCreation: 1 RC

(The Promise of Eden)

In the Beginning . . .
Epilogue

On the morning of the seventh day, the world was recreated in its original image, from the deepest ocean, to the highest mountain and all the fields in between. The Sanctuary of the Leight was a brilliant gem. The sky pure and blazing in azure, the mountains fell next from the heavens. The deep shades of sapphire and amethyst covered only at the tops by the pristine white snow. The trees of pine began midway down; like a dark emerald that lightened as it reached the less condensed woods to the open fields and beyond. The whole of the Earth was renewed, Hér water and air pure. All signs of pollution and the taint of the Darkeness removed from Hér. Shé sighed, a warm breeze washing over the land. Hér time had come, Shé was once again whole. A thousand, thousandths years of peace had finally come to the world, to Eden.

* * * * * * *

I walked out onto the balcony from our room. From my view, I knew that the sun was coming up over the Rain'Dai Mountains to the east. The sight would be breathtaking; it was one that I was quite familiar with these days. The rainbows could be seen, even from here, their permanent beauty forevermore a reminder of the loss and success that we had all gone through. This was my favorite time, the quiet before the day began.

* * * * * * *

It had been nearly six months since life had begun to return to the Earth, to Eden. After my sacrifice, the Earth had been snuffed out in an instant and in no more than a second, reborn. All of us had stood before the Sight of the Creator, each soul faced with our choices and our destinies. We had all been given a choice that day. We could travel on to Heaven, or as a gift, remain on Eden as a Reign of Peace began. Enjoying a life and existence of Plenty, with no fear of need or suffering.

Many of mankind choose to move on, their new journeys only beginning as they embraced the Leight of the Creator and Heaven. Even a large number of the faery had chosen the higher path. My own parents, their faces, their choice to move on. And a sister that I had not known my máthair carried. But another group chose Eden. We were made up of faery, humans and other magickal creatures that wished to remain behind. The Paradise of Eden was now our Sanctuary. The planet, so much larger now that all of the hidden realms had been freed, was only populated with a few hundred thousand. Animal and ocean life, filled aplenty.

Gods' Message was so complete and perfect. Standing before Hím, in Hís eyes, Hís last words to us. "Í have so many children, spread far and wide, so many in need. But Í will still be here, Í have always been here."

Then Hé pulled me to Hím, and the Creator put Hís hand to my womb and said, "ALWAYS BELIEVE." And Hís love surrounded us in a blanket of warm leight as Mother Earth washed Hér cleansing breathe over us in our return home.

* * * * * *

I looked over my shoulder as I heard Gable approach. He put his arms around me as I leaned back into his embrace. His hands came to rest on the large swell of my abdomen. Underneath, lay God's Promise for our future. Finally, the perfect Béing created; the blend of faery, human and Angel, the best of all creations. Six months into my pregnancy now, both of us could feel the faerylings life, as it responded to the touch of our joined hands.

*

"Gable, I've been meaning to ask you something. That day, in our place, when I awoke and went flying, I came to rest at the foot of a tree. There was something really unusual about it. It was a mighty, majestic weeping willow, its arms extended at a great birth. It appeared that a great golden fruit grew from it. But I know that willows do not bear fruit." I turned to look at him. "Do you know of which I speak?"

He stared at me for a long moment. His actual mind was blank as I searched him for an answer.

"You saw the *Tree*?" He finally asked, his voice was near reverence.

"Yes." I said, somewhat hesitantly.

He shook his head. "I know of it. But no, I have never seen it with my own eyes. It is the Tree of Knowledge. The first Tree of Eden. After the fall of Adam and Eve, it was forbidden to ever be seen again."

The shock of it cursed through me. "Of course, the flaming swords at the entrance to the bridge. The Guardians to the entrance of the Garden of Eden." I said with reverence. The olde and forgotten memory coming forward. "What . . . what of the fruit Gable?"

"When Adam and Eve left Eden behind, the Creator stripped the Willow tree of its fruit, for it had allowed the first sins to be born. From that day forth, the tree bowed over in tears for its own loss at the folly of humans. Forever weeping, it became known as the weeping willow. But the Creator was not a cruel Being and Hé knew that the willow was as devoted to Hím as it had always been. So the Creator spread out the offspring of the great tree, knowing that one day, it might find its place once more."

"It bows no more." I said, for though it had reached far and wide, the arms had been extended Heavenward and its leaves had been long and flowing, the only extension of its self, to Grace the grass beneath.

* * * * * * *

"Is Caitrin already there?" I asked him a while later.

"Yes, she is already at the gate. How does she know that he will come? He could have chosen differently. None of us found him as we stood before the Creator. It has been so long." He said. He felt fear for her, for Caitrin, for the chance that she would be incomplete.

"No, he will be wherever Caitrin is. Obviously, there were things awaiting him with the Creator." I said.

"How are you so sure?" He asked me.

"Soulmates follow each other wherever one may go." I said, as I turned in his arms for the heat of his kiss, the floodgate opening and my senses erupting in passion.

* * * * * * *

Caitrin stood at the open gate, waiting. He would come, she knew it. Each day, more arrived at the Keep. Those that had chosen to remain and live here in peace. She watched as the sun rose higher. From the distance, she saw a cloud of dust that rose along the pathway. As the minutes drug on, she could make out the progression of faery and humans as they approached the Keep. Even two Centaurs were amongst them. There was at least twenty here, this was a larger group. She looked, unable to identify anyone at this distance.

She was dancing with restraint as they finally come close enough for her to make out faces. Most appeared to be adults, but none bore a resemblance to him. She could feel her disappointment mounting, when a young faery at the back of the group caught her attention. He couldn't be more than eight or nine, and as he drew nearer, a smile lit her face.

He'd come! Here was the face that she remembered, the one that she'd always known. "RandelfSon, it's me, it's Caitrin. You've finally come home." She ran into the faerylings arms, his grip holding her tight. She pulled back her face, tears of joy shimmering down her cheeks.

He smiled at her and taking her hand, they walked back through the open doors of the Keep. Looking down at her once more, he laughed, his answer a mere reply. "Of course I came back; I said I loved you after all."

And they lived . . . *Happily Ever After.*"

The End

www.ingramcontent.com/pod-product-compliance
Lightning Source LLC
Chambersburg PA
CBHW030323020726
47493CB00004B/1138